An Uncommonly Festive Fiasco

Hannah Hendy lives in a small town in South Wales with her wife, their daughter, and two spoilt cats. A professional chef by trade, she started writing to fill the time between shifts. She now writes cosy crime fulltime, a dream job! She is the author of the bestselling cosy crime series, The Dinner Lady Detectives, published by Canelo Crime and Canelo US. Hannah is represented by Francesca Riccardi at Kate Nash Literary Agency.

Instagram - @hannahhendywrites

Facebook - @hannahhendywrites

Twitter - @hendyhannah

Website – hannahhendywrites.com

Also by Hannah Hendy

The Dinner Lady Detectives

The Dinner Lady Detectives
An Unfortunate Christmas Murder
A Terrible Village Poisoning
A Frightfully Fatal Affair
A Gravely Troubling Discovery
An Extremely Unlikely Death
A Curiously Convenient Demise
An Uncommonly Festive Fiasco

An Uncommonly Festive Fiasco

HANNAH HENDY

First published in the United Kingdom in 2026 by

Canelo Crime, an imprint of
Canelo Digital Publishing Limited,
20 Vauxhall Bridge Road,
London SW1V 2SA
United Kingdom

A Penguin Random House Company
The authorised representative in the EEA is Dorling Kindersley Verlag GmbH.
Arnulfstr. 124, 80636 Munich, Germany

A CIP catalogue record for this book is available from the British Library.

ISBN 978 1 83598 160 3

Cover design by Ami Smithson

Printed and bound in Great Britain by Clays Ltd, Elcograf S.p.A.

Look for more great books at
www.canelo.co | www.dk.com

1

In loving memory of Uncle Eddie, who travelled the world, but is off on the next big adventure now.

Chapter One

Ittonvale community hall bustled with a fervour that hadn't been seen since the Christmas festival the year before. The numerous food vendors had begun to prepare for the evening's entertainment, and the air was filled with a myriad of conflicting aromas. Margery had never thought to wonder what mulled wine might smell like when mixed with popcorn, but now she knew. She wasn't sure if her life was much improved by the experience.

Stall holders busily set up their wares – snowflake candles and shiny baubles that Margery's wife, Clementine, had been raring to throw her money at. She'd even gone so far as to enquire about the price of the snow globe filled with strawberry creme Quality Street chocolate. Luckily Clementine hadn't discovered the stall that printed children's handprints and footprints onto large ceramic baubles, or she would have probably demanded that they turn around and bring both their cats down to the hall for the evening.

The dinner lady team busily dragged crates and crates of food and mince pies through from the car park. It was so full of vans that Margery had barely been able to park the school minibus in the vendors area. She had promised Sally, who had taken on the role of a stern-faced parking warden even though she was the hall's treasurer and had no real power at all, that she would return to move it after they had dropped everything off. She had already decided she would do no such thing. The tiny sliver of rebellion felt fantastic. It was Christmas after all, the time to 'treat yourself' – the mantra Seren always repeated while opening a new Terry's Chocolate Orange.

They had nearly needed to walk there after Mr Evans had refused to give up his use of the school minibus for the Summerview school netball team's special winter tournament, but then Rose, Summerview's headteacher, had had a quiet word with him. Clementine hadn't questioned the sudden change of heart when he had come to drop the keys to them in the kitchen, but Margery had noticed his shaking fingers and decided that it was probably better she didn't ask.

The dinner ladies' area still needed a bit of careful décor but was mostly ready. Gloria had desperately tried to spruce it up with the few sad bits of tinsel they had brought with them, and Seren had nearly died several times falling off a ladder sticking the mistletoe to the ceiling. Ceri-Ann had settled down on the floor to make paper trains, which meant she hadn't been able to do her designated job of sweeping and mopping the room in preparation, and Karen had needed to mop around her. In the end, though, they had managed to make it look quite festive.

'Christ, the weather's terrible!' A man lurched through the door towards them, brushing rain from the shoulders of his leather jacket. His dark hair had probably been slicked back anyway before the rain could have even had the chance to wet it. It hung down to his shoulders in calm waves that looked effortless but Margery knew must take a full routine to maintain. His chiselled face was twisted in annoyance, but he still managed to look infuriatingly handsome, his jaw sharp enough to make the expression seem intentional. 'You doing the food for the bands? I'm the singer of Apex Void.' He held out his arm and pulled back his sleeve to show off his pink artist's wristband.

'You've come to the right place,' Margery said, already beginning to shovel potatoes onto the plate for him before handing it over to Clementine to add the turkey slices.

The man wasn't wrong about the weather. It was unexpectedly miserable, even for December. Heavy rain had been falling on and off and the black sky was still threatening another round. The weather report on Margery's phone told her that more was due, so it was lucky they had arrived at the hall in good time. The mince pies never would have made it inside in one piece in their fragile cardboard packaging.

'Mike!' someone yelled from behind the man as the door swung open again. Mike rolled his eyes so dramatically that Margery worried for a moment that they might roll away underneath the trestle table.

'What now?' Mike turned and snapped as Kevin, who Margery had met earlier in the day, approached.

Where Mike was tall and slender and carried himself with the air of someone who knew they were very good looking even though they were much too old to be as handsome as they thought they were, Kevin was the opposite. The zip of his coat strained over his chest, and his round face was red with annoyance.

'You're not supposed to be eating,' he puffed. 'You're supposed to be getting up on stage for sound check. How are you going to sing after you've eaten your weight in roast potatoes?'

Mike had already taken the plate from Clementine and was helping himself to gravy from the soup kettle at the end of the serving table. 'Yeah, yeah, yeah. Give us a minute! For crying out loud, you'd think this was Glasto, not some dingy little town event. No offence, ladies…'

Margery felt the atmosphere in the room change as the dinner ladies and event staff turned to listen, cutlery screeching against plates. It was one thing to think something like that, but it was quite another to say it in front of the people who were helping to put the show on.

'You're embarrassing yourself,' Kevin hissed at him under his breath. Margery was close enough to hear every word. Clementine hadn't been but was quickly shuffling her way over so she could eavesdrop too.

'There's no one here, mate,' Mike snapped back, stuffing another roast potato into his mouth. He wasn't wrong, even though he was much ruder about it than Margery would have been. Most of the vendors were here, and the hall staff and, of course, the dinner lady team had been here all day preparing the green room food, but there were very few actual visitors. There could have only been about twenty people in total, and both halls could have comfortably held over a hundred. 'Half the bands haven't even turned up.'

'A gig is a gig,' Kevin said, in a voice that suggested he had reminded Mike of that many times before. 'Think of it as a chance to practise that new guitar solo.'

'No one's here to hear it!' Mike said, his mouth full of potato.

He walked over to the nearest bin and tipped the contents of his plate into it before Margery could point out the food waste bin. He slammed the plate down on the nearest table before storming out. Kevin shook his head but followed him anyway.

Before anything even more dramatic could happen, Rose swept into the green room. She was followed by

Ittonvale school's head of drama, Rhonda Blossom. Both wore matching headbands and scarves, looking more like performers than any of the bands did, and they were both followed by a tiny dog.

'Good news, Margery,' Rose said, picking her Jack Russell terrier up and putting him on the nearest trestle table. Jason the dog began to tiddle closer to the roast turkey on his little legs. Rhonda's dog Ada Bones looked on in jealousy. 'The volunteers rota for tonight and tomorrow has Rhonda and I down as kitchen help!'

'Kitchen help?' Gloria cried from behind them. She came out of the kitchenette to look at Rose and Rhonda in horror. 'Whyever for?'

'That's just what the volunteers rota says,' Rose said, her mouth turning upwards in a perfect imitation of a very pleased frog. 'So that's what must be done. What shall we begin with? Perhaps tidying up this mess...' She waved a judgemental hand over the neat Christmas cracker display Ceri-Ann and Gloria had spent forty-five minutes putting together.

They were lucky to have the use of the hall and the kitchenette for the staff and band meals. The food vendors for the public had to bring everything with them in their vehicles and store it all away from the hall. The green room was usually a storage area, so although it was big enough for them and a few tables, it wasn't ideal. Margery assumed that it would be even worse for food vendors in the smaller hall. At least they would have windows to look out of, she thought, looking around at the bright strip lights along the ceiling and the ugly flat-screen TVs on the plain panelled walls.

'Do you not have a drama class to coerce into doing a Christmas concert?' Clementine asked. 'That one we watched last week can't possibly be the only thing you're putting on this year.'

Rose glared at her. 'I'll have you know that that was the best concert Dewstow has seen in an absolute age, Mrs Butcher-Baker. The best *A Christmas Carol* since the Muppet version. Everyone said so.'

'Come on,' Gloria said, escorting Jason gently back into Rose's arms. 'I'll show you where the dishwasher is.'

'Oh, well, I thought I'd be better at serving or icing a Christmas cake or something,' Rose spluttered. 'I could fold some napkins into swans? Oh, but that's not particularly festive, is it? Maybe I could look up a video of how to make a snowman…'

'Have you ever done any napkin art before?' Margery asked.

'Well… no,' Rose admitted, finally taking Jason from Gloria and following her out of the room. 'But it's just napkins, Margery. How hard can it be?'

Sally entered the room, finally having relinquished her duty as car park tyrant. A cloud of gloom followed her. Alongside Doug, she was in charge of organising most of the events, though Margery hadn't seen much of Doug yet. Sally was a tall and thin woman, with a striking but angular face and a nose that reminded Margery of a bird beak. She could only have been in her fifties, but she held the joyless energy of a Victorian ghost who had unfortunately died of dysentery.

'This is a disaster,' Sally hissed as she reached them, grasping for a plate and helping herself to a sliver of turkey so thin it was almost translucent. 'Friday night is always the worst night anyway, and we were counting on door sales to make the numbers up. At this rate, we won't sell enough tickets to cover the costs.'

'You know why, don't you?' Rose said, reappearing again behind Margery and folding her arms haughtily, any effort to collect dishes forgotten completely. 'It's because you don't have a play on. Now, if Friday night was a Christmas concert then that would be a sold-out crowd. You ought to speak to Rhonda about it. Between us we could whip something up for next year, I'm sure.'

'I quite agree,' Rhonda called from across the room. She nodded so vigorously that Ada Bones ended up nodding too with the movement. 'But Ittonvale has three sold-out performances next week and I don't want to strain the students' voices.'

'Oh no, of course,' Rose said, clasping a hand to her chest in horror. 'I feel the same about my stars...'

Rose's so-called stars were a group of Year Elevens who could just about remember the words and the melody to Rose's bizarre retelling of *A Christmas Carol*, which for some reason ended in a full firework display that was only barely visible from the school hall.

'How bad is it?' Margery asked Sally, who was glaring between Rose and Rhonda, if only to get away from discussions about Rose's drama groups.

'Dreadful,' Sally said. 'I organised all these food vans and whatever to come from all over the place, and there's hardly anyone out there to order from them! Some of the vendors have come all the way from the big city...'

'London?' Clementine gasped.

'Weston-super-Mare,' Sally tutted, before her voice rose again hysterically. 'Worse still, the bands are all refusing to do their sets tomorrow. Mouldy Lemon is finishing their set and then they're leaving, and Barbara's Notebook have already left! They're saying we haven't paid them, but Elliot paid the invoices weeks ago. I can't get any of them to stay, even after I promised them extra tickets from the raffle. And speaking of the raffle, is anyone even going to be here to win the prizes? I've got an entire case of cava and a bird table to give away!'

Margery hadn't heard of any of the numerous singers and bands, but she was sure it would still be entertaining to say the least. Most of the stalls and food vendors were Christmas themed and she was sure the bands would be in the same vein. She was hoping to hear at least one terrible cover of 'O Holy Night' before the weekend was over.

Sally poured the tiniest drizzle of gravy over her paper-thin slice of turkey, before storming back out of the room again. The green room did seem dreary to Margery, who had always thought that the festival seemed a bustling and busy affair. She had been sure the green room would be quite exciting. So far, the bands had already come and gone and there was no one left to order anything. They waited another hour and then packed everything away, clearing the trestle tables and cleaning the crockery.

'Come on,' Margery said, once Karen and Sharon had finished mopping the floor. 'Let's go and watch the final band.'

Karen and Sharon whooped in excitement, barely removing their aprons before leaving with Gloria and Ceri-Ann. Margery took Clementine by the arm and they followed behind their colleagues.

Apex Void were making their way up onto the stage. Mike was missing, Margery presumed hiding behind the gaudy reindeer decorations before making his big entrance. The rest of the band were either reindeer or elves, which would have been much more fun if they didn't all look so miserable. Kevin stood to the side, glaring at them all with a big false smile glued to his face. Margery found it unnerving how he could look both supportive and furious at the same time. Sally and Doug stood to the side of the stage, Sally looked as annoyed as she had done when they had seen her in the green room. Doug, the hall organiser, seemed sullen, his face drawn. He wore a festive ensemble of a Santa hat that hid his greying hair, and a snowman-themed waistcoat tied neatly around his rounded waist. It was an outfit that should have brought its wearer an unprecedented amount of Christmas cheer, in Margery's opinion. Maybe the low ticket sales were bothering him as much as they were Sally.

The weather outside looked worse than it had, much worse. Rain pelted the windows so hard that Margery couldn't see the car park through them. The dinner lady team had debated leaving, of course, before the weather got too bad. Margery oversaw a democracy, after all. They had decided in the end to stay, purely on the reasoning that running the festival green room was a highly sought-after position among the town's caterers. There had already been a harshly worded letter sent into the *Dewstow Free Press* from their rival canteen at Ittonvale Comprehensive school.

Margery chose to see it as a sign of their success catering Seren's wedding among other things. The fact that they were being paid for the weekend was a marvel in itself. She never would have thought to take the money, but Rose had demanded that she take it and save it for the dinner ladies' end-of-year staff party. They usually just had a few picky bits at someone's house, but this year they could afford to go to a real restaurant.

Finally, Mike appeared from behind them all, the crowd turned to see him hurry in, slinging his guitar around his neck as he went. He rushed to the front of the stage, nearly tripping over the length of the red trousers he wore, the bobble of his Santa hat flinging around dramatically.

'Are you ready to rock?' Mike yelled into the microphone, quite unnecessarily. He sounded a bit out of breath to Margery. Perhaps he had underestimated the distance from the hall doors to the stage.

There were so few people gathered that he could have probably whispered it to the same effect. There didn't seem to be a single actual guest here, everyone watching was either a food vendor or a weekend volunteer. Mike had a point about it not quite being Glastonbury. He looked more than slightly intimidating with the pointy guitar strapped around his neck, and the scowl he wore told Margery he was probably remembering better gigs.

The band burst into noise, the guitars and drums rising to a crescendo, all distortion and cymbals. The lead guitarist played a lick that sounded very much like the beginning of 'Rudolph the Red-Nosed Reindeer', and Margery found herself tapping her feet along. The guitars rang out, and the drummer counted off on the hi-hat while Mike gyrated, the long white beard bouncing around on his chest. He stepped forward and yelled into the microphone, 'One-two-three-four!'

At which point, the lights went out and so did the amplifiers, leaving the drummer playing along to nothing but the gasps of the small gathered crowd.

Chapter Two

'Right!' Arthur Mugglethwaite yelled from the stage twenty minutes later. Margery knew him quite well, he was on the school council and was notorious gossiper Martha Mugglethwaite's husband. He was a welcome sight in the chaos, both halls were still dark and lit only by the torches and phones held by the crowd. Arthur's hi-vis 'Head Volunteer' vest reflected the beams. 'We're working on the electric and we should have the emergency lights on any moment now. This is just a temporary setback while we wait for some answers…'

Margery glanced at the large hall windows out into the darkness. There wasn't much to see, the glass being pelted as it was by heavy rain and the reflection from the phone lights being held up by the crowd, but she could tell the wind was dreadful from the sound of it whooshing past the building. Outside, someone struggled along the front of the building, fighting the gale, their coat almost like a cape, whipping out behind him.

There was a noise to the side door and Margery watched as Doug finally made it back inside. He was soaked through, water dripping from his head and running down his face into his eyes, which were wide and desperate. Sally met him at the door, reaching for him, but he whispered something to her and she stormed out of the hall like a train. Doug rushed up the steps of the stage towards Arthur. They exchanged hurried whispers and even through the gloom Margery could see Arthur's face fall. He sidestepped so Doug could stand at the front of the stage.

'There's no need to worry,' Doug began, twisting his hands together. Drops of rainwater continued to drip from his hair and roll down his face. 'I've just been out and, well… it's just that the road outside is currently impassable.'

The crowd began to murmur among themselves. Margery and Clementine exchanged a worried look.

'What do you mean?' someone called from the crowd. Margery was sure it was Rose's voice, she turned to see Rose behind them cradling her dog, Jason, in her arms. 'We've got to get home, some of us have dogs to feed!'

Doug held his hand up for silence, which he didn't get. Instead, he had to shout louder over the rumbling of his audience. 'The large oak tree by the car park exit has come down and blocked the road.'

'My God!' Karen wailed from behind Margery. 'We drove under that tree only a few hours ago! We're lucky to be alive!'

Sharon burst into tears and Karen put an arm around her.

'At this time, the police have asked us to stay put. We can't leave the building for our own safety. I just got off the phone with them,' Doug continued, waving his phone in explanation. Margery began to feel a cool panic roll down her spine at being trapped. She willed the feeling away. They were perfectly safe inside the hall. 'But rest assured, that's just a safety measure. I'm sure we're not in any real danger.'

'We'll walk around it, then!' someone else screeched. Margery looked around and saw to her surprise that it was Martha who had yelled. 'A smelly old tree can't keep us here. I'm claustrophobic!'

'We can't go out there,' Ceri-Ann told her. 'Have you not seen the film *The Mist*? What if the power's gone out because the sky is filled with monsters?'

'No monsters!' Doug chuckled cheerily before his face fell again. 'But the road is a mudslide, and it's freezing to ice. It's practically a death trap.' The water dripping from his raincoat had quickly become a puddle underneath him. 'When I spoke to Sergeant Davis, he assured me his best team is on the way, and they've called for help too, but until the storm stops, they can't do much. He's assured me that it will only take a few hours.'

The room finally hushed as everyone took in the information. Arthur looked mortified standing behind Doug. He looked between Doug and the crowd, his brow furrowing.

'What if someone needs an emergency appendectomy?' someone else cried and the hall descended into whispering again.

'I'm sure we can just have a little go of the operation ourselves,' Doug said, with a much too cheery grin for Margery's liking. 'Listen, there are plenty of drinks left at the bar, everyone gets one free with their wristband! And food vendors can stay open, so let's eat, drink and be merry. It's the happiest time of the year, after all!'

'And what, play some music off our phones?' a bitter voice called. It was definitely Rose this time. Doug's smile faded briefly, but then he put it back on.

'What we all need is a little drop of Christmas spirit!' he cried, smiling much too wide and showing too many teeth.

'I'd love a Christmas spirit,' Margery heard Rose mutter behind them. 'There'd better be flavoured gin at that bar.'

Doug lunged for Apex Void's keyboard, which was still set up on the stage along with the rest of the band's equipment. 'How about a little Christmas sing-song? "Rudolph the Red-Nosed Reindeer", come on, everyone!'

He launched himself at the keyboard, the keys clacking as he pressed them. The hall remained quiet, except for the murmuring of the crowd.

'Oh,' Doug said, backing away from the keyboard sheepishly. 'Of course, there's no power.'

The lights flickered back on suddenly, leaving them all under the horrible artificial glow of the ceiling strip lights. Margery put her hand up to her eyes, squinting at the sudden change in brightness as the Christmas lights around the bass drum on stage began to flash on and off manically. The doors creaked back open and Sally re-entered the hall, looking pleased with herself.

'I'll leave it to the professionals. Apex Void can continue now the back-up electric is on,' Doug said with a grin, forgetting all about the keyboard entirely. 'Thank you, Sally.'

Margery looked over to where Apex Void had gathered by the makeshift bar, they hadn't wasted a moment before getting a drink each. Mike looked furious at the suggestion that they needed to perform.

'Or... you know...' Doug stammered, probably having seen what Margery had. 'We'll put on some music!'

On stage, Doug slapped his hands together in glee, rushing over to the DJ booth. 'I Wish It Could Be Christmas Everyday' began to blare through the hall. Margery and Clementine exchanged a worried look at Doug's blasé attitude. He couldn't surely expect them all to just stay here? There must be a plan for the rest of the evening. Arthur shook his head too, obviously thinking the same as Margery.

The residents of the hall began to gather by the bar. Margery didn't know what to do after that. She wasn't good in groups and didn't fancy pushing through the crowd to get a drink. There didn't seem to be anyone manning the bar. Instead, it had become a free-for-all of people grasping for whatever they wanted.

'Listen, you must never ever tell anyone what I'm about to say,' Clementine said, in a low whisper. 'But I think at least a few of us should stay sober. I thought Gloria might, being a good stern Catholic woman and all that but…' Margery turned to look over to where Gloria and Ceri-Ann were happily opening a bottle of Prosecco, the cork disappearing into the air with a pop.

'Where's the party animal I married?' Margery joked. Clementine grimaced.

'Listen, I like a Frangelico of an evening as much as the next person,' Clementine explained. 'But the power's already gone out once, hasn't it? What if something else happens and everyone's too trollied to notice and then the rain comes through the hall? We'll all be washed away! If we're sober and awake then we can sort some boats. I'm not sure how… maybe everyone can sit in one of our big oven trays, we'll work out the details later.'

Clementine wasn't wrong, even if she was being a bit hyperbolic about the solution. The events of the day were already unprecedented, even given their very full history of strange events occurring in their presence. Who was to say it wouldn't get worse before it got better? It wouldn't hurt to stay sensible, and she wasn't really in the mood for a big night out anyway.

'Hiya!' a voice said. Margery looked up to find Elliot, the owner of Wrapmasters, looking down at them eagerly and holding a tower of takeaway containers. 'Would you like some chicken skewers? It seems a shame to waste them, but I mean, hardly anyone turned up and I cooked a load of stuff earlier thinking it was going to be packed.'

'Ooh yes,' Clementine said. 'We've been wasting away here!'

Margery chuckled, remembering the sheer amount of Yorkshire puddings that Clementine had eaten while they had packed the food away earlier. Clementine took a box and opened it excitedly. Margery took one too.

'Thank you so much, Mr...' Margery began, tucking into the chicken gratefully.

'Call me Elliot,' Elliot said with a smile. 'It's no trouble. Might as well try and enjoy ourselves if we're going to be stuck here!'

'Oh, Elliot,' Margery exclaimed, realising she knew the name and piecing the information together. 'I am sorry, you were the one emailing me for the booking! I didn't realise it was you. You're the person who booked us?'

'Yeah, that's me,' Elliot said with a grin. 'I do most of the bookings for the events now. It gives him and Sally the time to get on with better things, you know?'

'Well, that's nice of you,' Clementine said, through a mouthful of rice and chicken. 'At least it's more exciting than the last festival. The only good thing about that one was Father Christmas's beard falling off halfway through his entrance.'

'Doug was supposed to be Santa tomorrow so there's still time,' Elliot said with a laugh. Margery wondered if many children would arrive to visit the Santa's grotto out in the hallway. The store cupboard had been transformed into Santa's lair, though Margery hadn't visited it properly and didn't have much intention to. She had thought it was impressive, though, when she had passed it briefly earlier, all cotton wool and papier mâché that formed the entrance, leaving a doorway to enter by. It probably wouldn't be busy in this weather, it would be a long and boring day for Doug. 'At least most people managed to escape before the tree came down. I bet they won't pity us, having to sleep on piles of kitchen towel!'

'I bet there's a first aid kit we can take the foil blanket out of,' Clementine pondered. 'Maybe if it's big we can cut it into bits and all share it. Ooh! What about the fire blanket?'

Margery chuckled. 'It's looking like we'll all have to share that at this rate.'

'Yeah, I'm hoping I don't run out of stuff before we get rescued,' Elliot said with a chuckle. 'If that happens then anyone who actually paid the pitch fee to be here will get first choice of chicken.'

'What do you mean?' Margery asked, pausing with her fork halfway to her mouth.

'Between me and you,' Elliot lowered his voice to a whisper, 'I've been trying to nicely get rid of a vendor who was told they didn't have a spot here, but I'm not sure how to do it politely...'

He hadn't even finished speaking before the room was plunged into darkness again. Elliot sighed, sounding so tired Margery felt endlessly sorry for him. Worry overtook that quickly. No power surely meant no heating and no lighting and that couldn't be a good thing.

'Elliot!' a stern voice called from across the hall, interrupting them. 'There you are.'

Elliot startled in surprise before relaxing when he saw it was only Sally holding a torch. She made her way over to him, the beam cutting through the darkness.

'Where have you been?' she snapped. 'Come along now, I need you to help me with the electrics.'

'What do you need me to do?' Elliot asked, his eyebrows raising in alarm. 'I don't know anything about electrics. Surely they're difficult to fix?'

'No, difficult is telling your ten-year-old daughter that Geri Halliwell has left the Spice Girls,' Sally said in a dismissive tone. 'Do you know how many times we had to listen to "Viva Forever" that year? Now come along…'

Sally left, not even turning back to check that he was following her. Elliot turned to Margery and Clementine, wincing in apology, but then he plastered a smile onto his handsome face. 'Have a good evening, ladies. Duty calls.'

He followed Sally out, leaving Margery and Clementine alone again.

–

Margery wasn't entirely sure what Doug's version of 'a few hours' was, but an hour later it had become clear that they weren't going to be rescued tonight. As Clementine had predicted, the event had turned from mild Christmas festival to chaotic pub lock-in. They had both taken a glass of sherry and left Ceri-Ann and the rest of the dinner ladies enjoying a baby-free evening with Rhonda and Rose, who were all far too many wines in to hold a conversation with at a reasonable volume.

There was no choice in the end but to hunker down in the green room and hope for rescue the next morning. The bed of tea towels and aprons wasn't particularly cosy, but somehow Margery found herself drifting off easily into a shallow sleep. The Christmas music from the other room had joined her as she crossed over into the other realm, making her dreams flicker and twist with images of fairy lights and snowflakes. She was still very dimly aware of what was happening around her, but restful enough to not feel the need to get up.

There was a bang that made Margery's eyes fly open. She lay in the low light for a moment, listening to Clementine snoring next to her and the creaking of the building. The party hadn't shown any signs of stopping when they had walked past the main hall earlier, but it must be over now – the music had stopped and she could no longer hear the group's off-key singing. The power had gone off again a few hours before, which Margery had thought would wind things down, but had only seemed make everything much more of a ruckus, lit by battery-powered Christmas lights and phone torches.

The narrow window that ran along the top of the wall behind them lit the room in a purple overtone, night leaving as morning arrived, but still dark. It must be at least four in the morning. Margery lay on her back and listened to the soothing rhythm of Clementine's breathing. She moved a hand over to place it on Clementine's back so she could feel the air leaving her, in a way that was both familiar and comforting. Margery thought it was always strange to see someone asleep when you weren't expecting to. Unintentional vulnerability laid bare. Even someone you had slept next to for decades. Margery didn't always feel her age, could often swear honestly that she only felt thirty-five in her head, but she definitely felt sixty-five today after sleeping on the floor.

'You shouldn't have done that.' A voice sounded through the open doors of the green room. Ceri-Ann and Seren must have left them open. 'Why couldn't you just leave it alone?'

'I had to,' came another man's voice, higher and shriller than the first.

Margery realised that she knew the voice, but she didn't know it well enough to place it. Finally, they either gave it up or took the argument elsewhere and Margery shut her eyes again, willing for a drop more sleep. Things were quiet for a few minutes, and she found herself dozing off. Then, there was a crash.

Margery sat up with a start. She realised through a wave of confusion that the green room lights were on, the power must be back. She put her hand to her chest, willing her heart to calm down as she realised that the noise had come from a door somewhere out in the hallway, over the low thumping of the music that had returned. It went off as soon as it had come on, whoever was nearest to the speakers probably pulling the plug. Clementine was still asleep, but that wasn't unusual. She could have slept through an earthquake and the tea towel she had wrapped over her eyes made for a good makeshift eye mask.

Margery crept past her to the light switch and turned the light off. Something was happening in the hallway. She peered out into the corridor just in time to see a figure rush out of the grotto in a blur of red. She didn't get a good look at them, just of their back and the bobble of the Santa hat they wore as they disappeared through the nearest door, which slammed behind them. Margery couldn't imagine that it was Doug running around at this time of night with the Santa outfit on and imagined that he would be furious to find out that it had been worn. It was enough for Margery to go back into the green room and shut the door tightly again, shaking her head in annoyance at the drunken revelry.

Chapter Three

'This is a nightmare,' Clementine said, as they watched the breakfast queue build and build. It had already left the green room and begun snaking around the corridor and almost into one of the halls. 'It's worse than being at work. Why did we agree to do this again?'

'Well...' Margery hesitated, trying to think of some good in the situation and finding none. 'We didn't realise that there'd be a big storm, and we wouldn't be able to escape the place, did we? And Rose kept telling me how good it would be for the school's reputation. I didn't feel like we had a choice.'

Margery was frustrated. There had been no sign of Doug all morning, which was annoying Margery no end. If this had been her event, she would have been trying to make people comfortable with the situation, not sloped off out of the way just when people needed reassurance. If the weather was bad enough to down a power line, then was it bad enough to affect the building's roof? Would their cars all be able to withstand the wind? The storm certainly didn't show signs of stopping any time soon. When would they be rescued? Surely the police would have to evacuate them soon. There were a lot of questions and no one around to answer them.

Ittonvale community hall could only be accessed by driving down a winding lane that could be tricky for traffic as it was, it was a narrow one-way track that would have been steep for the minibus at the best of times. They had practically careened down it yesterday afternoon and Margery wasn't sure how they'd traverse it now, especially with a tree blocking the route. All the other food stalls were still closed. So much for helping Margery and her team with breakfast. Margery hadn't seen the owners of The Spice Girls since earlier yesterday evening, so they must have escaped. Margery wondered if you were supposed to think of the puns and silly names for things before you opened a food business. Everyone here seemed to have thought of the silly name first and then arranged their menu around it afterwards.

'We're going to run out of coffee,' Gloria hissed as she brought in another steaming flask of hot water from the boiler. 'We can't run out of coffee, Margery, not after last night. Seren tried to climb the Christmas tree. It took three of us to get her out from under it after she knocked it over. I thought she might have to wear it as a hat for the rest of the weekend...'

Seren did look like a person who had spent an evening knocking Christmas trees down. She was an unfortunate shade of white this morning and she still had remnant strands of tinsel lining her ponytail. Gloria said Sally had forced them all to go to bed in the end. Margery suspected that they would have all been up for much longer if she hadn't, though she wasn't entirely sure where they had all slept.

'I think I saw a vending machine full of energy drinks in the entrance,' Margery said, wringing her hands together. 'Perhaps we can get the key from Doug and serve them instead?'

Margery's brain was much too tired to think of any other solutions this morning. Even without the disturbance that had got her out of bed, the noise of the wind had kept her awake for the rest of the night and the green room's fire escape door had clanged and clanged against its hinges constantly, as if someone was desperately trying to claw their way into the building. She should really tell Doug or Sally to get that looked at. Sally was currently nursing a coffee and a roll on the table across from them, so Margery decided that it could wait for a while.

'Could the other food businesses not help us out at all?' Rose asked, glaring at Mrs Bell, who was next in the queue. She put a very small sliver of turkey onto the plate, which Mrs Bell took with a look of dismay. 'Surely they'd do well to see what stock they have left. I mean, this isn't really breakfast, is it? Unless you usually eat turkey sandwiches for breakfast. I, myself, do not. The cranberry sauce is quite cloying at this time of the day.'

'You'd think so, wouldn't you?' Margery said, not hiding her sigh. 'I don't think any of them are up yet.'

'Drank the bar dry, didn't they?' Ceri-Ann said, much too judgementally for someone who was wearing a pair of sunglasses and was as ashen-faced as Seren. 'I should know, I helped them do it.'

'Weren't you drinking some sort of caffeine-based cocktail?' Rose asked her. 'I'm sure I saw you with an espresso martini. Surely you're raring to go today?'

'No, no, no, not me!' Ceri-Ann said breezily. 'You're thinking of someone else.'

'You made me one,' Seren piped up from where she was serving stuffing balls to a confused-looking member of Apex Void. 'It was delicious.'

'You!' Gloria cried, pointing a finger at Ceri-Ann. 'You used all the Kenco! That was a catering-sized jar, it makes four hundred coffees!'

'I don't know what you're on about, mate.' Ceri-Ann shook her head, the sunglasses wobbling with the movement. She hid the steaming mug of coffee she was holding behind her back.

'This is a terrible day,' Gloria said with a sad huff of air, looking at Ceri-Ann like a mother would look at their disobedient teenager. 'It's worse than the day we had to help Karen sell her house.'

'We got the asking price for it, didn't we, though?' Karen piped up, then she and Sharon high-fived each other.

That had been a particularly bad day, Margery remembered. Each time a prospective buyer had entered through the front door with the estate agent, Karen and Sharon had run through before they entered each room, hiding things that might reduce the property value. Margery and Clementine had been left hiding in the shed, each holding a pet that Sharon thought would look untidy. It had been made much more difficult by the fact that Jenkins, Karen's cat, and Percy, Karen's dog, obviously hated each other and had not decided to become best friends in the confined space. The rest of the team had squished into Margery's car with bags of washing and other things that Karen hadn't had time to put away that morning. On the front seat she had squashed a life-size cut-out of Pedro Pascal, which usually lived in Karen's spare bedroom. Karen had never forgiven them for accidentally creasing one of the corners.

Before anything more could be said, there was a scream from the corridor outside the room.

'What was that?' Margery asked, as Clementine grasped for her, her hand closing around Margery's wrist tightly.

'Someone who realised we've only got teabags, probably,' Gloria said, still shaking her head at Ceri-Ann, but smiling all the same.

There was another scream, more painful than the last, a terrible wail that was so panicked and high that it made the hairs on Margery's arms stand on end. They followed the noise into the corridor, where a crowd had gathered. Margery saw where the scream had come from immediately.

Mrs Bell was standing to the side of the sign pointing to Santa's grotto, her face covered by her hands. The colourful cardboard door was hanging open now. Martha Mugglethwaite was trying to comfort her, but Mrs Bell's eyes were drawn only to the entrance of the grotto. Margery craned her neck to see what the upset was, just catching a glimpse of the legs that lay on the floor inside. Arthur Mugglethwaite shone his torch inside, illuminating the figure lying on the floor, legs crumpled horribly underneath them.

'Father Christmas!' Karen shrieked from behind Margery. 'Who'll deliver the presents now?'

Whoever it was, they were wearing a fake white beard, and the red Santa outfit Margery had seen briefly the night before, his face white and his eyes open and unseeing. His hands were gloved and lay at his sides. The sight took Margery's breath away, leaving her gasping for air. It must have been Doug she had seen sprinting towards the hall in the Santa outfit he had been meaning to wear today, but who had he been running from?

'What happened?' she found herself asking. Mrs Mugglethwaite raised her head to meet Margery's eyes.

'Thank goodness you're both here,' Mrs Mugglethwaite cried. She left Mrs Bell and rushed over to the gathering crowd and began to usher them back. 'Let the detectives through!'

'What?' Margery asked in alarm. Clementine shook her head.

'You are detectives, aren't you? The police are still working on the road,' Mrs Mugglethwaite said, as though that made any amount of sense. 'You're the next best thing. I hope you've got your investigation notebook with you… I'm sure we can find a pad and paper if not—'

'Sorry,' Clementine said, interrupting her. 'You can't possibly believe that we're as good as the police. Are you mad?'

'A man's been murdered here,' Mrs Mugglethwaite said, gesturing to the body as though Clementine might have simply not seen it. 'And not just any man, a man dressed as Santa. This could be a Christmas-related crime for all we know.'

'A Christmas…' Margery began. 'Martha, have you lost your mind?'

'You've heard the detectives!' Mrs Mugglethwaite screeched again over her, even louder than the last time. Arthur stood next to her, wringing his hands, the torch forgotten. 'Everyone out! Someone bring them a pencil for the investigation!'

The crowd began to disperse. Margery shared a worried look with Gloria and Ceri-Ann as they passed by them.

'Christ, Martha,' Clementine said. 'If I wasn't a bit deaf already, then I would be now. I'm being serious, what do you expect us to do?'

'I don't know,' Mrs Mugglethwaite said, her voice haunted. 'But that's why we need you to sort it.' She stumbled backward and leaned against the nearest wall, putting her head in her hands.

'Let me through!' The voice came from behind them. Sally pushed her way through the leaving people, stopping as soon as she clapped eyes on the body on the floor of the grotto. She rushed over and dropped to her knees in front of him, grasping for the man's wrist.

'No,' Sally said. 'No, it can't be... he can't be dead. He was so young!'

Young? Margery thought. Doug hadn't been young, unless Sally considered mid-sixties to still be brimming with the promises of youth. She herself did not, and Clementine was constantly bemoaning the fact that neither of them would be able to die young anymore. Arthur knelt next to Sally, patting her shoulder gently. He looked up and caught Margery's eye. He beckoned for them to follow him and led them out of the corridor into the empty green room. Sally's sobs seemed to follow them, rattling through the halls.

'No one could have got in or out of here last night,' Arthur said as soon as they were out of earshot of anyone else. His face was white and drained. 'If they did, then they would have been seen by the police at the top of the hill. I've been on the phone with Detective Symon of Ittonvale police, do you know him?'

'Know him?' Clementine snorted. 'We practically keep him in work.'

'Well, he says he can't get down,' Arthur explained. 'Hang on.'

He took his phone out of his pocket and began to ring out.

'How are you calling someone?' Margery gasped, thinking of her own phone, which had been a useless paperweight since they had turned onto the road down the hill to the hall.

'I'm calling using the Wi-Fi,' Arthur explained, gesturing into the air as if at all the invisible internet waves.

'Detective Symon speaking,' Symon said across the phone's speaker.

'Hello, Symon!' Clementine cooed, taking the phone from Arthur. 'Do you want me to get Ceri-Ann on the line?'

'The body!' Margery hissed.

'Oh right,' Clementine said, her eyes widening. 'Look, Symon, you can't be serious.'

'I'm sorry, but I am,' Symon said. 'That storm last night took out three trees on the way down to you alone. We're stretched thin trying to sort it all out. Ittonstow doesn't even have power back yet. I've had about four million phone calls from the village residents. God forbid none of them can boil their kettles this morning.' He took a deep breath. 'Obviously I want to get you all out, I don't like that Ceri's down there trapped, but Sarge already sent anyone who can help other places. You're all okay, aren't you? No casualties? Apart from the obvious I mean.'

'There'll be more casualties soon, Symon,' Clementine huffed. 'I've only got one inhaler with me.'

'Well,' Symon said, sounding to Margery like he was trying not to smile. 'Try not to use it all at once.'

'What should we do in the meantime, Symon! Should we arrest someone?' Clementine said, her mouth so close to the phone that her lips practically brushed it as she spoke.

'Just hang on until we can get down there,' Symon said. Even over the bad signal Margery could hear the wind whipping past his head. 'We've got every free officer from Ittonvale and Dewstow trying to sort this and manage the traffic from the nearby road, and the fire brigade are trying to get here with the gas and electric companies.'

Margery took the phone from Clementine. 'How bad is it?'

'Er…' Symon paused as if processing how to explain in a way that didn't cause them all to panic. 'The tree took out the power line, which is quite bad anyway,' Symon explained. 'But the thing is, it was rotten inside and in the roots. The roots came up and broke one of the gas supply pipes. The gas people have made it so you won't all… you know… explode in a fireball immediately. Sorry, probably could have picked my words a bit better, but there's still a lot to do to get it safe enough for you to leave.'

'Gosh, I knew the weather was bad, but not that bad,' Margery said with a frightened gasp.

'Yeah, thing is, it wasn't the weather that did it,' Symon said, his voice hanging ominously over the distance between them. 'We think someone pulled the tree down with a vehicle. We found a chain that would have been wrapped around the trunk of the tree. Whoever did that was lucky, mind. If it hadn't been rotten then they'd probably have pulled the tow bar off their car. Worst case scenario it could have fallen on them.'

'What?'

'All the stuff that was supposed to be under the ground… um… well it's out of the ground now. I'm surprised you couldn't smell the gas from the broken pipe down in the hall, it still stank when I got here,' he explained. 'Someone pulled that tree down on purpose, but we don't know why yet. I bet you could find out a bit more if you asked around. That bloke didn't just drop dead, did he? Arthur's going to send me some photos of the body and we'll see what we think.'

'Forget all that, how long will it take you to clear it all?' Clementine asked. 'We really need to get out of here, Symon. You can't leave us here with someone who's died!'

'Been murdered, more like,' Arthur said darkly, not bothering to look up.

Margery winced, realising that in her panic she hadn't even thought to ask how the man had died. She left Clementine and Arthur behind and went back out into the corridor, peering into the grotto at the body. She stared at his open eyes, the stupid fake beard covering his face. Gingerly she crept forward, taking in the horrible sight. Elliot's rugged looks were forever gone, his face was white, and his tongue hung from his mouth over his pale, dry lips. There was an egg-shaped bump on his forehead that looked like it had been moulded on with papier mâché as part of a student's art project. Margery took a step back, trying to find any words and gasping at the surprise of his face. She had been convinced the body was Doug, not suspecting for a second that it might be Elliot. No words would come. Just a horrible sick feeling that she knew she would never really escape from, no matter how much distance she could put between herself and it.

'That's murder,' Clementine said, from behind her. 'He didn't hit himself, did he?'

'No,' Margery agreed. 'Someone must know something.'

They shared a frightened look. Margery turned to gaze at the floor to the windows to the car park, the sleet battering the glass as the wind howled. Whoever had killed the man was still in the building with them. More than that, if the tree hadn't fallen by accident, the killer must have chopped it down to trap them all here with them. A roll of terror made its way down her back at the thought, turning her legs to jelly.

Chapter Four

It did feel as though they might be well out of their depth with this one. For one thing, when they usually helped solve an investigation it was not without the help of the local police force. Even when the officers involved had not wanted their help. This was a strange and frightening anomaly. Margery found herself wishing that Symon had been at the festival the night before. If it had been his rest day, he probably would have come down to see how Ceri-Ann was getting on. He would have brought baby Nick with him, though. Margery found her face falling even further at the thought of the toddler being involved with all this mess, and an unaccounted-for murderer still among them. Maybe. They hadn't proved if Elliot had been murdered or not yet, though Margery agreed with Clementine that the head injury might not be innocent. Still, there was no obvious murder weapon to be found and nothing much more to clear up. Yet, Margery couldn't get the image of Elliot running down the corridor away from someone out of her head, and she had shut the door and not intervened. She tried not to think about it too much, the guilt would swallow her whole otherwise.

'Do you ever get the feeling that we've bitten off more than we can chew?' Margery asked Clementine.

'All the time,' Clementine said with a grimace. 'I know Symon wants us to help, but who are we to meddle, really?'

'You love meddling,' Margery reminded her. 'You could win an award for meddling.'

'I don't always! For example, I would never meddle with time, Margery,' Clementine said gravely. 'You can't meddle with time. You might end up killing a dinosaur and then not be born or end up getting the bubonic plague or something, no, no. It's much better just to go along with it all.'

Even Margery, who had known Clementine for over four decades, didn't know what to say to that. Margery tried to think of what Symon might do next if he was down here with them and came up short. Surely Symon would have a good plan and wouldn't waste time before jumping in. Would he interview people first or shut the crime scene down? It was hard to say. Margery assumed he would have had an entire team with him. It felt very lonely just her and Clementine.

'Right, first things first,' Clementine said, changing the subject entirely as they marched back towards the green room. 'Let's find Doug and see what we can put in place to support everyone… Gosh, what a horrible thing. Then let's see what we can find out from interviewing people. There might be CCTV or something like that on site.'

'There isn't!' Sally called from behind them.

Her voice was a bit too smug for Margery's liking and not helpful at all. Margery usually had a bit of patience for everyone, even Mrs Mugglethwaite when she was in the middle of a rant about the price of postage stamps now that she had retired and didn't get her post office discount.

Today the very limited drops of patience that Margery did have had already evaporated with the breakfast debacle.

'Are you sure?' Margery asked her, trying not to sound as snappy as she felt. 'There's really nothing?'

'I told Doug we needed to install it,' Sally explained with a fleeting wave of her hand. 'More than once a group of yobs has left all their rubbish strewn all over the car park overnight. If we had cameras, then we'd have had them all arrested by now. Doug's too tight to get any and now look what's happened.'

Her reaction made Margery's stomach churn horribly. You couldn't surely compare a dead body with littering as far as crimes went.

'Where is Doug?' Margery asked. She looked around in confusion. 'Do you know if he knows?'

Sally shook her head. 'I don't, unfortunately. He must be around here somewhere, though, what with us being trapped here like zoo animals.'

With police permission, Arthur and a small group of others had taken it upon themselves to move Elliot's body into the chest freezer at the back of the building. Margery wondered if that would ruin the police's DNA testing or whatever else they did, but Arthur had seemed more concerned that the body would inevitably begin to rot the longer it stayed in the hall. Margery had watched the group carry Elliot out, wrapped in the tablecloth from his stall, and felt sick. The dinner ladies luckily hadn't had too much in the chest freezer and had been able to move it into the smaller fridges in the kitchenette. It brought back horrible thoughts for Margery, of their poor kitchen manager Caroline and how she had died in the school's walk-in freezer all those years ago now, Margery and Clementine almost befalling the very same fate. They had been lucky to escape then, but Margery didn't feel lucky now. All the shine had gone out of that first victory now that they had needed to repeat it more times than she liked to think about.

The spot inside the grotto where Elliot had lain still had a dark patch on the carpet where his head had been. Margery knew that if she went into the hall and approached his stall, it would all be clean and ready to go for the day. All she would have had to do was throw some chicken onto the electric kebab grill and in an hour she could have begun serving customers. The futility of it struck her. She wasn't sure how old Elliot had been, but he couldn't have been past his early thirties.

'Can you not call Doug for us?' Margery asked Sally. 'He should really know what's going on. He's in charge of the hall.'

'I've already tried to,' Sally grumbled. She looked worried, Margery thought, though they all had the tired look that Margery usually associated with camping and early morning holiday travelling. Sally looked particularly weary, the bags under her eyes dark and pronounced. She continued, 'He didn't answer, his phone was either off or had no signal.'

'You asked Elliot to go with you when we were talking to him last night,' Clementine said to Sally. She winced at the sound of his name. 'Did anything happen then?'

Sally looked like she didn't want to tell them, her mouth puckered up, pronouncing the wrinkles. 'We needed to organise the rest of the food and drink and establish a routine call between us and the police. Obviously we don't know how long we'll be here, and we don't want to run out of anything. It probably seems very silly to you, but we can't be running out of soap and toilet paper, can we?'

Sally looked as though she might cry for a moment, closing her eyes tightly for a second. The tears didn't fall.

'Of course, the only person who's paying any attention in helping to save anything is Mrs Bell and she's severely outnumbered by selfish ingrates,' Sally said, folding her arms tightly against her chest. 'I need Doug to get up from wherever he's nursing his hangover and sort this out. We need to talk about what we're going to do with Elliot, I need Doug to call his family. I don't know where the emergency contact details are kept or their phone numbers and I can't get into Elliot's phone because it's got no battery and I don't know the password even if I can get it back on, and maybe I shouldn't be trying to call them anyway. Doug employed him, he should contact them.' Her voice cracked and Margery felt the pang of guilt at questioning someone in distress.

Before Margery could comfort her, Sally's face warped back into the sour expression it had held before.

'What did the police say to you?' Sally asked, her eyes narrowing in suspicion.

Margery found herself feeling a bit taken aback in the sudden change in questioning. 'Detective Symon asked us to ask around and see if we can find out what happened—'

'I don't want you causing trouble,' Sally said. 'Poking about when we've got people to look after. If you want to be helpful then you should get planning an evening meal. That'll raise morale.'

'We weren't planning on causing trouble,' Margery said at the same time as Clementine scoffed.

'There's been a murder,' Clementine told Sally, stressing the word out a little too far.

'No, there has not,' Sally said with an indignant snort. 'Not on my watch.'

Even Margery paused for a moment.

'You can't possibly think Elliot's death was an accident?' she asked, thinking of the wound on his forehead. A young man didn't drop dead like that for no reason.

Sally made a small, strangled noise in her throat. 'That remains to be seen,' she hissed, her voice lowering to where it could barely be heard under the wave of people talking. 'I won't have you inciting a panic...'

'There'll be a panic if someone else is murdered,' Clementine assured her. 'The person who killed him must still be here.'

Sally didn't bother to respond, instead, she stormed away, rushing through the double doors and letting them slam behind her. It would have been much more dramatic if the doors weren't on soft-close latches, Margery thought.

They let her go, there would be plenty of time to ask her questions later. They hadn't heard from the police again so Margery assumed that they would still be here for a few more hours. She was beginning to worry that they might be here much longer than that. For all of Clementine's joking that they might miss Christmas trapped in the hall, time was ticking on. Her mind filled with worry still when she thought back to Sally's aggrieved expression. The police had asked them to help, so they must. That was what Margery told herself. It was not entirely soothing.

'Christ...' Ceri-Ann began from behind them, her head snapped to Clementine as Clementine's mouth opened to tell her not to swear. 'I mean... Christmas, look at that weather!'

Margery turned to see where Ceri-Ann was pointing and realised that she could barely see through the window as the rain continued to hammer against the glass. The building must have been getting a real pummelling. She hoped Symon and his team would be able to get them out soon. She didn't much fancy being trapped inside the building if it flooded.

'Ladies, did any of you see anything out of the ordinary last night?' Margery asked the dinner lady team. They all shook their heads.

'No,' Gloria said, then paused. 'Well, I mean, I did see some things I never thought I'd see…' They all turned to look at Seren, who still had tinsel in her hair. 'But I didn't see Elliot.'

'Did anyone?' Margery wondered out loud.

'We should retrace his steps, we'll probably find Doug on the way,' Clementine suggested. 'And at the same time we should look for a murder weapon. That bump is right in the middle of his forehead. I'm no forensic expert, but he obviously didn't get it from a fall.'

Margery nodded, they were both good ideas. They would have to ask around to get a good picture of where he had been the evening before. After leaving them to go with Sally, Elliot must have spoken to at least a few others in one of the halls. He probably spent the evening with everyone else and joined in with the revelry. The building simply wasn't big enough for him to have been on his own for long. There were two good-sized halls either side of a large reception area full of tables and chairs. The larger hall contained a stage where the bands had been playing, and the smaller had a bar built into the back wall. There was a big enough kitchenette at the back of the hub, which contained a double oven and a single undercounter fridge.

In a forgotten corner at the back of the hall lay a chest freezer, big enough to hold a day's worth of catering. The green room was out of the way, past the toilets and out of the public eye, but that was it. Hardly anywhere to sit and ponder your thoughts for the evening.

Margery suddenly thought back to the Santa outfit she had seen the night before. Why had he been wearing it? He certainly hadn't been earlier in the evening and Doug had been due to wear it today for the Santa's grotto. Had it been Elliot storming through the corridors and waking people up? Surely no one would have killed him for that, though, even if it had been maddening at the time. There was the argument that she had overheard. That had seemed off. But Margery thought someone must have seen something.

'Where is he?' a man's voice bellowed from across the hall, making both Margery and Clementine jump.

Mike was soaking wet, his hair dripping into his eyes and running down his face. The water rolled down his leather jacket onto the floor as he stood in an awkward hunch-like posture, as if that would stop it. His hand grasped the front of Arthur Mugglethwaite's shirt.

'Have you been outside?' Arthur was babbling, his hands trying to pry Mike's from his clothing. 'You shouldn't have been outside, don't let my wife see you out there!'

Arthur had been busily trying to keep the peace and stop his wife from leaving all morning. Margery had seen her trying to open the fire escape more than once. On her second attempt she had made it three steps before her umbrella had turned inside out and forced her back into the building.

'I can do whatever I want,' Mike barked.

'No, you can't,' Clementine said, stepping up to confront him with no fear at all. 'We've been told to stay here by the police and to not leave the building. Which part of that don't you understand?'

Mike gave Arthur one last sour look before he finally let go of the front of his shirt. Arthur staggered backward into Martha's arms, clutching his chest where Mike had held him.

'Who are you looking for?' Margery asked to distract Mike and let Arthur get away.

Mike glared at her too, before his face softened again. 'Kevin, obviously. You seen him?'

'No, not since last night,' she told him.

'How can he possibly go missing in a place this size?' Mike asked, throwing his hands up in exasperation.

'I don't think he's missing,' Margery said, her eyebrows raising in surprise.

That would be outrageous if it were true. Nobody was supposed to leave, and Margery didn't see how they could have. Not properly, anyway. Not with the downed tree and the danger of being electrocuted or killed in a gas explosion. Anyway, there couldn't possibly be two people missing, not in a hall. It was big, of course, but not big enough to lose anyone. Kevin would be wherever Doug was, she decided. It made sense and they had seemed to be friends from what little conversation she had seen them have.

'Did you check outside?' Clementine asked Mike. The question seemed futile as she gestured at the water dripping onto the hall floor from Mike's jacket.

'I went to see if he was in the van,' Mike said with a scoff at his soaked clothes. 'He's not. Wasted journey.

I'll have another look in the gents. He's got to be here somewhere.'

He must be, Margery thought. Though if he wasn't, she was very intrigued to know where he had gone.

Chapter Five

The hall had only just managed to calm down. Arthur was over in the corner being comforted by his wife. Martha had decided to give up on escaping for now, though Margery had caught her glancing over at the nearest fire escape longingly more than once.

Mike had disappeared as quickly as he had arrived, stumbling away and leaving a puddle behind him as he went. They had watched him go, listening to the squelching of his big black and silver boots. Margery had noticed them the day before because they had seemed oddly shaped. She had thought it was because she wasn't used to seeing cowboy boots on anyone older than the Year Eleven students gearing up for a family holiday in Ibiza, but it was only now watching him walk away that she realised that they must have had a concealed heel. They made him walk in a strange manner, almost having to lean backward to keep himself upright. Margery wondered how many inches taller they made him.

Margery didn't hold any judgement in the boots. She had always thought that it should be allowed for men to soothe their own insecurities the way some women did. Margery had spent enough time looking at the ever-growing constellations of lines on her face in the harsh lighting of their bathroom mirror over the years to know that you couldn't always help what worried you.

And she didn't think herself a particularly vain person. She imagined that if you had noticed something about your appearance that you didn't like and was not easily changed then you might well spend the time and money to correct whatever you thought was the issue. The only problem was that there could be so many things to worry about: your weight, your height, your teeth. Margery was glad that she was able to put it to the back of her mind most of the time, helped along by Clementine's constant comments about Margery's supposed radiant beauty. Margery had often wondered over the years if Clementine needed a new prescription for her glasses.

Mrs Bell had already returned to her mince pie and craft stall and was sitting quietly to the side drinking a glass of something and fiddling with the wreath she was making. Bits of wire and artificial holly littered the floor underneath her chair. She was so tiny, she was half hidden behind the boxes and boxes of Tesco's premade mulled wine. Margery gave her a wave as they made their way over. Mrs Bell had been the only craft seller who hadn't given up and gone home early, the rest had disappeared, leaving only a few strands of tinsel behind. Margery was sure she regretted that now, though she didn't look much worse for wear after finding Elliot's body. Margery didn't know her that well, but Mrs Bell had lived in Ittonvale longer than Margery had been alive and they had spoken at many of the town's events over the years.

Mrs Bell smiled at them as they arrived at her feet. 'I know you,' Mrs Bell said, the gap-toothed smile warming her face. 'You're the ladies who helped my friend Vivian.'

'Sort of,' Clementine said at the same time as Margery said, 'In a way.'

'You've come to ask me about the young man,' she said in a croaky voice, the grin disappearing.

'Yes,' Margery said, not feeling it wise to sugar-coat anything. 'I'm sorry you saw that…'

'I can't remember his name,' Mrs Bell said softly, giving them both an apologetic smile. 'I'm afraid I didn't see much, just… you know.'

'Elliot.'

'Oh yes,' Mrs Bell gasped, raising a finger in the air and tapping it to her temple as if that would help her remember next time. Margery wasn't sure it would. 'I was just walking back from breakfast and I thought it would be nice to see the presents for the kiddies, so I popped into the grotto and there he was.' She gestured at the floor dramatically with her hands, then her fingers returned to the wreath.

Margery nodded sympathetically. The police would surely be able to get more information from the grotto than any of them would with their eyes alone and so it had been taped off ready for Symon to come and inspect it. Margery didn't want to ever have to step foot in it again.

'I'm afraid I didn't see anything else,' Mrs Bell said. 'Did you want a glass of wine?'

'Oh, no,' Margery said. 'Thank you, though.'

'All right,' Mrs Bell said. 'Ooh, actually…'

'Yes?'

'I heard them arguing,' Mrs Bell whispered, but she didn't elaborate.

'Heard who, Mrs Bell?' Margery asked.

She always tried to be especially nice to Mrs Bell, who hadn't had the easiest life by all accounts, even when the conversation was so slow it had become infuriating. From what Clementine had told her, her husband had died young and Mrs Bell had never remarried, nor did she have many friends. She ran her stall, and she came to town meetings, but she didn't speak much. In fact, she never as much as made a peep most of the time. Sometimes Margery wondered if it was because she had forgotten how to hold a conversation over the years or if she had always been like that.

'Doug and Elliot, of course,' Mrs Bell said, lowering her voice to a hushed whisper.

'When?' Margery asked, leaning in to listen. She wondered if that was the argument that she had overheard before she had got up to shut the green room door.

'Last night,' Mrs Bell told her with a fierce nod. 'And now he's dead. A shame, a terrible shame.'

He was dead, Margery thought with a pang of sadness that welled up suddenly. It was a shame.

'Gosh, it's terrible you heard them arguing,' Margery said gently. 'Did you know Elliot well?'

'I did.' Mrs Bell nodded, picking up the artificial holly from the floor next to her and inspecting it. 'I used to babysit him years ago. We…' Mrs Bell trailed off, her eyes dropping down at the wreath on her lap. She tutted softly, it was tinged with sadness at the memory she must have been thinking of. 'We were going into business together, Elliot and I. Such a shame…'

'I'm sorry to hear that,' Margery said quietly, though she wondered what sort of business Mrs Bell was talking about. It seemed an enormous undertaking to start something new at her time of life. Margery wasn't sure that she would have the guts to do the same if she were in Mrs Bell's shoes. Especially as Mrs Bell hadn't seemed to remember Elliot's name a moment ago. A flicker of confusion edged along the outskirts of her mind. Mrs Bell couldn't be in the best of health if she couldn't remember the name of a work partner.

Mrs Bell waved a hand dismissively. 'It is what it is, dear.'

'Was it a catering business?' Margery asked.

Mrs Bell nodded. 'Yes, I was the main investor in what was going to be our new company. I can't imagine it will happen now.'

'Will you get your money back?' Margery wondered.

Mrs Bell gave a shrug so small it wouldn't have been noticeable if Margery hadn't been standing so close to her. 'We'll see.'

Clementine cleared her throat. 'Do you know what they were arguing about?'

'Money,' Mrs Bell whispered. 'It's always about money, isn't it?'

'I suppose it is,' Margery said, thinking back to the cases they had been involved in. Many of them had been about more than money, but she didn't think Mrs Bell would want to know that. Most people wouldn't want to know how frivolous the reasons to take someone else's life could be.

'I suppose we'll have to go to the funeral,' Mrs Bell said, with a sad sigh. 'I hope it's at a crematorium. I don't like graveyards. They feel a bit too much like window shopping at my age.'

Mrs Bell guffawed at her own joke. Margery didn't know if she should laugh too or grimace.

'Right,' Margery said, when no other words would come.

'You'll let me know if you find anything out?' Mrs Bell asked. 'I want to be the first to know. I was the first to find Elliot, after all.'

Margery assured her that she would try her best and Mrs Bell went back to her wreath making. Margery and Clementine might as well have been rendered invisible. They shared a look and then rejoined the hall.

Margery was about to suggest to Clementine that they try talking to someone else when there was a noise behind her.

'I think I can help you.' Margery turned to see the owner of Keep Rollin' sidle up to them, a glint of something in her eye.

Margery and Clementine had been briefly introduced to Jade by Sally on their arrival, and they had seen her setting up her stall, of course. But there had been no time to formally visit her or try her sandwich rolls, which Ceri-Ann had told them were all named after bands from the early 2000s. Jade was around the same age as Seren, with the exasperated look of a millennial who had very recently been forced to get rid of their skinny jeans and ankle socks. She was still wearing her chef jacket, her black braids pulled back tightly under the patterned bandana.

'I've got some information for your case,' Jade said, lowering her voice. 'I think I know who killed Elliot.'

'Really?' Margery gasped, leaning in closer.

Jade nodded. Her face lit up, but in something closer to malice than Margery liked. She tried to work out what that meant, deciding in an instant that she wasn't sure she trusted Jade at all.

'Jacob and Elliot argued last night,' Jade said, barely concealing a smile. 'I bet Jacob was the one who killed him.'

Margery found her eyes widening at the accusation. She hadn't spoken much to Jacob, but he had seemed quiet and mild-mannered when he had been setting up his food stall the day before. Though she had thought that his food might be more style than substance, he had certainly gone to great lengths to look the part with his leather apron that matched the colour theme of his stall.

'What makes you say that?' Clementine asked, matching Margery's thoughts without a single word passing between them. 'I've argued with lots of people, I've never killed any of them. Even if they deserved it!'

Jade stumbled at that, her brow furrowing as she thought. 'Well, it's suspicious, though, isn't it?'

'It is,' Margery said, trying to placate her enough to continue the conversation. 'But what was the argument about?'

Jade looked as though she wanted to lie, but instead she shook her head. 'I'm not sure. I saw Jacob go into the hall last night and then I heard Elliot arguing with him.'

Maybe that was the argument she had overheard as well, Margery thought. Someone must have argued with Elliot before they killed him. You didn't just kill someone. Unless it had been a random murder, which she didn't believe it could be. This was not the sort of place for random murders. If someone killed Elliot, even by accident, they would have a reason for wanting him dead.

'All right,' Margery said, at the same time as Clementine asked, 'Where's Jacob, then?'

'He was over by his stall,' Jade said, waving a dismissive hand over towards it. 'I'd best get off. You'll let me know what he says, though, won't you?'

She sauntered away back to her own stall, turning the sign that listed her sandwiches away from view as she went. Margery and Clementine watched her go. She seemed much too pleased with the idea that Jacob had killed Elliot, without much proof. Margery wondered if they should believe a word that she said. It was one thing to be suspicious of someone's activity the night of a murder, but quite another to immediately accuse them.

'She knows more than she's letting on,' Margery told Clementine. 'I think she has an ulterior motive for telling us about the argument. I know an argument happened, because we heard it, obviously. But she seemed very pleased to tell us and I don't like that. It felt more like she wants to get Jacob in trouble for something rather than help the investigation. She's got no proof that he killed Elliot, has she?'

'She did, and I agree with you,' Clementine said, scratching her chin. 'I wish I hadn't slept through it all, I might have been able to help you work out what was said. But it's a start, isn't it? Something to go off so we can solve this before we run out of crisps.'

'I'm more worried about Seren running out of her vape liquid before she risks going out for a cigarette,' Margery said, glancing over to where Seren was looking forlornly out of the window at the atrocious weather.

Seren was holding her lighter in one hand and puffing on the vape pen with the other. The strawberry-scented smoke curled up into the air sadly, the full cigarette pack still visible through the pocket of Seren's apron.

'Let's go and have a chat with him anyway,' Clementine said, taking Margery by the arm.

They wandered over, finding Jacob sitting down by his stall, which was empty, all of the charcuterie tidied away from the built-in refrigeration. Margery had found it a strange option for a winter festival when she had seen the stand the night before. She could see it being brilliant for guests after a wedding ceremony while the bride and groom went to have photos, but it didn't seem to really have a place here at the winter festival, which was more hearty soups and seasonal crafts. Elliot must have agreed, putting it right in the back corner away from everything else. Margery could tell that Jacob must be a bit peeved by that. When they had first seen the stall the day before, he had been sulking, twiddling his handlebar moustache with his fingers and looking over at the huge Serrano ham on its stand with sadness in his eyes. Margery had wondered briefly if the ham was just for display, but it did have a huge knife sitting next to where it waited on the stand. She wondered how much meat you could get from the huge bone. It certainly seemed big enough to feed the entire hall. The ginormous ham was gone now, along with the knife, and everything else was boxed up as well, leaving only the empty service fridge.

Margery had seen Jacob and Elliot talking in front of Jacob's stall yesterday while they had set up but hadn't paid it much attention at the time. Now she wondered if they had been arguing then too. Jacob certainly hadn't seemed in high spirits, but she had never met him before and didn't know if that was usual. You couldn't accuse someone of murder simply because they were grumpy. Jacob was scrolling through his phone mindlessly and looked up in excited anticipation when they approached.

'Hiya,' he said with a smile in a strong West Country accent that reminded Margery of childhood holidays in Burnham-on-Sea. 'You all right?'

'We are,' Margery said, finding herself unable to quite return the expression, the day much too dire already. Jacob didn't seem particularly perturbed that Elliot was dead, as he sat grinning at them. 'How are you?'

'I'm all right, mate,' he said. 'Wish I'd updated my insurance, though, you know what I mean?'

'I imagine you spent a lot of money on stock for the weekend,' Margery sympathised, thinking of the walk-in fridge packed with food for the festival back at the school. They hadn't been sure of the storage situation in the hall and Karen and Sharon had been due to pick up what they needed for today's meals that morning. It was not meant to be. Margery had been running through what she would do with leftovers in her head, plotting it all out for future meals. She could probably still freeze most of it, if they could get back in time to do so anyway. That didn't seem certain at the moment. They had heard nothing more about the tree situation since they had spoken to Symon, and Elliot's death was sure to hold things up even longer.

'Between us…' Jacob lowered his voice. 'This weekend was my last hurrah really. I said to myself when I booked it that if it didn't go well, then I'd have to look for a proper job. Looks like I'd better get my CV ready when I get home.'

'Gosh,' Margery said. 'Are things that bad?'

Jacob nodded. 'Couldn't be worse. This really isn't what I signed up for,' he said with a sigh. 'I think I've bitten off more than I can chew here.'

'Is there anything we can do to help?' Margery asked.

'Do you know anyone who'll buy all this food?' He gestured to his stall, which was covered up for the night. 'I was worried I didn't have enough, but now…'

He trailed off, but Margery wondered exactly how much financial trouble he was in. That could be a lead, maybe Jade was right in her suspicions. They had been wrong before, though, and Margery decided that it was not good to immediately jump to conclusions. Especially when you had people actively arguing and causing trouble, like Mike.

'Is it okay if we ask you some questions about Elliot?' Clementine asked him, changing the subject. Margery watched his brows raise in surprise as if he hadn't considered that he would be asked.

'Yeah, of course,' he said. He put his phone away and jumped up from his seat in anticipation, clapping his hands together. He was tall in a gangly way that was upsetting to Margery, like a plant that had desperately grown upwards searching for sunlight, much too quickly to support its own weight. 'Exciting, I've never been questioned as part of a murder before! What do you want to know?'

'Where were you last night?' Margery asked, thinking it best not to beat around the bush when trying to pry for information. For once, they had the total permission of the police to ask questions and everyone involved was trapped inside a building with them. It was an opportunity too good to miss out on with a single moment of hesitation.

Jacob raised a hand to gesture around the room.

'I was here,' he said with a shrug, looking at both of them with amusement crinkling the corners of his eyes. Clementine rolled hers.

'Fine, where were you when Elliot was murdered?' Clementine asked, trying a different tack.

Margery had been wondering to herself how Elliot hadn't been found until the morning. They couldn't have been the only people to hear the argument he'd had with Jacob or whoever. Surely if they had all heard that, then someone must have heard Elliot being murdered? Maybe he hadn't been killed in the grotto, but put there afterwards? But if that was the case then surely they would have seen or heard his body being moved.

'Well, I dunno because we don't know when he died, do we?' Jacob said, shrugging again as if the answer was simple. 'But for most of the night I was having a drink with Ryan and Mike,' he added, with a sigh that told her he thought that was very obvious as an answer. 'Ryan's my mate.'

'Who's Ryan?' Margery asked, feeling annoyed with the sheer volume of people she didn't know already.

'He's the bassist for Apex Void and Mike's the singer,' Jacob explained, not knowing that Margery and Clementine already knew who Mike was. 'We were in the other hall all night. I fell asleep under the stage.'

He laughed suddenly, nearly causing Margery to jump in surprise.

'God, only Mike could get me to do shots of vodka,' he said, with another chuckle. 'Bit stupid seeing as we can't even go and get a hangover McDonald's.'

'Can he vouch for you?' Margery asked.

Jacob nodded, turning his head.

'Mike!' he yelled across the hall. Margery whipped around to look where he had shouted. Mike had dried up somehow and was sitting with his head in his hands, but he looked up at the yell. His face still carried the look of someone who had drunk a very large and very old glass of milk.

'What?' he yelled back.

'Was I with you all night?' Jacob screeched.

'Yeah!' Mike shouted, giving a thumbs up and then folding his arms around himself sulkily.

'What about your argument with Elliot?' Clementine asked.

'I didn't argue with Elliot,' Jacob said with a shrug. 'I barely know him, why would we argue?'

'Well, Margery heard someone argue with him,' Clementine said. 'And then we were told it was you.'

'Not me!' Jacob said with a grin. 'Who'd you hear that from?'

'Jade,' Clementine told him.

Jacob chuckled again, but there was no humour in it this time.

'She's my ex,' he said. 'I bet she told you about the tomatoes too. She's had it in for me since then…'

'The tomatoes?' Margery asked, feeling her eyebrows raise.

'Yeah, she reckons I stole her secret sundried tomato marinade recipe,' Jacob explained. 'She uses it for her Blink-182-themed sandwich, Mozz My Age Again?'

'All right,' Margery said, feeling more confused than when they had first started asking him questions.

'Yeah, it is all right.' Jacob shrugged. 'It's mozzarella, sundried tomatoes that she makes into this tapenade thing and then basil, which you mash with a pestle and mortar. You have to mash it very precisely, three times one way and then four times—'

'Did you steal the recipe?' Clementine interrupted before Jacob could explain Jade's entire menu.

There was a pause. Jacob rubbed the back of his neck, looking away sheepishly.

'Well, maybe, but that's not reason enough to tell people that I killed someone, is it?' He scoffed. 'Makes you wonder what she's hiding.'

It did, Margery thought. Why would Jade do that? This was a serious thing, you couldn't just blame whoever you decided had annoyed you the most. Unless she had genuinely thought that Jacob and Elliot had argued. Margery wondered who she had really heard if not them. You would think that she would know her ex-boyfriend's voice quite well. Margery could have picked Clementine's voice out blindfolded from half a mile away, probably.

'I don't talk to Elliot anyway, not even to argue with him,' Jacob said with a dismissive roll of his shoulders. 'He's a dick.'

'Did you used to speak to him a lot, then?' Clementine asked. 'You must have at least a little to know that he's… that word. You just told us that you barely know him.'

Jacob looked upwards for a moment, the annoyance clear on his face. Then he sighed gently. 'You didn't hear this from me…'

'Go on,' Margery said.

'I've been avoiding him for ages,' Jacob said, dropping his voice so that only they could hear him. 'He's in charge of organising the festivals for next year and between us, he hasn't done a very good job of it.'

'Do you know where Doug is?' Margery asked.

Jacob shook his head. 'Nah, but he came in through the fire escape last night and left water everywhere and mud! I had to clean it up, proper slip hazard it was.'

He sat down and went back to his phone, scrolling through in a way that told Margery that his side of the conversation was over, but she knew that couldn't possibly be all he knew. Either Jade was lying about the argument, or Mike was covering for Jacob. There was something hidden behind his blue eyes and she intended to find out what it was.

Chapter Six

They left Jacob to it, though Margery suspected that they'd be back at some point for more concrete answers. It left them meandering aimlessly through the hall again.

'Now what?' Clementine asked.

'We really need to find Doug,' Margery suggested with a shake of her head. 'He's got to be here somewhere. He must have a better idea of what's taking the police so long to get down here.'

Clementine sighed. 'I feel like we've looked everywhere we can think of already.'

They had already been into the bigger hall, so they made their way through the reception towards the smaller one.

'How long are they going to keep us here?' Margery asked out loud, more to herself than anyone else. 'Surely they'll need to come and rescue us at some point.'

'Hopefully they'll evacuate us before Christmas Eve,' Clementine said as they walked. 'We'll miss out on picking up our turkey from the butcher. And Maria's supposed to be coming down! I tried to text her to tell her we're trapped but I've got no signal.'

Margery had no signal either and she was worried about more than texting Clementine's sister. Luckily, she had been able to use the hall's Wi-Fi last night to email their across-the-road-neighbour Dawn Simmonds and ask her to pop in and feed the cats. She knew Dawn had got the message because she had already emailed back a selfie of Crinkles with a brand-new bow stuck to her head and her face smashed up against Dawn's, who was smiling such a huge smile you could see where her dentures met her gumline. Margery just hoped that Dawn wouldn't use this unsupervised time in their home with free rein over their house keys to rearrange their furniture or teach Pumpkin how to use the washing machine. She wouldn't put it past her. That reminded her that Dawn's choir were supposed to be performing at the festival tonight. She wondered if it would happen. It did look doubtful. Dawn hadn't been in the hall the night before because she had been at home ironing her costume. She may well have had a lucky escape.

'The school's Christmas dinners are next week,' Margery said finally as they entered the other hall. She thought about how busy these few weeks were going to be anyway, without all the things that had gone awry. Saturday morning had ticked away as it was, and now with all of this going on it wasn't certain that they would be back to work on Monday morning.

'I know,' Clementine said with a nod. 'I helped you roll ten million stuffing balls to put them in the freezer.'

'I really wanted all this event stuff to be packed up so we could start again right away,' Margery said, worrying her lip with her teeth. 'That's why we didn't put ourselves down for Sunday. Ittonvale school canteen were supposed to be swapping with us tomorrow night.'

'Try not to worry too much,' Clementine said soothingly. 'What will be will be.'

It didn't look as though Doug was in the second hall either from a fleeting glance. Margery scratched her head. The lights had so far only come back to the main hall, leaving the other rooms dark and unsettling. Luckily, there were plenty of candles and battery-powered Christmas tree lights to light the way.

'Have you seen Doug?' Clementine called to Rhonda, who was sitting with Rose.

Rose had given up all semblance of helping the dinner ladies to do anything, volunteers rota be damned. She was busily feeding Jason and Ada Bones the last of the turkey from last night's 'simple roast', which Margery always forgot needed nearly every pan and dish in the kitchen to make. Lunch had very much become a 'help yourself to what's left' sort of situation and Rhonda's was a paper plate of stale Yorkshire puddings.

'No,' Rhonda said. She wiped her skirt, crumbs of Yorkshire pudding flittering to the floor. 'But I'd like to give him a piece of my mind. You'll let me know when you find him?'

They agreed that they would and began the search again. The thing was, Margery thought worriedly as she looked around the hall, there weren't many places to search to begin with. It seemed crazy to believe that they would find anything to prove what had happened to Elliot. They had already searched his food stall, which had been cleared of anything more than the catering equipment. Where was Doug hiding? Surely there was nowhere to hide. And there was Kevin as well. Mike had obviously looked everywhere he could think of if he had been out in the car park looking for him.

Between the group, they had already looked in all of the storage rooms and the toilets and everywhere else Margery could think of. She decided to have a short break, going over to Mrs Bell's mulled wine stall, which she had reopened at some point and was now serving tea and coffee too, though Margery didn't know where she had got it from. There was still a selection of her famous mince pies proudly on display, the pastry so pale still that they might as well have been cooked using the warmth of the winter sun in the car park. Mrs Bell was nearly the same colour as her mince pies. Her skin was almost translucent under the harsh overhead lights of the hall. They gave her an almost ethereal glow.

'Margery!' Clementine called.

Margery rushed over to Clementine. The hall hadn't taken long to descend into a medieval bartering system and the raffle prizes had all mysteriously gone missing. Margery had been sure she had seen a member of Apex Void drinking from a bottle of cava with a red bow and a raffle ticket attached to the neck. Margery noticed Jade out of the corner of her eye. She had put up a sign that promised her secret tomato recipe to others in exchange for a fresh T-shirt. In the other corner, Rose was in full performance mode.

'Get your full toiletries package here!' Rose bellowed. 'Roll up! Only a small donation needed, and all the profits go to the Ittonvale and Summerview school drama departments!'

Rhonda added a very small smear of toothpaste from the travel-sized tube to the bassist of Apex Void's finger. Margery stared jealously. The dinner lady team hadn't had any toothpaste or toothbrushes that morning and had resorted to sharing the mint Aero that Seren had been saving for a special occasion. What that occasion could possibly be, she hadn't said. Ceri-Ann had remarked sadly that she would sometimes skip flossing her teeth as a treat and then she'd promised them all that she would never take basic dental hygiene for granted ever again.

'This is daylight robbery,' the man scoffed, looking down at the toothpaste. But he paid anyway, tapping his phone to the card reader that Rose held out to him.

Margery wondered if that was the best use of the remaining communication that they had with the outside world but decided it was best not to go against Rose. If for no other reason than the fact that they'd need to buy the package themselves if they were here much longer, and it wouldn't do to be blacklisted. Rhonda gave the man a very short spritz with the aerosol can of deodorant and then beckoned forward the next person in the queue.

'Have you got any batteries?' Ceri-Ann asked as Margery noticed her. She and Seren were sitting on the floor, trying to get the portable radio from Karen's survival kit to work.

'No,' Margery said, watching them curiously. 'What are you doing? Trying to call for help? Or speak to Symon?'

'Oh, God no,' Ceri-Ann said, winding the radio again by the handle. 'I'm trying to get some music going so I can keep doing Whamageddon.'

'Is that the thing where you try not to listen to "Last Christmas" by Wham! until Christmas Day?' Clementine asked finally after a pause. 'You did it on karaoke last night, didn't you?'

'Yeah, I'm doing an alternative version where you have to listen to "Last Christmas" at least once a day because it's obviously the best Christmas song,' Ceri-Ann explained, as if what she was saying was perfectly sensible. 'All me and Symon's mates are doing it and I can't let Chantelle beat me. She heard it eleven times yesterday because she works at Tesco in Ittonvale. Symon said he went in there to buy a meal deal just in case it came on, which is cheating if you ask me, while I'm trapped here listening to Rhonda and Rose singing hymns while robbing people blind. I said, "You're lucky we aren't engaged, Symon, because I wouldn't marry you anyway now…"'

'Rose could sing it to you,' Clementine suggested. The idea made Ceri-Ann look ill for a brief moment.

'Ah, I really wanted to win this year,' Ceri-Ann said with a sigh.

'What's the prize?' Clementine asked.

Ceri-Ann beamed. 'It's a seven-inch vinyl single from the first release of "Last Christmas" in 1984!'

'You don't have anything to play it on, do you?' Clementine asked, her brow furrowing. 'Why didn't you say before? I bet we've got an old record player up in the loft.'

'Could you not play it on your phone?' Margery asked.

Both Ceri-Ann and Seren shook their heads sadly.

'Wouldn't count,' Ceri-Ann began, whooping as the radio burst into life. Seren and Ceri-Ann leaned in to listen, their faces almost pressed together in their eagerness.

'Come on, let's go and have a cup of tea and a sit-down,' Clementine suggested to Margery. 'We'll feel better after a bourbon biscuit or two and I'm not really in the mood to listen to anything Christmassy.'

'*You'll* feel better after a biscuit, you mean,' Margery said, though she smiled at her anyway.

'Listen, the list goes: you, the cats and then bourbons, as you well know.'

They managed to find a cup of tea and a quiet corner of the hall. They sat down on fold-out chairs next to the largest of the artificial trees, the twinkling lights reflecting off the plastic baubles in a pleasing way that reminded Margery of cold winter evenings and advent calendars. The biscuits eluded them. The entire catering box of them Margery knew she had packed had disappeared somewhere. Margery suspected that Rose had a say in that but didn't feel like arguing with the woman. She was sure that if she wandered over to where Rose and Rhonda were holding court, then Margery would find the custard creams and bourbon biscuits removed from their pre-portioned packaging and laid out for sale for about sixteen pounds each.

Margery briefly wondered if that was what would happen to society at large if there were ever a large-scale apocalyptic event. All bartering and pillaging. Clementine often bemoaned the fact that they lived too far away from a big city. 'We'll have to get straight in the car and drive directly towards London as soon as we hear the nuclear warning if we're going to be lucky enough to die in the first blast,' she had said numerous times over the years. 'I don't know about you, but I'm not boiling water for anything but a cup of tea. We'll take the cats with us and a couple of deckchairs. It'll be a fun final day out!'

Clementine had begun to fiddle with something at the bottom of the wall.

'What's that?' Margery asked, as Clementine's fingernail scraped against the flaking plaster. There was something sticking out from a hole in the skirting board and jammed behind the radiator, though she couldn't see what it was.

'No idea,' Clementine said, in a way that told Margery she knew exactly what she was trying to do. 'It looks like there's a wire loose here.'

'Well, should you be touching that, then?' Margery asked in alarm. 'What if you get electrocuted?'

'No, no, don't worry about that.' Clementine chuckled, still tugging at the wire. 'My clogs are rubber, aren't they? The electricity will just shoot straight through me into the ground. That's what it does.'

'That's not how electricity works at all,' Margery said, putting down her mug so she could try and stop her. 'And you're sitting on the floor… and you're not wearing your shoes!'

'It's not *not* how electricity works,' Clementine said with a grin, giving the wire another tug. 'Who are you? Benjamin Franklin?'

'Do you not remember when you kept fusing the house because you kept trying to plug in that broken hairdryer?'

'I do,' Clementine said sadly. 'My hair was dry by the time I'd got the ladder out of the shed and turned all the fuses back on.'

'You're ridiculous,' Margery told her, reaching for her arm.

Clementine batted her arm away, 'Don't touch me because we'd both die if it does kill me, and you're too lovely to die here.'

Margery rolled her eyes. She was about to tell Clementine that she seriously shouldn't be rummaging around in a wall when the wire suddenly gave way. The skirting board popped open just enough that the end of the wire was visible, the rest hidden behind the radiator. Margery murmured in interest at what Clementine had uncovered.

'Oh!' Clementine said, looking very surprised to still be alive. 'See, I knew it wasn't going to kill me!'

Once Clementine had pulled enough wire through it became clear what it was. A string of skull-shaped fairy lights. They didn't come out easily from behind the radiator, Clementine had to tug them free.

'Well, they're interesting, aren't they?' Margery said as Clementine held them up to inspect them. 'I mean, perhaps not for our Christmas tree, but…'

Clementine bemoaned that you had to flick through sixteen different settings on their tree lights before you found one that didn't make your living room light up like a school disco. Margery was just glad that they had replaced the old fire hazards that they usually threw on the tree.

'Mr Fitzgerald would have liked them, wouldn't he?' Clementine said agreeably. 'Why were they behind the radiator, though? That seems a bit more than odd.'

It did, Margery thought. She stared at the skirting board suspiciously as though if she glared at it long enough the wall would crumble to reveal more of its secrets. The hall certainly seemed to contain more than enough mystery to be getting on with.

'I haven't seen lights like these before,' Clementine said, looking down at the bundle of wire and bulbs lying on the floor in front of her.

Margery picked the lights up by the string. They were the newer sort of lights, safer than the old style, so they couldn't have been behind the radiator for that long. It was certainly a style choice, you definitely didn't see many skulls with Santa hats on. Especially not in light form. 'They're not normal Christmas lights, are they? We wouldn't have them on our tree.'

'Why not?' Clementine said. 'I quite like them, actually, they're growing on me. Maybe we should borrow these once we've worked out why they were in the wall?'

'Where would you put them?' Margery asked curiously.

'On the cats' Christmas tree!' Clementine explained. 'They love a skull.'

That wasn't not true, but Margery wasn't sure where in their tiny two-bed terrace they would fit a smaller Christmas tree for the cats, it was barely big enough for their full-sized plastic tree and all the other assorted items they had gathered over the years. Margery sometimes felt sorry for whoever had to clear the house out once they were both dead. She suspected they would leave it all to Ceri-Ann to sell for baby Nicholas. Maybe she should put a date in the calendar for a few years' time to begin sorting it all out, throwing away the old Argos catalogues and the half-finished tins of paint. After they had both turned seventy, maybe. She was sure she had read about that process somewhere, Swedish death cleaning. She couldn't remember what it was called in Swedish, but it had always seemed like a good idea to her. You came into the world with nothing, and you would leave it much the same. There was no use holding on to things as they reached the inevitable conclusion.

'What should we do now?' Margery thought out loud. There didn't seem to be many options.

'Well,' Clementine said, scratching her chin. 'We could go and question everyone again to see if anyone's had any more ideas about the murder weapon and then we can ask about this set of lights. Maybe it's from a set or a pack. We'll need a few of them for the cats' Christmas tree, won't we?'

'I can't see what good asking about the murder weapon again would do,' Margery said. 'Other than make people annoyed at us. If they aren't already. Tensions are running quite high in the hall, aren't they?'

'That's an understatement,' Clementine chuckled. 'Gloria told me that Sally accused her of killing him with our kitchen rolling pin, which is funny, isn't it, seeing as she told us that Elliot hadn't been murdered...'

'I don't think the murder weapon is going to just jump out at us,' Margery told her as they walked back through the hall doors. 'I think if whoever did it was clever enough to get away until now then the weapon is probably well hidden, or might have even been taken away from the building.'

'Yes, and if someone did use our rolling pin they could have just rolled it away across the car park,' Clementine said thoughtfully. 'Though I suppose that's a long shot, isn't it?'

It was an understatement at the very least.

Chapter Seven

There was nothing left to hang around in the hall for, so they re-entered the green room, where the dinner lady team were lounging. Margery thought that they all looked quite relaxed for a group that had very recently seen a dead body and were trapped in a building and cut off from the rest of the world. She supposed that was a good thing. The alternative was blind panic.

'I'm just saying I don't think it's autograph-worthy,' Ceri-Ann was saying while Sharon and Karen scoffed.

'Of course it is!' Karen said. 'Just because he's not as famous now doesn't mean we shouldn't get him to sign something for the canteen. We aren't going to meet anyone more famous, are we? Taylor Swift isn't going to land her jet on the school playground, is she?'

'Yeah, and even if she did, she'd probably only want a takeaway piece of cornflake crunch and pink custard before leaving straight away,' Sharon butted in loudly. 'She's a very busy woman, she hasn't got time to sign oven trays for us—'

'But what's the point of it if the students don't know who he is?' Gloria tutted. 'No, I'm with Ceri-Ann on this one. It'll just be a weird squiggle on an oven tray. You can't hang that up. Environmental health will have a field day if they see it at work.'

Karen looked sadly at the large oven tray with the Sharpie pen scrawled over it.

'Who did you ask to sign it?' Margery asked, looking over at the tray curiously.

'Mike from Apex Void,' Ceri-Ann said, her voice holding back a definite scoff. 'Was he even big when you were younger? They weren't as good as Wham!, were they?'

'I don't know, really,' Margery said, tapping her finger to her chin as she tried to remember. 'I don't think I had any of their records or anything like that. I wasn't really into thrash metal. Clementine was, though, when I met her she had a nose piercing… It had a safety pin through it!'

The team turned to look at Clementine, who shrugged.

'Why are you all so surprised?' Clementine said. 'I could have been in a band! I'm annoyed by everything enough to write angry lyrics. I had to get rid of the piercing, though, my mother hid my house key one day and wouldn't let me in until I took it out. She said it was unsightly, but I think she was just annoyed I'd taken it out of her sewing kit.'

Karen shook her head. 'Apex Void have changed genres since the eighties, though! Mike's like the only original member left.'

'Yeah, they changed genres because it's a cash grab,' Ceri-Ann said. She pulled out her phone and began to scroll through it. 'Look at this terrible version of "Last Christmas" they did the other week. I've been looking through their other stuff as well. They're obviously trying to go viral. But it's not what that band used to sound like at all.'

She held up her phone and put it down on the table so they could see, all crowding around it. Onscreen, Apex Void burst into a much too upbeat version of 'Last Christmas'. Mike wore the same Santa outfit he had been wearing on stage the night before and the band were all dressed as reindeer. It was fine, as Christmas cover songs went, but Margery didn't think any of them looked like they were enjoying themselves. Some of the issue was that all the other members of the band were a good twenty years younger than Mike as Karen had said.

'Where have you two been?' Gloria asked as the video played. Karen and Sharon bobbed their heads along with it.

'Doing our jobs as detectives,' Clementine said with a gleeful grin. Margery rolled her eyes.

'Found anything?' Gloria asked. 'I'm getting a bit bored, which I never thought I'd have to say during an ongoing murder investigation.'

'Me too,' Ceri-Ann said with a sigh. 'And I miss Nick. My mum's been video calling, though. He's having the greatest time at Nanny's. I bet he won't want to come home.'

'I'm having a nice time,' Seren piped up. She was still tapping along with her foot to the Apex Void video that was still playing. 'It's nice to spend time together, isn't it? Like a family.'

'Are you mad, Seren?' Gloria asked, turning to her with her lip curled up in disgust. 'How much more time can we possibly spend together? We do every day at work and then I see at least one of you pretty much every weekend. When does it end? With our deaths? When will that be?'

Possibly sooner rather than later, since there was still a murderer running around, Margery thought dimly.

'It is sort of nice,' Karen said.

Sharon nodded. 'Like a little holiday.'

'Yeah, exactly!' Seren grinned, though her face fell just as quickly. 'Except there'd probably be more food on a holiday… but remember when we went away for Rose's hen do, that was great, wasn't it? We've been saying for ages we should all get together again out of work. Maybe an all-inclusive to Gran Canaria or something?'

Margery thought about Rose's hen party and the week's holiday that had built up to it, it had been fun. Even though they had of course ended up embroiled in an old town saga and nearly imprisoned by St Martin's-on-the-Water's local police force. Still, a good time had been had by all in the end.

'If we all get out of here alive, we'll all book to go away together in the summer holiday break,' Margery said, hoping she would get to keep her promise.

She turned back to the video. Onscreen, Mike was thrusting his hips in a horrible way to the beat. His guitar was forgotten in his hand and the Santa hat on his head was bobbing around so much it was amazing it had stayed on. Maybe he'd glued it on for the day, Margery thought to herself. Or used Velcro. The shot changed to the drummer, playing an elaborate momentary drum solo before Mike appeared again. There was something absolutely horrendous about Mike's gyrating. Margery didn't think that anyone her own age should attempt to move their body in that way. It couldn't be doing any good to his aging hips.

'Wait,' Clementine said, gesturing to the phone. 'Quick! Wind it back.'

'You can't wind back a phone video,' Ceri-Ann said, but she replayed it with a tap of the screen.

'Look, Margery.' Clementine pointed at the screen. Ceri-Ann looked too, quizzically.

'Oh!' Margery said. She turned to Ceri-Ann to explain. 'We found some lights hidden in the hall that look exactly like those.'

The scene had changed to the band playing outside in a car park. The skull-shaped lights were around the bass drum, flashing different colours.

'Oh wow.' Clementine whistled. 'Were they on the drum kit last night? I can't remember.'

'Not the same exact ones, though, surely?' Margery wondered out loud. 'Why would they be hidden in the hall? That video wasn't filmed here, was it?'

'Doesn't look like it,' Clementine said. 'Ooh, let's go and ask Apex Void where they got them from!'

'Shouldn't you be finding the murder weapon?' Gloria asked. 'Only I'd like to go home at some point soon. I've got mince pies to make with the kids.'

'Yes, we really should,' Margery said, getting up from her seat. 'I'm not sure how, though. We haven't found anything that could have killed him yet. Come on, Clem, let's go and have another look.'

Clementine followed Margery back into the main hall. There was still no sign of Kevin, but Mike and the rest of the band were sitting in the corner still. Laughing and joking, it was a complete turnaround to the angry man who had almost attacked Arthur not even an hour ago.

'What can I do for you, love?' Mike asked as they got closer. Margery found herself growing annoyed by the smarmy look on his face. How could he think he could act how he had and then just switch back on the charm immediately after? They had all seen his little outburst, after all. 'I'm not signing anything else for your ladies, I think that's got a bit out of hand. If you want to set up a private VIP meet and greet, it can be arranged – for a price, mind.'

'Oh no, thank you,' Clementine said quickly. Margery saw Mike's face fall for a moment before he put the mega-watt smile back on. The veneers were much too big for his mouth. Margery wondered how he kept it closed while he slept, perhaps he taped it shut. 'We just wanted to know, where did you get the skull Christmas tree lights from?'

Mike didn't say anything. Instead he stared at Clementine, blinking at her in confusion.

'They were in your music video,' Margery offered in explanation.

Mike ahhed in acknowledgement. He shrugged. 'I'm really not in charge of stuff like that. I just turn up and sing.'

Something else crossed his features for a fleeting second. Margery realised she had seen the look a moment earlier when Clementine had asked him about the lights, but she couldn't quite put her finger on what it was. She was usually quite good at reading people, but Mike seemed to be acting. Maybe the look underneath his smile was distress or anger, it was hard to tell.

'That video was Kevin's stupid idea,' Mike said, shaking his head at the thought of it. 'He's always trying to find new ways to get a new audience. Not going to happen, I keep telling him that. We need to concentrate on the tunes, not try and get kids now to listen to us. We're way past it in their eyes, but we've still got another classic album in us. Our fans will love it. Kevin keeps reminding me that the fans are getting on as well and popping their clogs.

Look at you, you're probably about the average age of our fanbase.'

Margery decided to ignore that, Clementine didn't seem to have noticed the dig.

'You really don't know where they're from?' Clementine asked. 'Don't you get any say on what your videos look like? I thought you were the star? Margery's allowed to choose what goes up in our kitchen at work.'

Mike flicked a hand dismissively. 'I didn't dress that set, did I? I just turn up and perform. That's all I want to do. You need to talk to Kevin about where he got them from, I dunno.'

'Where is he?' Margery asked.

'I still don't know,' Mike sighed. He looked around like Kevin might suddenly materialise. 'I wish I did.'

'Have you told Kevin your concerns about the band?' Margery asked.

'Of course I have,' Mike scoffed. 'But he doesn't listen to me, does he? Just gets my contract out and shows me where I signed on the dotted line. I'm just the face and all that. He reckons he's the brains. I'm not so sure, none of his schemes have worked recently, have they? Not when we're still doing gigs like this... er... no offence.'

'None taken,' Clementine said cheerily.

Mike looked down at his watch. 'Now, if you'll excuse me...'

'Somewhere to be?' Margery asked.

'I told my wife I'd call her at two,' he explained. 'She'll get funny if I miss it. I know she thinks we're probably all just having a jolly in here, but it's getting a bit weird, don't you think? Best to hold on to some sort of normality.'

'Getting a bit weird' was the very least of it, Margery thought. And Mike had been the main perpetrator with his temper tantrum – after the discovery of Elliot's body, that was. They were only a few steps away from having to sell their kitchen equipment to Rose to buy the vending machine snacks she had hoarded.

'When you see Kevin, tell him I've got a bone to pick with him,' Mike said, his face souring. 'I can't believe he's just dumped us here.'

–

'Well, back to the drawing board on the lights, then, and we're no closer to finding what Elliot was hit with,' Clementine said as they made their way through the halls and back to the green room. 'And I don't like that all the people who might have answers are missing. Where's that band manager, for one?'

'I don't know,' Margery admitted. 'Could he be with Doug?'

'Well, they don't seem to be anywhere else here,' Clementine grumbled. 'Is there a chance they might have left?'

'I don't see how,' Margery said. 'But maybe they're outside?'

They reached the other hall and Margery looked out of the huge windows at Apex Void's van in the car park. The snow was gathering over the vehicles parked. The windscreens lay thick with it, reminding her of cotton wool stuck to a homemade Christmas card.

'Let's go and see if he's in the band's van,' Margery said, suddenly feeling much braver than usual. 'I know he wasn't there when Mike went out, but maybe he is now? Or he might have left something to explain where he's gone.'

'Yes, good idea! Then let's search Elliot's van,' Clementine said with a pleased grin. 'He must have had one. How else would he have got all of his equipment here? Everyone has a van except us with the school minibus. I hope it sitting in the car park gets rid of the smell of teenagers' feet. All I could smell was socks on the way here.'

Checking Elliot's van was not the worst idea that they had had, Margery thought. Maybe it would give them some insight into why he had been killed in the first place.

'But the keys?' Margery began. Clementine smiled.

'Arthur put them in a bag with the rest of Elliot's valuables when they moved his body,' she explained. 'We'll just have to ask him for them.'

Chapter Eight

It had pained them both to put their shoes on and traipse out into the cold. Margery could only thank their lucky stars that their footwear was the polyurethane clogs they usually wore at work and they were non-slip, though it didn't stop her toes from freezing inside them. Arthur must have been under the impression that they were really detectives because he had given over Elliot's keys without asking even a single question.

Margery wondered why. Surely there was some sort of protocol when things like this happened. Sally certainly seemed like the sort of person to take things very seriously, perhaps she wouldn't have been as happy to assist them. Doug seemed the same way. A stickler for the rules. They were different people written in the same font, as far as Margery was concerned. There must have been a folder full of risk assessments somewhere in the building. Margery knew that obviously there couldn't possibly be one for when a member of your team was murdered while dressed as Father Christmas, but there may have been something similar to use the guidelines of. She made a mental note to update her own kitchen records as soon as they were allowed back out into the real world.

Even as bundled up as they were, Margery could still feel the wind battering her face through the scarf wrapped around her head. She didn't dare take a moment to see if

Clementine was okay, she wasn't sure she would be able to remain standing if she did. To think that they could have spent the entire time at home watching the rain pound against their own living-room window, cups of coffee in hand and joined by the cats. Margery had always had a bad feeling about taking the job on, but she had reasoned that her concerns lay in the workload. It was a bit gratifying to realise that she had been right, even though it wasn't for the reasons she had thought it would be.

Clementine led the way. Margery followed, the wind whistling horribly in her ears and the ground slippery with sleet and snow. Her vision narrowed down to Clementine's orange raincoat. She reached out a hand to keep a finger on her, shuffling along behind. Clementine reached the van door and fumbled with the keys. It unlocked with a clack that Margery could barely hear over the weather. Clementine managed to get the door open, and they climbed inside. Margery's kitchen clogs slipped on the step up and she nearly fell back. Clementine grasped for her arm, saving her before she could fall onto the cold tarmac, which might as well have been an ice-skating rink.

They sat back on the van seats, panting as Margery slammed the door shut for a temporary reprieve from the cold air. The windshield instantly fogged over, though they wouldn't have been able to see through the thick layer of ice resting on the outside of it anyway. Margery found an unexpected wave of claustrophobia wash over her at the idea of being shut away, unseen from the rest of the world. They hadn't told anyone apart from Arthur where they were going and she had felt uneasy about that even before they had got to the vehicle.

'Well,' Clementine gasped, 'I certainly wish I'd taken a few ice-skating lessons after that.'

'Or, in the very least, tried rollerblades,' Margery said as she tried to catch her breath. She stared out of the passenger-side window at the snow falling. Even if there was something to find, it would be much more difficult to see now, under a layer of fresh snow.

'I think our luck's run out,' Clementine said gloomily. 'How often does it snow, really? Once every few years here? We're right by the Severn, it's usually too mild for snow like this. It's usually just a sprinkle at worst.'

'Yes,' Margery said. 'We did have that big storm a few years ago, but I don't remember it being this bad.'

'There was no bread left at the supermarket.' Clementine laughed. 'Remember Martha and Dawn fighting over the last tin of tomato soup?'

Margery smiled at the memory. 'Yes, and Dawn lost her grip on it and went careening into the eggs.'

She reached out and opened the dashboard, rummaging around inside.

'What are we looking for exactly?' Margery asked as she searched. Clementine had begun to peer through the side storage next to the steering wheel, pulling out takeaway leaflet after takeaway leaflet.

'I don't know. Anything, I suppose,' Clementine said, looking as confused as Margery felt. 'More fairy lights, a written admission of guilt for stealing some sort of tomato sauce recipe. Honestly, Margery, these people!'

'I don't think Jade would have blamed Jacob for killing Elliot just because Jacob stole her recipe,' Margery thought out loud. 'Surely not? And we don't know what motive Jacob would have had.'

'People have killed for less,' Clementine said darkly before making a noise of triumph. 'How about this?'

It was a printed letter with the *Ittonvale Community Events Committee* header, and it was signed by Doug. Margery scanned through it. It was a brief but informative letter promising Elliot that Wrapmasters would be receiving the peak slot at the upcoming Ittonvale summer festival as part of their agreement and to keep up the good work with organising the rest of the food stalls.

It surprised Margery that Doug would so brazenly give Elliot preferential treatment, even if he was one of the organisers. She wondered what their agreement had been for Elliot to receive such an accolade.

The summer festival was almost as big of a deal as the Christmas one in Ittonvale, even if Margery didn't like it as much. To have the best food truck slot would be a coveted thing indeed and there would have been questions about Doug's blatant nepotism with Elliot. Margery wondered if all the traders inside the hall were really telling the truth on how they felt about Elliot. A thing like that could certainly cause some rivalry if it had been discovered. Margery thought back to Jade and her faux concern. There was definitely something more to it all. Jacob had said he didn't know Elliot well in the same breath as he had condemned him as a bad person.

'I thought Elliot was in charge of booking events?' Clementine said, reading it over her shoulder. 'Why is Doug sending him letters like that? This would cause a lot of bitterness if the wrong person saw it.'

'I thought so too,' Margery said, handing the letter back to Clementine. 'It's a shame we can't find Doug. He's got a lot to answer for, hasn't he?'

Clementine nodded agreeably. 'Where is Doug? It's strange, Margery.'

'I wonder if he managed to leave somehow?' Margery suggested. She turned back to the window. There were no tracks on the ground except for their own recent shoe prints. No one could have gone anywhere recently. The snow would have given them away. Anyway, the police were waiting at the top of the hill trying to fix the electrical situation and the gas lines and remove the tree. Margery was sure they would have had some questions for anyone making their way up the hill.

'Look at this,' Clementine said. She held up a clipboard she had pulled out of the driver's side door. 'A map of the food vendors.'

'Interesting,' Margery said, giving it a brief once-over. Without context, it didn't tell her much.

'Yes, look!' Clementine stabbed a finger at one of the back corners of the diagram. 'That's where Jacob is…'

'Yes?'

'Yes, but he's not listed on this map, is he?' Clementine said smugly.

'Ooh!' Margery gasped, realising that Clementine was right. There was no mention of the charcuterie stall on the map. 'Remember what Elliot said about certain people not paying their way! I bet he was talking about Jacob. He didn't pay for his spot, turned up and Elliot was trying to get him to leave, maybe?'

'I agree,' Clementine said with a firm nod. 'Well, Jacob might have more to tell us, then.'

'I think we ought to bide our time and not let on that we know,' Margery said. 'It might be more useful information that way.'

Clementine nodded again in agreement.

'Should we go and look at the band's van now?' Clementine asked.

Margery considered it. There was nothing else in the front of Elliot's van, apart from a few sweets in the console and a first aid kit in the dashboard.

'Let's look in the back of this one first,' she said.

She opened the van door and then stepped back down onto the pavement, trying to be careful and holding on to the passenger side door gingerly. She slid the side door open, letting it slam into the runners. There was not much inside. Elliot must have taken all his equipment into the hall with him. There were a few boxes of premade flatbreads and a few cartons of cooked chicken breast, which Margery thought were probably still fine to eat. It was certainly colder than a fridge out in the car park. She handed a box of each to Clementine. They might as well take them back into the hall. Elliot was no longer around to ask for permission.

Margery had been certain that Doug and Kevin were hiding out here somewhere in one of the vans together, but now it seemed a silly idea. Surely they would need to run the engine for the heating at some point and the van batteries and petrol wouldn't have lasted. Without proper equipment, she couldn't imagine anyone having a comfortable night. You could easily die if you weren't prepared for this weather, either from the cold or from carbon monoxide poisoning from your own engine running and the heating on full blast with not enough ventilation. It had been cold enough in the hall the night before, though the power was back on for now. Margery wasn't sure how, perhaps Sally was somewhere behind the scenes running on a massive wheel to keep it going.

'Anything?' Clementine asked.

'Maybe,' Margery said, shining her phone torch into the back of the van.

'What's that at the back behind the boxes?' Clementine said, pointing behind Margery.

Margery looked where she was gesturing. She reached up and moved the box, it slid away, light and empty. But then something caught her eye. She reached in and grabbed the plastic string, pulling it out towards her and realising as she did so what it was. The skulls in Santa hats looked even less appealing in the gloom of the van. Margery turned to show Clementine her find.

'Were they Elliot's lights all along?' Clementine asked, taking them from Margery and inspecting them. They certainly looked the same as the ones in the hall. 'It's a shame we can't ask him where he got them from. Weird, though. Why were the other ones behind the skirting?'

Margery shrugged and put the lights back, hoping that Clementine would have forgotten all about them before they got out of here at last.

'Is there a way in which Elliot could have accidentally hurt himself? Fallen over and hit his head, perhaps?' Margery wondered. 'No one seems to have heard or seen a scuffle or anything that would indicate he fought back.'

'No,' Clementine said. 'But I don't think he could hit himself on the head hard enough to bruise like that and then just lie down on the floor to die. It doesn't seem possible.'

Margery agreed with that. Even if you desperately tried to hold your breath until you died, you would only be able to do it till you lost consciousness. Then the lizard part of your brain would kick in and you'd be back to where you were initially. It certainly didn't seem possible to give yourself that sort of head wound without tremendous force.

They closed the van up and walked carefully over to Apex Void's van, laden with boxes of chicken and bread. It worried Margery that she didn't know what to do next, or what to make of the letter Elliot had received from Doug. Hopefully they would be able to ask Doug a few questions once they'd returned inside. The band's van was locked, as she had suspected it would be.

'What now?' she asked Clementine through chattering teeth.

Clementine shook her head. She put the box she was holding down on the cold ground and then stood on her tiptoes to better look in through the back window of the van.

'Nothing in there,' Clementine said, even as Margery joined her, gaping in through the windows.

'There's a sheet on the floor,' Margery said. 'But I can't see anything under it.'

The sheet looked as though it was probably used to cover the band's equipment while they travelled. She stepped down from the van. Short of breaking into it, Margery wasn't sure what more they could do.

A jolt of motion from across the car park caught her eye. Someone in a red coat making their way around the building, bright as fresh blood against the white walls.

'Where is she going?' Clementine asked. She put her hand up to wave and Margery grasped for it.

No one was supposed to leave the building, not even them. Jade must have had a reason to. It was better that she didn't know they were here as well. Margery pulled Clementine behind the nearest vehicle, and they watched Jade struggling as her heeled boots slid on the wet concrete. She walked with purpose, striding along as fast as she could and disappearing around the building.

'Should we follow her?' Margery asked, knowing that they should. It was their only option after finding out so little from the vans.

Before they could, Jade was marching back. She had pulled her hood over her head, but Margery could tell from what little she could see of her face that she was worried. It didn't quell Margery's own fears at all.

Chapter Nine

Margery and Clementine had run out of people to ask where Doug was, and no one seemed to know anyway. It was as if he had disappeared off the face of the planet, a thing that was impossible in Margery's opinion. He couldn't have disappeared into thin air, they just couldn't be looking hard enough. Clementine had suggested she summon Symon on her phone and ask if they had seen him. Symon had not and neither had his team, and he assured them that he had a team watching footage of all the traffic cameras in the area to see if they could spot Doug.

In a fervour Margery suspected was brought on by having too much free time, Clementine had begun to inspect all sorts of places. Even the ones that didn't hold any hope of housing a fully grown man. She lunged from cupboard door to cupboard door and searched under tables as if Kevin or Doug would be discreetly squished underneath one. She even very briefly stood on a chair and peered up into the suspended ceiling, Karen and Sharon each holding on to one of her legs to support her. Margery thought they must be missing something. Her head reeled with worry. Before Clementine could start looking under the coffee mugs in the kitchen cupboards, Margery finally managed to force her to sit down for a break.

Margery had been busily trying to organise what remaining food they had left while the others played with some of the battered board games they had found. The Monopoly box hadn't had enough players' pieces and Clementine had won the coin toss to be the top hat. Everyone else was using a teaspoon that Seren had written their name on in permanent marker. It wasn't the least confusing way to play as the spoons didn't all quite fit on the board, but Gloria was still winning by a mile, nearly every square containing one of her hotel pieces.

'Doug and Kevin have got to be somewhere,' Clementine screeched for the thirtieth time that day, her hand wrapped around the handle of the mug of tea Karen had made her. She had become more and more shrill as the upset went on. 'I just wish we knew where. It's weird! Why would they hide?'

'Maybe Doug killed Elliot,' Ceri-Ann suggested. 'Killed him and then did a runner.'

'Would he have killed his own employee, though?' Margery asked.

Ceri-Ann laughed. 'Are you telling me that you've never wanted to strangle one of us? What about that day that Clementine forgot to defrost the bread for World Book Day?'

'Yes, and we don't know what their relationship was like, do we?' Clementine said, rolling the dice and then moving the top hat. 'Maybe they didn't like each other. Maybe Elliot hadn't got the bread out of the freezer in time for an event and Doug kept bringing it up years and years later…'

Margery wasn't sure about that, but she supposed that there was no proof either way. The thing was, there had been nowhere to run to.

'There were lots of coats in the cloakroom,' Seren piped up, her face falling as she counted her remaining Monopoly money. 'Doug showed me where to put mine when I got here. Maybe he's hiding in there? He would have needed his coat to go out. Maybe he went and put it on and then decided to have a little sleep.'

'You've had a coat this entire time and you've been sleeping on the floor without anything?' Gloria asked, looking at Seren with confused dismay. 'You could have used it as a blanket or a pillow, Seren. You had carpet burn on your face this morning.'

'Oh, I don't want to crease my coat,' Seren said chirpily. She passed Gloria the last of her money. 'That's why I hung it up.'

'I'll go and have a look,' Margery said, pleased to have an excuse to put down her clipboard. 'I don't think he could still be asleep, not with all the commotion that's been going on, but we haven't got any better ideas. He certainly wasn't hiding in any of the kitchen cupboards.'

Margery went out into the hallway and opened the door to the cloakroom, though you couldn't really call it that any more. It had been stripped bare. Most people had taken their coats back out to wear already. Margery found Seren's coat and put it over her arm to bring back to her. Doug had certainly not been hiding in the cloakroom, then.

Margery dragged Doug's coat from the peg and held it up to inspect it. Doug must still be in the building if his coat was here. He wouldn't have left without it, not with the weather the way it was last night. There was something heavy in the front pocket. Doug's phone. Margery slid it out of the coat pocket and clicked the side button. The screen lit up, but she couldn't unlock it without the passcode. How odd. It was one thing to disappear, but without even stopping to take your phone… A flicker of worry began to flash on and off in her mind like a bulb that was rapidly burning out. What had Doug done to warrant disappearing like that? The answer could be as simple as Doug had killed Elliot and then made a run for it, not worrying about any of his belongings on the way. Margery made her way back to the green room, worrying the phone in her hands still.

'Anyone know how I could unlock this?' she asked the dinner ladies as she arrived.

Clementine gasped, looking up from her seat. 'Is that…?'

'Yes,' Margery said. 'It's Doug's phone.'

The dinner ladies all oohed, crowding around it. Karen took it from Margery and examined it, holding it up gingerly with her index finger and thumb.

'Let me have a go,' she said with a grimace. 'Maybe it'll explain where he is.'

'It is strange,' Margery said as Karen began to tap at the screen. 'Most people are glued to their phones, aren't they? I certainly don't know many people who would leave it for such a long time in a cupboard. You'd think he would have taken it with him wherever he's gone.'

'Not me,' Clementine scoffed. 'I never use my phone! I can't abide the things…'

'You're playing solitaire on yours right now.' Ceri-Ann gestured to the phone in Clementine's hand.

'Well, someone's got to beat my high score,' Clementine said with a roll of her eyes.

'I'm in!' Karen cheered with glee. 'His passcode was one, two, three, four!'

'Have a look for a message or something,' Clementine suggested. 'Maybe he messaged someone and told them what his plans were.'

'Oh yes,' Gloria said, the sarcasm dripping from the words. 'I'm sure he wrote down exactly how he killed Elliot and why…'

Karen nodded enthusiastically. 'I bet he did!'

'This has been a sh… I mean… bad weekend, hasn't it?' Ceri-Ann said, catching Clementine's eye before she could say the word. 'I thought it would be a bit cheerier than this, what with Christmas ten minutes away and whatever. I guess it's made me more thankful for what I've got, though.'

'And me,' Gloria said with a sigh.

'Me too,' Margery said, thinking of their warm, cosy house and the cats and Christmas Day with Clementine and her sister, Maria.

She thought of all the build-up to Christmas at the school and exchanging Christmas cards with the team, seeing the students' faces light up with excitement on the last day of school term. The dinner ladies going to watch the last school Christmas concert as a team and singing along to the carols. Even seeing their traditionally prickly neighbour Dawn Simmonds outside the house on Christmas morning was usually a calm exchange of well-wishing. All of it seemed to have been sucked away with Elliot's death, leaving the world a very beige place. No one had even bothered to turn the decorative lights back on in the hall today. The trees sat in darkness, the tinsel ominous in the dim light. The trees seemed less festive for some reason, Margery couldn't quite place why. They seemed to be missing something.

‘I’ve got a three-litre bottle of imitation Baileys from ALDI at home, especially for Christmas,’ Seren said sadly, interrupting Margery’s thoughts. ‘I just wish it could be here with us.’

They all nodded agreeably at that.

‘Found something,’ Karen said, holding the phone up so Margery and Clementine could see it. The screen displayed a video, though nothing much was happening.

‘All right?’ Margery asked.

‘Listen,’ Karen said, hushing her.

Barely audible above the rustling was a low murmur of conversation. The video had been filmed inside Doug’s coat or pocket, Margery realised.

‘You can’t do this,’ an angry voice said. ‘You won’t get away with it.’

‘I can do whatever I want,’ Doug replied, his voice rising haughtily. ‘I run these events. I’ll have the band blacklisted if I want to and you couldn’t do anything about it. Who’s going to believe you?’

The band, Margery thought. She exchanged a surprised look with Clementine as she realised who the other voice was.

‘You can’t,’ Kevin said over the tinny phone speakers.

Doug must have started filming because he had known that the conversation would descend into a slanging match, Margery realised. What had Kevin been up to?

‘All this over a sandwich,’ Doug scoffed. ‘Don’t be so ridiculous.’

‘It’s not just a sandwich,’ Kevin said, his tone rising in desperation. ‘It’s a Rollin’ Rollin’ Rollin’ sandwich and it’s a special Apex Void-themed menu. You know that. We’ve put months of work into it!’

'Well, Jade hasn't paid for her stall space so unfortunately Rollin' Rollin' Rollin' won't be at the summer festival this year,' Doug explained. He seemed calm, but Margery could hear a faint hint of trepidation in his voice. 'We've filled all the spaces now. Elliot's got another sandwich company coming. Pete's Meats, do you know them?'

'Pete's Meats!' Kevin scoffed. 'Do you want to give everyone botulism?'

Margery could almost see him throwing his hands in the air in outrage, though the video remained dark and viewless. 'Jade paid Elliot! She told me when she'd done it, and I gave her our share of the holding fee…'

'Does she have any proof?' Doug asked. 'A bank statement?'

'She said she paid cash,' Kevin said. His fury sounded like it was waning. 'Elliot only wanted cash. She said he was supposed to give her a receipt, but he said he'd run out of printer paper for the invoices.'

'Well, we've got plenty of paper here,' Doug said. 'Are you sure that she hasn't just taken your money? I had one of her sandwiches earlier and believe me, it wasn't all that…'

'You're lying,' Kevin said, his voice breaking into a stutter with anger.

'I'm not lying,' Doug scoffed. 'It was the one called Linkin Pork, I'm not sure I got the reference—'

'I don't mean about the sandwich! Someone's lying about the money,' Kevin interrupted Doug. 'And it isn't me and I trust Jade. Why would she lie? She wants this space at the festival as much as we do.'

'Well, why would Elliot lie?' Doug asked. 'His job is to book the best caterers and entertainers that he can get. Why wouldn't he book Jade and Apex Void?'

'I don't know,' Kevin said, after a pause. 'But that's what's happened.'

'I don't think so,' Doug told him firmly. 'Now if you'll excuse me...'

'You're unbelievable,' Kevin barked. 'I'll never forget this, Doug. Just you wait! You'll get yours, you'll see!'

'You're arguing with the wrong person,' Doug told him calmly. 'You should go and ask Jade for the money back, before she can waste it all on stock for her stall.'

'Jade isn't the problem here, your employee is!' Kevin yelled. 'I'm going to go and give Elliot a piece of my mind right away.'

'Don't,' Doug snapped. 'Let me deal with Elliot.'

Kevin laughed bitterly. 'You know he's in the wrong here! No, I'm going to go and talk—'

'Kevin,' Doug said, his voice low. 'I said I'd sort things out with him. Leave it to me.'

Kevin didn't dignify that with a response. There was the sound of footsteps and Doug sighed angrily and then it was over.

'Well,' Clementine said. 'That didn't sound very innocent, did it?'

'No,' Margery agreed. 'What's this about Elliot taking people's money? No wonder Kevin was angry.'

'In cash at that,' Clementine said. 'Very interesting. Do you think Kevin might have attacked him right after he left Doug's office?'

'Maybe,' Margery said, nodding.

Kevin had certainly sounded angry enough for a fight from the video, but that didn't mean that he had acted on his rage. The thing was, it was very hard to tell if he was a vengeful person or not when he had disappeared from the face of the earth. Margery thought that he would probably have a lot to say for himself when they caught up with him. His disappearance was becoming more and more infuriating by the hour. Symon hadn't come back to them, which meant that he hadn't found him either, and the police would have seen him trying to slip past them the night before. It was mystifying.

'We didn't pay a fee to come here, did we?' Gloria asked, Margery almost jumped at the interruption. She had been so invested in her own thoughts that she had nearly forgotten about the rest of the team.

'No,' Margery said. 'They paid us.'

That was what made Kevin and Doug's argument all the more confusing to Margery. Why had the dinner lady team been paid to come when others had needed to pay a deposit?

'I think we ought to up our search for Kevin,' Margery said with a sigh. She felt very tired all of a sudden. 'He can't be far.'

'We really need to find Doug too,' Clementine said. 'We obviously aren't looking hard enough.'

Margery didn't think that was it, but she kept her thoughts to herself for the moment.

'Oh no!' Margery turned to see Ceri-Ann desperately tapping at her phone screen.

'What's wrong?'

Ceri-Ann looked horrified, her mouth hung open in such a panicked way that Margery felt a wave of worry roll down her spine.

'The Wi-Fi has gone off!'

Chapter Ten

The loss of the internet was a deep slash through all of their wellbeing. There was nothing left to distract them from the isolation of the hall. Clementine had initially scoffed at the revelation. 'You youth and your phones!' she had exclaimed, chuckling at the situation until she had realised that her own phone battery had died halfway through a game of solitaire. Ceri-Ann paced the room, the phone in her hand now essentially a very expensive paperweight. Margery knew that while Clementine had immediately decided that Ceri-Ann must be disappointed that she couldn't post on social media, the upset was more likely about being cut off from Symon and Nick, Margery wasn't a mother, but she could imagine how horrible that would be. The phone signal here was notoriously bad anyway, the hall being out of the way in the countryside, the Wi-Fi been the last flickering connection to the outside world. She wanted to reach out a hand and comfort Ceri-Ann but knew it was best to let her pace.

Martha had arrived before anything more could be discussed about the video they had seen on Doug's phone. She had been beyond excited to drag them away from their group and summon them to the kitchenette, where Arthur waited for them, though Arthur didn't look pleased at all to see them – quite the opposite. Margery felt her heart drop. It was bad enough that Doug hadn't reappeared yet and Elliot's murderer was still probably somewhere in the building.

'Are you all right?' Margery asked Arthur, her senses tingling that he was very annoyed. She tried to ignore the bubbling excitement coming from his wife, but it proved too difficult a task.

'You've got to talk to…' Martha lowered her voice to a volume usually only heard by fleas and ants. '…the police.'

There was a pause as Margery and Clementine tried to work out what she meant.

'Okay?' Clementine said. 'We have spoken to them already, though. You were there, do you… do you not remember? It was this morning…'

'Yes, of course,' Martha said, her beaming smile falling for a moment. 'But haven't you found anything else out?'

'Well,' Margery said, thinking of the accusations in the video on Doug's phone and the letter from Doug to Elliot in Elliot's van. 'Sort of.'

Martha clapped her hands in glee at that. 'I knew you would! You see, Arthur, this is why I've hired the dinner ladies in the past. They get the job done! Not like some people I could mention…' She gave Margery a conspiratorial wink that she didn't quite understand.

'All right,' Clementine said. 'But how are we going to talk to them without phone signal or the internet?'

'Symon's on my radio frequency,' Arthur said, tilting his own radio to show them both.

'Why have you got a walkie-talkie?' Clementine asked. 'What are we, twelve?'

'I'll keep watch!' Martha called as she left the kitchen and shut the door behind her. Margery found herself smiling despite everything, imagining Martha acting like a club bouncer while simultaneously listening with her ear pressed up tightly to the door frame.

'Symon, come in, over,' Arthur said into the radio. 'I've got a report here from the dinner ladies.'

'A report from the dinner ladies?' Symon's voice came over the radio, crackling like pork skin in an oven. 'All right, yeah, what have they got?'

'They're here now to tell you themselves,' Arthur said, nodding in the self-assured way that Margery knew infuriated Rose at governors' meetings. 'I'll let them tell you more about it.'

Arthur handed the radio to Clementine, who looked down at it with wide eyes. There was a pause.

'You didn't say "over",' Clementine said. 'Over.'

'I don't need to,' Arthur told her. 'You've got to tell him what you've found out.'

'Practically nothing in the ten minutes since we last messaged him,' Clementine said with a dramatic sigh. 'Over.'

'Well, tell him that.' Arthur gestured to the radio.

'Symon, we don't know anything,' Clementine told the radio, talking to it much too closely.

'You need to hold the button down,' Arthur said, waving at it in annoyance.

'Let me have a go,' Margery said, taking it from Clementine and speaking into it. 'Symon, it's Margery. The band's manager, Kevin, is still missing, and so is Doug the organiser.'

'Over!' Clementine said, from over her shoulder.

'Yeah, we haven't found them either,' Symon said. Margery could hear how tired he was, even over the crackly line.

'We went out to the car park to look, but we couldn't see them,' Margery told him.

'That was a good plan, though,' he said. 'Did you find anything else useful?'

Margery thought about it. 'Actually, we think that one of the food vendors isn't supposed to be here...'

'Who!' Arthur stuttered with outrage. 'Tell me and I'll go and...'

'And do what?' Clementine interrupted him. 'Kick them out? We're all trapped here together and let's be honest, it doesn't really matter now. It's better if they don't know we know.'

Margery agreed.

'Do you think Elliot was killed by a weapon?' Margery found herself asking out loud, despite feeling squeamish at the question but wanting to change the subject before Arthur and Clementine could properly argue. 'Could he have fallen over and hurt himself?'

'I don't think so,' Symon said. Margery could imagine his face going pale behind his freckles. 'Not from what you said. Arthur said it looks like blunt trauma to him.' Arthur nodded grimly. 'God, I wish we could get down there. Forensics would be able to tell exactly what killed him in like two seconds.'

'I haven't seen any baseball bats lying around,' Clementine said with a grimace. 'And he's got a huge bump on his head.'

'Almost certainly a head wound that killed him.' Arthur nodded.

Margery wasn't certain.

'It didn't look that bad,' she said.

'Certainly a head wound,' Arthur said in his best smug school councillor voice.

'Oh, and the Wi-Fi has gone out,' Clementine told Symon.

'That's weird,' Symon said. 'Is the power on, though?'

'Yes,' Margery told him.

'I'll check and see if there's an outage or something,' Symon said. He sounded defeated to Margery's ears. It made her suspicious.

'Did you find anything more out about the tree?' Margery asked.

'No,' Symon said. 'I mean, yeah, someone pulled the tree down. But it was rotten in the middle and it all came up. An accident waiting to happen, though, I reckon. It could have come down at any time…'

'Deliberate, then?' Clementine asked. 'Or did someone accidentally knock it with their van on the way to the hall?'

'I don't think so,' Symon said. Margery could almost imagine the bemused look on his face. 'Definitely pulled down with the chain, but actually some of it looks like it was cut.'

'Cut?'

'Yeah, but the big bit of tree that fell has all these chops in it,' Symon said. 'Like whoever tried to chop the tree down couldn't manage it so they gave up and pulled it up.'

'Could a theoretical axe or something like it have been used to hit Elliot?' Margery asked. 'Have you found what they were trying to chop it down with?'

'Not yet, but we will,' Symon said. 'Or you will, I guess. I thought it might be in the car park somewhere and the snowfall has covered it, but we can't get down there to look.'

'Should we go and search?' Clementine asked. 'Only it's quite cold now, Symon, and we didn't think to look earlier.'

'No, don't worry,' Symon said. Margery could hear him thinking over the line.

'What is it?' Margery asked him.

'It's just, I don't know if we're going to be able to get to you today,' Symon said. 'Everyone's going to have to stay in the hall again, and I don't think that'll go down well, from what Arthur told me.'

Like a lead balloon, Margery thought.

'The road's nearly clear, but they're still working on the gas lines,' Symon explained. 'I bet it'll be either evening or tomorrow morning first thing, that's what they're aiming for, anyway.'

'We can't do that,' Arthur said, at the same time as Margery and Clementine gasped with horror. 'You don't know what it's like down here, Symon. To say we're descending into madness is an understatement.'

That explained why he'd made them make the call to Symon, Margery thought.

'Yes, we'll have all gone mad by then,' Clementine said, but she didn't sound quite as displeased. There was a gleeful note in her voice. 'There's got to be another way.'

'It gives us more time to find the killer,' Margery said.

Clementine turned to stare at her in disbelief. 'What? You're usually trying to stop us finding the killer!'

'What have we got to lose? We're stuck for the time being anyway,' Margery said with a shrug. 'If it gets really bad we can call Symon back up and see where they are with the gas lines. Like Symon said, the road is nearly clear and it's just the lines that are the danger. Maybe he can manage to get someone down to help us, on a… erm… snow plough or something.'

'They might have to jump it over the big hole in the road,' Symon said quietly.

Clementine sighed, rubbing a hand over her brow. 'Do you think whoever did this knew the damage it would cause, Symon?'

'Yeah, I think so,' Symon said. 'They must have had some idea, or why do it? I don't know if they knew about the gas though. Maybe Doug does? He's been in charge of the building a long time.'

Another reason to find Doug, Margery thought to herself. The door opened and Sally entered, her face a perfect sneer that twisted her features into something horrible.

'So, we're all staying put a bit longer, then?' Sally asked. There was a glint of something harsh in her eyes.

'I told you this was important police business!' Martha called from the doorway. Margery suspected she wouldn't be asked to do security for any events in the near future.

'Sally,' Arthur said, looking as though he wanted to surrender his post and throw his radio to her. 'Where have you been?'

'I could ask you the very same thing,' Sally said. 'Tucked away in here with the *detectives*.' She said the word distastefully, as though it had caused her to crack a filling. 'Have you forgotten who's in charge now, Arthur?'

'Doug…' Arthur began. Sally shook her head and then gestured to the hall.

'Where is he, then?' she said, her mouth rising in a sneer. 'Not here, and if he's not here that means I'm in charge. You might be head volunteer, but I'm on the payroll!'

'Well, the police have told us to stay put,' Arthur said. 'Are you going to go over their heads?'

'No, of course not,' Sally spluttered, her face almost purple.

'Well, then I say we call a meeting, let everybody know what's going on. It doesn't do any good to keep people in the dark. Look at all the resource hoarding that's happening already!'

Sally glared at him. 'If that's what they've said, then that's what we'll do, but I need to be informed about these things, Arthur!'

'Yes,' Arthur said, hanging his head. 'Yes, well, I think we just got carried away.'

Sally stepped forward as though she might challenge him, but the power went out, plunging them all into darkness. Margery found herself rubbing her brow in annoyance. How much longer could this go on?

-

The stage was lit with candles that had been donated from Rhonda's Christmas crafts table. They littered the top of the stage and the floor below it, casting shadows that danced along the ceiling. 'Donated' was possibly not quite the right word. Rhonda didn't look pleased about it at all, her face the bitter sneer of someone who had been forced to eat several lemons. Perhaps she had, Margery thought cheerfully. You could only hope for a bit of good news at times like these.

Sally still seemed as furious as she had been, but she had finally agreed to call the meeting and had been very useful summoning the troops. It made Margery feel grateful that Sally hadn't been present for any of the rest of their talk with Symon. She certainly wouldn't have been happy that they hadn't left it to her to call all of the shots and it was no good stepping on her toes now.

'We're working on getting the power back on,' Arthur stuttered from the stage, his arms tucked tightly around his own torso.

'What did you say? Make sure you're projecting your voice!' someone called from the back of the room. Margery had a horrible suspicion that it was Rose.

Margery had never seen him so flustered. For one, Arthur usually seemed to be able to withstand all sorts of dire meetings with good humour, having taken the reins on the council since Mr Fitzgerald had died. Even Martha looked worried, standing to the side of the stage clutching a tea light in her gloved fingers. The heating had gone off with the power and the hall was so cold that Margery could see her breath billowing into the air. She pulled her coat tightly around her with folded arms and huddled closer to Clementine. The rest of the gathered crowd bunched together alongside them for warmth, shivering as if they were all one body.

Margery wasn't sure what the candles were made from, but they flickered ominously, occasionally billowing dark smoke into the air of the hall and making her need to cough. The mixture of Christmas scents was giving Margery a headache, and she knew she couldn't be the only one. The gingerbread and peppermint scents curdled in the air and created something horrible and new. She was grateful to them for the warmth they gave off but felt that there were far too many to not be some sort of fire hazard.

Sally stormed up the stage steps and stood next to Arthur, almost slamming him out of the way. She was the only one who didn't look particularly cold, in her huge puffer coat and thermal hat and gloves. Margery eyed the gloves with envy, her own fingers frozen down to the bone and beginning to ache. They usually ached anyway, arthritic as they were, but the cold did nothing for them. The pain rattled down her fingertips and into her torso, a pin cushion of aches.

'Unless you've been living in an alternate reality to this one…' Sally said in a loud, clear voice. It could have rivalled Rose's best assembly voice. Perhaps there was a place for her in Rose's adult-only drama group. '…then you've noticed that once again we have no power. We've working on restarting it with the back-up generator. Until then, we all need to pull together to help each other.' Sally cast a stern eye over the audience, lingering for more than a moment on Rose and Rhonda. She continued. 'I want to see us all working together, not taking advantage of the situation.'

Margery turned to look at Rose, who was avoiding meeting Sally's gaze and hiding something that looked suspiciously like a bag of gloves behind her back.

'How are they going to get the power back on?' Clementine whispered to Margery. 'There's no electricians here, are there? No one useful at all for this situation. We could all make you a nice sandwich, but that's no help, is it? Not without the bread for it.'

'How are you going to get it back on?' Mike called over the crowd, echoing Clementine's thoughts.

Sally continued to smile the big fake smile but didn't immediately answer. She didn't know, Margery worried. They were trapped here for another night with no heating, no Wi-Fi and no electricity. It could be devastating. It was cold now, but the temperature would drop even further tonight. They would all have to pull together if they were going to remain well.

Arthur made to leave the stage and Martha rushed to meet him. In her hurry, Martha bumped into Mrs Bell. Mrs Bell flung the scented tea light she was holding into the air and wax splattered onto the floor like great globs of spilled soup. Margery watched as she scuttled to a stop, kicking one of the jar candles as she went. It rolled away, still lit, underneath the curtain that ran along the front of the stage. It was a very dramatic reaction to an accidental nudge, Margery thought, but then again, Mrs Bell was quite elderly. It must have really surprised her.

'Ooh, sorry,' Martha cried, almost lunging back to steady Mrs Bell herself. 'Are you all right? Butterfingers!'

'You mean butterfeet,' Sally said, looking down at Martha, who was still half on the stage staircase and half off it, with her hand around Mrs Bell's wrist. Mrs Bell was still blinking in surprise. 'Someone go and get the fire extinguisher, please!'

Before a single person could move, there was a sudden yelp from somewhere beneath Arthur and Sally. They looked down at their feet in surprise. Margery couldn't see anything there except the soft glow from the candle, which seemed to be growing underneath the stage. The fire was spreading. There was another screech, unmistakably of pain.

Margery gasped as a figure crawled out from underneath the stage, flames licking their clothing. They screamed as they rolled around on the hall floor, trying to put the fire out, the coat they were wearing blazing, the flames casting a shadow of the flailing person on the ceiling. The gathered crowd stepped back, some screaming, some trying to move away from the fire. The scent of the burning coat and hair was enough to snap Margery into action. She lunged forward and threw her own coat over them. The dinner lady team joined her with their own coats. The person's flailing arms appeared from beneath the pile, clawing their way back to the surface and pulling themselves to their feet as Seren returned with the fire extinguisher. She held it up, pulled the pin out and aimed where the smoke was coming from. It erupted into a stream of foam and water, covering the entire front of the stage and the person lurching in front of it.

'Kevin!' Margery heard Mike cry from the back of the room. 'Nice of you to finally join us!'

Kevin hunched over, coughing and spluttering, soaking wet and the sleeves of his coat still smouldering. Arthur reached for his wrist, but Kevin stumbled back from him. He didn't wait for a moment longer before he made a break for it, leaping across the hall far too fast for someone who had spent more than a day hiding underneath a stage.

Before anyone could stop him, he had reached the sliding doors and pulled one open, stumbling outside. The crowd gasped as if they were one body. Margery found herself being jostled as everyone tried to get closer to the window to watch him go. She made it to the glass and stared as she saw the last of Kevin disappear into Apex Void's van. The taillights came on, but she couldn't hear the engine over the noise of the torrential rain. The wind whistled through the still-open sliding door, burning her eyes.

'He can't be planning to leave,' Clementine said with a gasp. 'Symon said the road isn't clear yet and anyway we're all witnesses to a murder, aren't we? The police will want to talk to all of us.'

Margery didn't need to answer, Kevin showed them exactly what he was planning to do. He sped across the car park in the van, narrowly avoiding hitting several parked cars, and hit the hill that led up and out. He made it a fair way up and then the van began to struggle. For a moment Margery thought it was stuck in place, but then it began to roll backward, and it didn't stop.

There were only a few moments before the group with their noses pressed against the hall windows realised what was about to happen and everyone rushed away from them. The van had lost control, the wheels turning uselessly as it flew backward at speed. Margery screamed along with everyone else as the van narrowly missed the hall windows and collided with the main doors with a terrific crash. She didn't wait for Clementine, instead, she rushed out into the hallway. Glass smothered the floor, the entire back windscreen was gone for good, the doors buckled and lying open. Kevin clambered out of the back of the van with great difficulty, clutching his side and moaning, shards of glass pouring from him and sprinkling to the floor.

'Did you mean to do that?' Mrs Bell piped up. 'One of us could have opened the door for you.'

Kevin spluttered, holding his hands to his chest. A glint from something inside the buckled back doors of the van caught Margery's eye. Among the wigs and instrument cords lay an axe, flecks of wood still clinging to its teeth.

Chapter Eleven

Margery and the rest of the dinner lady team swept up what broken glass they could with the kitchen broom, piling it away into the glass bin. There was not much they could do about the van wedged in through the main doors, letting the wind in. Gloria had suggested that they take the cardboard left from their arrival and tape the back windscreen up, which kept some of the wind out, but not all. It whistled up and down the hallways and dropped the temperature inside even further than Margery could have imagined. Ceri-Ann had borrowed the police radio to ask what Symon's ETA was. They couldn't stay here much longer, not with the building as it was. Who knew what structural damage had been caused by the van? There was a possibility that the entire thing might come down with them all inside it, though Margery reasoned that at least they would be warm if they were wearing the building.

Once the clean-up had been sorted, Margery and Clementine returned to the main hall. Kevin was sitting with Sally as they entered, though he didn't seem to be talking much. Sally was leading the conversation as he sulked, arms folded tightly to his chest. Rhonda had stepped in to perform first aid and strapped his wrist up tightly with bandages, possibly too tightly – Margery could see where his fingertips were beginning to turn blue. He had been tremendously lucky to not be severely hurt, the glass could have ruptured an artery. Margery was glad that the building hadn't turned into the final resting place for two people. Kevin didn't seem too worse for wear, his ego more bruised than his body. The axe had been left in the van, ready for Symon to examine it when he got here. Margery wasn't a forensic expert, but even she could tell from the wooden splinters stuck fast to the teeth that it had been used recently. It would be down to the police to identify if it was the axe that had cut down the tree in the car park, but Margery had a sneaking suspicion that she knew what the answer would be.

'We should talk to him about Doug,' Clementine whispered to Margery. 'After all, he's probably the last person who saw him and we have their entire argument recorded, don't we?'

Margery considered things. 'We'll have more leverage if he thinks we've actually spoken to Doug and not just… well… stolen the man's phone. Let's be careful not to let that slip.'

Clementine nodded. 'I agree.'

They began to make their way over. Margery bumped into Mrs Bell as they passed her. The old woman grasped her elbow with bony fingers.

'So sorry, Mrs Bell,' Margery said, reaching out to steady her by the elbow. Mrs Bell still wobbled for a second before she settled. Clementine had already rushed off towards Kevin and Jade without so much as a glance backward.

'I don't trust him,' Mrs Bell muttered under her breath. 'You can't trust a man with a sword, Margery.'

'I quite agree,' Margery said politely. 'Er… which man?'

'The man with the pig's leg,' Mrs Bell said cryptically.

Instead of staying to explain what she meant, Mrs Bell lurched away again, leaving Margery scratching her head in confusion. She hoped Mrs Bell was okay, the weekend was beginning to take its toll on everyone, but it wouldn't do to induce a case of delirium among the most elderly of them all.

'Oh my God, now what?' Kevin groaned as Margery and Clementine arrived at his seat. 'Is it not bad enough that I've only got half an eyebrow now and what's left of my beard smells like burnt Christmas dinners! Can't you leave me with what's left of my dignity?'

'I think you look very nice,' Sally said, so sweetly her voice was almost sticky. Margery noticed her hand on his knee. 'It makes you look rugged. I do love a man with scars!'

Kevin ignored her in favour of glaring at Margery and Clementine. 'What do you want?'

'Have you seen—'

'I told you, I don't know where Doug is,' Kevin said. 'What more do you want from me?'

'We know where Doug is,' Clementine said. Margery nodded along, trying to not feel bad about the lie.

'Really?' Sally asked in a curious voice. 'Well, can you ask him to do some work? There's no time for shirking. There's plenty to do here. For one, he can break up that nonsense going on with Rose and Rhonda…'

'He showed us a video of the argument you had last night,' Margery told Kevin, ignoring Sally entirely. His cheeks went red.

'Of course he was recording that – I knew it!' he snapped, throwing his hands in the air. 'That's just like him to be a snake. Well, I think I was very justified in what I said, so I don't care.'

'He said that Jade hadn't paid for her stall at the summer festival,' Margery began.

'Rubbish!' Sally said, holding up a hand. 'I saw Jade's invoice, she paid up all right. Paid extra, even. Always a bit too keen, that's her problem.'

'Then why did Doug say she hadn't paid?' Clementine asked. 'And why was it so important to you, Kevin? It was Jade's money, wasn't it?'

Kevin groaned. Sally patted him on the shoulder and he sighed, obviously not wanting to tell them anything more than he had already.

'Fine!' he spat. 'I owe Doug money already, that's why it was so important to get Jade the pitch.'

'How much?' Clementine asked, her brow raising in curiosity.

'A lot,' Kevin said, his face darkening at the thought of it. 'Jade agreed to help me do a deal on the sandwich for a cut of the profit and I couldn't say no, could I? This is our livelihoods on the line, the band… and you know, it's all for a good cause.'

He turned to Sally, who smiled at him.

'Truth is, the band hasn't been doing well lately,' Kevin explained, wringing his hands together. His face was screwed up as if the confession was physically painful. 'I've been trying to get them more interest, but the world they came up in just doesn't exist any more. The last ten years have been a downward spiral, really. Ever since they did the big reunion gigs. That was probably the last tour that sold well.'

Sally opened her mouth, probably to compliment Kevin on his great band management, but Kevin turned away from her and folded his arms.

'That's why you've been doing the viral videos,' Margery said quickly before Sally could say anything.

'Yes.' Kevin nodded. 'I had to try. So far it's not been very viral at all. And the ones that have gone viral have been more of a flu than anything else. Lots of disparaging comments… Mike's past it, the recordings sound cheap, blah, blah, blah… you know what the internet is like.'

Margery and Clementine nodded at that, though Margery wasn't sure she did know.

'So, yeah, I did argue with Doug, but I'm a man on the edge,' Kevin said, rolling his eyes dramatically. It made Margery cringe. 'The band got an advance for the upcoming record that's due out next September and I've already spent it keeping us all going. There's nothing left to record with, I've already had to put it off long enough. The band are getting suspicious because I've had them practising in my garage, can't afford the practice room any more. I've got to try and recoup the costs somehow or I won't be able to afford the studio time.'

'Recoup the costs by any means possible?' Margery asked.

'No, of course not!' Kevin said. He ran a hand up to the bridge of his nose and squeezed. 'Just tell Doug that we need that slot, when you see him.'

They promised that they would, though Margery wondered when they'd be able to keep it.

'Listen,' Sally began. 'There's obviously been some misunderstanding between Jade and Elliot. Unfortunately, we obviously can't ask Elliot about it all now, but I imagine it would have been easily sorted by a word from Doug.'

'That's why I went to him,' Kevin muttered. 'Fat lot of use that did.'

'You should have come to me,' Sally said, running her hand down his arm again.

Kevin gave an exasperated sigh, shrugging her off. 'Listen, why don't you give us a few minutes?'

Margery had wanted to ask Sally to give them a moment alone, but the look on Sally's face had told her she had no intention of ever doing that. She wondered if she would listen to Kevin. After a second, to Margery's amazement, she got up from her seat.

'I'll go and get you a lovely cup of tea,' she told Kevin. 'Ladies, no more questions. Can't you see Mr Smith has had enough of an ordeal?'

She sauntered away, leaving Margery to wonder if she'd had a personality transplant in the last thirty seconds or if Kevin just had some sort of bizarre magnetic hold over her. Margery wasn't sure if it was just because she was too homosexual to see things any differently, but she wasn't entirely sure what Sally saw in him. Kevin was either oblivious to her attentions or wasn't very taken with them either.

'We've been looking for you a while,' Clementine told Kevin, once Sally was out of earshot. 'I bet you've got some answers for us. Enough secrets for you to hide away with, anyway.'

'I didn't hide well enough, obviously,' he scoffed, the noise arriving from deep in his throat.

Margery found herself desperately trying not to roll her eyes.

'Anyway,' Kevin continued, his brow furrowed with anger. 'You'd never have found me if you hadn't accidentally lit me on fire.'

'How do you know that it wasn't purposeful?' Clementine said with a dramatic eyeroll. 'Wait here, Margery,

I'll go and get another candle. I'm sure Rhonda has got another scented one left somewhere. What scent would you like your pyre to be?'

'No, don't!' Kevin cried, flinching away from them. His greying hair was crispy around the edges, and his beard still held the smell of burnt peppermint.

'Why did you run?' Margery asked. She was still confused about that. If Kevin was as innocent as he said, then why bother?

'Well, why were you looking for me?' Kevin asked back, with the self-righteous indignation of someone who had not recently crashed a van containing an axe through a huge pane of glass. 'Can't a man just go for a little lie-down under a stage for a few days?'

'A little lie-down!' Clementine said with a dark laugh. 'You were under there with a pile of blankets and an entire catering-sized box of cereal that you stole, from us may I add! Creeping around under there in your nest like a spider or a rabbit… whatever hides underground…'

'Got to look after yourself,' Kevin said, looking away from her.

Margery shook her head in disbelief. She folded her arms and waited for him to say more, but he ignored her. 'There's got to be more to it than that.'

'All right!' Kevin snapped, finally sick of the silence. 'I was the first person to find Elliot's body.'

Margery waited a beat, so did Clementine. They had learned in recent years that the space of conversation might be filled by the person panicking to answer questions. Sometimes you could draw out more answers with a well-held silence. Margery had taken to the technique much faster than Clementine, who struggled to stay quiet about anything most days. Still, they were becoming a well-practised team. Kevin remained quiet.

'So?' Clementine asked. 'Why didn't you raise the alarm?'

Kevin looked confused. 'I don't know, I just panicked.'

He folded his arms around himself tightly and Margery knew he wasn't going to tell them any more about it. Still, it didn't hurt to ask.

'You found Elliot,' Margery said. 'But you just left him there?'

Kevin shrugged.

'Why was there an axe in your van?' Margery asked, deciding that they could no longer beat around the bush.

Kevin looked confused at that.

'What axe?' he asked.

'The axe in the van,' Margery reminded him, feeling her patience whittling down to nothing. 'Were you planning to cut down the tree with it?'

'No! Why would I?' he spluttered. 'Even if I did, it's not illegal to cut down a tree, is it?'

Margery wasn't sure of the legalities of it at all and didn't think it wise to argue that there was a strong likelihood it was illegal. Surely there had to be some repercussion for trapping them all inside the building.

'You can't think an axe brought down that huge tree,' Kevin scoffed.

Margery shrugged. 'Maybe not, but Elliot did have a head injury that could have been caused easily by the handle of an axe or something heavy like that – and anyway, your van does have a tow bar on the back. One of you could have used it to pull the tree down.'

Kevin shook his head, his lip turning up in disgust at the very idea of it.

'Well,' Margery said, trying a different tactic, 'did any of the rest of the band?'

'Yes!' Clementine said nodding vigorously in agreement, her voice filled with annoyance. 'Come on, out with it.'

'Really! We were in the building all night,' Kevin said. 'We must be being framed.'

'Who would frame you?' Margery asked, suddenly confused. 'And for what?'

'Elliot.' Kevin's eyes darted around to look anywhere but Margery's face. 'We owe money, well, the band does. Not me, you see… I won't be defaulting on my mortgage.'

'Only because the band are on the hook for the contracts they sign,' Margery said, shaking her head at his audacity. 'How do you sleep at night?'

'Very well! I've got to have an escape clause, haven't I?' Kevin snapped. 'It's my career, sometimes business is just business.'

'I don't think that's all there is to it,' Margery said, lowering her voice. 'I think you saw something that frightened you and then hid under the stage, leaving the rest of us to it.'

'Like a coward,' Clementine added, slamming her hand down on the nearest trestle table. It wobbled, dangerously close to folding in two.

'Wouldn't you?' Kevin scoffed. 'Elliot lying dead in the hall like that. Someone wanted a show!'

Margery had been about to give up the questioning as they didn't seem to be getting anywhere, but suddenly something snapped into place.

'What do you mean, "hall"?' she asked him. Clementine sucked in a breath as she realised what Kevin had said.

'Where Elliot was,' Kevin said. He wasn't even looking at her, his arms were still folded as he stared past her out of the hall windows behind them. He hadn't even realised the revelation going off in Margery's head. 'His body.'

He flicked a finger towards Elliot's stall, which was still barren and bare.

'When did you see him there?' Margery found herself asking from very far away, trapped in her own thoughts.

'About four in the morning,' Kevin said. He was staring at her now, his brow furrowed. 'I'm not going to lie to you, I panicked. I know it's not very gentlemanly, but I knew that the killer would be back. I went and hid right under the stage.'

'He wasn't found in the hall,' Margery told him. She watched the blood drain from his face in a way that would have been satisfying if it all wasn't so dire. 'He was found in the Christmas grotto.'

'Did I say hall? I meant grotto,' Kevin said. He leaned back against the window, his legs hardly able to keep up his weight. He couldn't look them in the eye, Margery realised with suspicion.

'Did you move his body?' Clementine demanded.

Kevin blinked at her, open-mouthed. 'No, of course not!'

Someone had, if what Kevin was saying was the truth, Margery thought to herself. Someone had killed Elliot and then moved his body to the Christmas grotto, only to be found the next day by poor Mrs Bell.

'But—' Margery began.

'I misspoke,' Kevin snapped. 'I've had a terrible ordeal and I said the wrong thing, okay?'

Margery wondered if that was really true, but she didn't think they would get much more out of him if they continued down that line of questioning.

'Where was everyone else?' Margery asked instead. That thought had been whirling in her head ominously since they had found Elliot's body. 'Was everyone in the other hall?'

'I thought I saw someone leaving as I was going to get under the stage,' Kevin admitted. 'The party was beginning to wind down in the other hall, I only saw Elliot because I came into this hall to grab my water bottle.'

'Who did you see?' Margery asked.

'Doug, I think,' Kevin said. 'He was wearing those white snow boots. No one else has those, do they?'

'You saw him?' Clementine asked.

'Yeah.' Kevin nodded. 'He was leaving as I came in.'

'He wasn't hiding under the stage with you,' Margery said. 'Where is he?'

'I really have no idea,' Kevin said.

Margery and Clementine exchanged a worried look. Margery had been wondering if that was the case. Symon and his team had been waiting on the only exit road, and it seemed mad that Doug would have made it up the hills through the woodland in this weather. Not in a storm. Though, if anyone knew the area, it was Doug. And if anyone knew the hall best it was Doug. Maybe there was a secret hiding place on site.

'Everything's going wrong,' Kevin sighed. 'I bet the summer events won't even happen now. You don't want to know how many tote bags and T-shirts with the Apex Void logo on I've ordered. Practically our entire fee for this weekend's gig. It's taking up all my garage space.'

He slumped back against the window again, but Margery found herself unable to raise even the tiniest droplet-worth of pity for him. Her well of empathy had run bone dry. How could you worry about future revenue at a time like this?

'So, you definitely didn't kill Elliot?' Clementine asked, her raised eyebrows showing off her disbelief. 'And you definitely don't know where Doug is?'

'Why would I kill Elliot?' Kevin asked. 'How will the band play the summer festival now? It's not going to go on, is it, not after this. That's money down the drain. We've got a Christmas cover record out – guess how many records we've sold?' Clementine opened her mouth to guess, but Kevin interrupted before she could. 'Sixteen! It's not worth the vinyl it's printed on. Christ, and I paid extra for the records to be green splatter glitter. We really needed this.'

Margery saw movement from the corner of her eye and turned to find Mrs Bell shuffling over to them, a smile on her face and a tray of squished mince pies in her hand. Kevin didn't wait for her to reach them. They all watched him shuffle away, rubbing his bandaged wrist. Maybe he had gone to find where Sally's promised cup of tea had got to. Margery suspected it was more to avoid further questioning.

Mrs Bell's face had fallen. 'Ooh, I just wanted to offer him a snack. It must have been terribly boring under the stage. I thought he might want someone to chat to.'

'What do you think?' Margery asked Clementine as soon as Mrs Bell had shuffled out of earshot again.

'I don't know if he killed Elliot,' Clementine said. 'But he's certainly got something else going on and I don't believe none of the band had anything to do with the axe. It was in their van! Symon will need to double check that they didn't use that when he gets here. Or they hadn't at least planned to use it for something. I don't know.'

Margery looked up at the ceiling as though the answers might be written there. There was nothing but rows of paperchains stuck to it with Sellotape. 'I really wish Symon was down here now. I really don't know where to go next with all of this. What did you make of Kevin's slip about Elliot's body being in the hall?'

'I don't know,' Clementine said, twisting her wedding ring around her finger nervously. 'Who would have moved Elliot's body? Why not just leave him there if you killed him? Were they trying to cover it up and didn't think anyone would find it? It wasn't a very good hiding place if so. That's what happened if what Kevin said wasn't a mistake and he's not lying. All this and we still don't know where Doug is and I really don't think that can be a good thing.'

For once, Clementine looked truly rattled.

Margery took her hand and held it tightly. 'Come on, let's go and find the others.'

Chapter Twelve

They passed Rose and Rhonda, who had already continued their trading, if you could really call it that. Rose had waited exactly eleven minutes after Kevin had careened back into the hall to restart. The worst thing was they were encouraged on by people desperate enough to rent a T-shirt or buy a teabag in a mug for seventeen pounds. Margery had a mind to report both of them to HMRC as soon as possible, though she didn't think that would be a suitable chastising for Rose, who would probably have the spare cash to pay the tax bill.

'I always thought I'd be a great cult leader, but turns out I just don't have the charisma,' Clementine sighed, gesturing at them as they passed. 'Look at Rose: she's taken it all in her stride. She's practically started a coven out there already. We've only been here a day. What will she get done by next week? We'll probably all be carving her face out of marble.'

It was true, Margery thought, and with Rhonda at that. If someone had told Margery last week that Rose and Rhonda would be putting their twenty-year-long disagreement aside for this then she never would have believed them. Rose had sort of forgiven Rhonda for stealing her job at Ittonvale Comprehensive school decades before, but they had existed alongside each other in a very tumultuous truce ever since. It was quite nice for them to make up at Christmas, Margery thought, joy to the world and peace on earth notwithstanding.

They finally arrived at the door to the green room and found the rest of the team. The day had become longer and more boring the more it went on and time seemed to have stopped completely, though the sun had begun to lower outside after passing the midway point. She watched its slow descent with interest through the window and felt guilty for being bored. She bet that Elliot would have given anything to be bored again.

However, the boredom gave her time to think. Had Elliot's murder been planned? The killer might well have known that Margery and Clementine would be here and so could have set up a lot of dead ends and red herrings for them to focus on to draw attention away from themselves. They had been dragged into things in that way before. Perhaps they should begin to try and make themselves less well-known for their proclivities. It was very rarely helpful. Most of the time it was at the very least a hindrance and at the worst of times it put them in grave peril. Then again, Elliot's murder might have been a spur-of-the-moment act of anger. There was no way of knowing yet.

Gloria was furiously trying to scrub her coat clean on one of the trestle tables, it had been useful to put the fire out but had suffered dreadfully for it. Karen comforted Sharon as she wept over the remains of her favourite windbreaker. Great glops of wax had run down it and there was a burn hole in one of the sleeves where the waterproof material had caught fire.

'What are we going to do if we need to evacuate the building or something?' Ceri-Ann asked. She folded her arms and looked down at her own singed winter coat.

The faux fur around the hood hadn't fared well against the wax from the errant candle. It stuck up like a lion's mane. 'I can't wear this. Not in front of actual people. What if someone wants to sign me up to be a model and then they see my coat and think that's how I wear it all the time?'

'We'll wrap ourselves in foil,' Clementine suggested. 'Or pay Rose eight million pounds for her coat. We'll pay by cheque and then she won't know it's bounced for days.'

'I used to love paying for things by cheque,' Karen said, sitting back with a smile at the memory. 'When I was nineteen I had a cheque book and I'd go and buy a new outfit in town on my lunch break with it when I only had six pence in my bank account until payday.'

'Those were the days. They don't even feel that long ago,' Sharon agreed. 'You could always go into the bank and ask them to make your overdraft bigger and they almost always would.'

'Yes!' Seren beamed. 'And if you couldn't be bothered to call in sick then you'd just come in the next day without telling anyone where you'd been and then tell your manager that you didn't have any phone credit or money for the phone box to call them… I mean, I'd never do that now, Margery!'

Margery laughed in spite of everything. The dinner ladies slipped back into their usual easy chatter. It had a familiar rhythm to it and reminded Margery of being at work, which, she had to admit to herself, was one of her happy places. Even in this new and murderous environment, her team stayed the same. It was like entering a warm kitchen on a freezing cold day. The lights flickered back on suddenly and they all whooped. Ceri-Ann held her phone up in the air as if that would help it find a signal, only to put it back down in defeat.

'We could talk to Jade?' Margery whispered to Clementine as the chatter continued. 'She owed Elliot money, didn't she? If you believe Doug rather than Kevin.'

'Maybe,' Clementine said, thinking about it. 'She was eager to get Jacob into trouble, though, wasn't she? Ooh, what about Doug's office?'

'The office?' Margery asked. She hadn't even thought of it before. Even when they'd been desperately searching for him. The office had stayed locked and silent, no signs of movement inside it. 'That's a good idea, actually.'

They made their excuses and crept over to it through the corridor outside the green room. Searching the office was much easier said than done. For one thing, the door to it was in a well-trodden area and for a second, it had a keycode lock on the door handle. Clementine would bend to inspect it and then two seconds later someone would come wandering into the hallway and interrupt them. Margery was sure that Arthur wouldn't mind them delving into the room – he would probably give them the code himself – but Margery suspected he didn't know it. Sally was a different story, Margery couldn't imagine that she would be happy to let them in, even for a very good cause.

'I think I know how to work it out,' Clementine said, jabbing at the combination lock with her finger. 'Look, not very secure, is it?'

Margery looked where Clementine was pointing and saw that three numbers were more worn than the others. She could almost imagine the fingerprints that had worn them away over the years.

'So, it's a combination of those three,' Margery said. 'Hmmm, start with number three first – it's worn all over, that says to me that it's the first number. The others are only worn to one side.'

Clementine began to try the numbers, flinching back from the keypad as the door behind them opened again.

'We're never going to be able to sneak into here,' Margery said, pretending they were deep in conversation as the guitarist of Apex Void wandered past.

'You have to push the star button first,' Ceri-Ann called from behind them, causing Margery and Clementine both to jump. Ceri-Ann was watching them with interest.

'We're just trying to…' Clementine began, giving up and waving a hand over the door lock.

'Important dinner lady business, is it?' Ceri-Ann asked, grinning from ear to ear. 'Need some help?'

'Oh, I see how it is,' Clementine scoffed. 'Just because you helped Symon cheat on all his detective exams, you think you can help us…'

'I didn't help him cheat. He read loads and loads of books about being a detective, Sherlock Holmes or whatever, mate,' Ceri-Ann said with a roll of her eyes, but her smile didn't fade a bit. 'Come on, let me help! What's the problem?'

'We keep getting interrupted while we're trying to open the lock,' Margery explained. 'We only want to see what's in here.'

'Say no more,' Ceri-Ann said with a wave of her hand. She turned to Seren, who had wandered out into the hallway holding a biscuit and looking incredibly pleased with herself. When she noticed Ceri-Ann's gaze, she hid it behind her back. 'Seren, do you think you could cause a distraction?'

'A distraction?' Seren looked as though she had never heard the word in her life. 'What do you mean? Me?'

'Ooh, yes,' Clementine said, nodding victoriously. 'Go in the hall and throw yourself on the floor, Seren.'

'You don't have to do that, Seren,' Margery said, feeling her eyes widening in alarm. 'Just maybe watch the door for us?'

'I know…' Seren began, looking pleased with herself. Margery could practically see the cogs in her head whirring. 'There's a karaoke machine in there, maybe I could start it up? It's all plugged in still from last night. The power's back on, isn't it?'

'Oh my God, yes, Seren!' Ceri-Ann cried in triumph. 'Gloria loves karaoke, get her to do a duet with you. Ooh, and then Rose will join in – she won't be able to help herself!'

Seren grinned toothily and scurried away to enact her plan. A few minutes later the distinct tones of 'Man, I Feel Like a Woman' blared through the closed hall door. Gloria came out of the green room, following the sound blindly, as though she had been summoned by Shania Twain herself. Ceri-Ann pointed towards the hall and Gloria clapped her hands together in excitement, rushing through the doors.

Margery and Clementine smiled at each other and then Clementine continued to try the different combinations. Gloria began to sing the second verse, obviously pleased to be asked to join in, and Clementine fumbled with the lock. She exclaimed with a yell when the door handle turned easily. The three of them slid inside and shut the door firmly behind them.

Doug's office was bland in its mundanity. It contained little more than a metal desk with a matching uncomfortable-looking chair and a filing cabinet. The bookshelf behind the desk barely held anything but a few files, all labelled boring things like *Dewstow Summer Fete 2000–2010*. Margery stood in the doorway as Ceri-Ann began to rummage through the filing cabinet, taking it in. Clementine sat down in the office chair. It swung around as she did so, and she began to search through Doug's desk. They all ignored the laptop sitting on it for now. Margery assumed it would have a password, though if it was similar to Doug's phone then perhaps it wouldn't be a hard one to crack. Doug might be the sort of person who thought that the internet was wishy-washy nonsense and passwords were futile, for all they knew.

Margery had half expected Doug to be waiting for them in the office. She had thought that perhaps this was where he was hiding out away from Sally and the rest of the rabble. In her mind, he had either killed Elliot and tried to run or decided he had finally had enough of the stress of it all and locked himself away.

Margery joined Clementine at the desk and looked down at the clutter in dismay. There were lots of photo frames arranged next to the laptop, all of Doug smiling at town events and shaking people's hands, along with several used coffee cups. The coffee had dried to the insides of them long ago, it was no wonder that they had struggled to find enough cups at breakfast. The rest of the clutter was mostly rubbish, but something caught Margery's eye. She picked up the dried orange slice next to a piece of wire and inspected it.

'What was this for?' she asked the room.

Clementine shrugged, Margery didn't know either. Perhaps Doug had been planning on joining Mrs Bell's wreath-making class at some point. Clementine opened the door to the desk, exclaiming with interest at what she found inside.

'Ooh, look, Margery,' she said, 'Tickets for the summer festival! Gosh, I wonder if that'll still go ahead now that one of the organisers has gone.'

'I'm sure someone will step into the role by then,' Margery said, feeling a sudden surge of sadness at the sight of the book of tickets. Perhaps no one would. It did seem like a big job, all the planning started months and months before. That's why she was surprised that it had taken so long for Doug to tell Kevin that Jade hadn't paid her deposit.

'Well, I'm not sure who'll do all the food now Elliot's gone,' Clementine said. 'Remember that letter we found that said Elliot was in charge of it at the summer festival? I wonder what will happen now.'

'I remember,' Margery said, thinking of the mysterious letter they had found in Elliot's van. There had to be something here that gave that more clarity. It couldn't just be a dumping ground for receipts.

'They aren't cheap, those tickets,' Ceri-Ann said from behind them, as Clementine pulled a stapler out of the desk and examined it carefully. 'We were going to go just for the Saturday but it's fifty pounds each. I asked Symon if he could get us in, police business or something, but he said that would break the code of conduct or something boring like that.'

'Gosh,' Margery exclaimed. 'That certainly seems pricey seeing as you have to pay for everything when you get inside anyway.'

She reached out and flicked through the tickets.

'Wait a minute,' she said. 'There's more than one of each ticket here. Look, they're numbered twice…'

'What does that mean?' Clementine asked, peering over Margery's shoulder.

Margery shook her head. 'I'm not entirely sure, but possibly they've double booked it to make more money? That seems suspicious, especially since we know that Kevin accused Elliot of stealing Jade's deposit.'

'Surely a thing like that must have a maximum capacity for safety,' Clementine suggested.

Ceri-Ann nodded, taking the tickets to look at them. 'Yeah, it does. The police usually help man it but Doug said he was hiring outside security next year.'

They all went back to their search. Margery went over to the Wi-Fi router sitting on the filing cabinet and turned it around. She thought she might be able to get it back on, the atmosphere in the building would surely be better if they could all play solitaire on their phones. She gasped in surprise when she saw that she couldn't.

'Someone's cut the power cord,' Margery said, lifting the remaining cord to show Ceri-Ann and Clementine.

'Oh my God, who would do that?' Ceri-Ann huffed furiously. 'Do they not want us to be happy? How can I tell Chantelle how many I'm winning Whamageddon by if I've got no internet.'

Clementine didn't answer, her attention was taken up by something over on Doug's desk.

'What's that, Clem?' Margery asked. She leaned forward to peek at the file over Clementine's shoulder.

'It looks like a diary planner,' Clementine said. 'Or a to-do list, something like that.'

Margery read over her shoulder, all little titbits of information. It did indeed look like a list of things left to organise for the upcoming events in the hall. Doug needed to source stacks and stacks of haybales for an autumn festival, and he hadn't yet managed to procure a Wild West-themed band. The margins were filled with phone numbers in small lettering, and notes to self. List after list of things to ask Sally to sort out and diagrams of where he thought the tombola should go for the summer festival.

'Look at this,' Clementine said. 'It's a list of deposits that were taken.'

Margery scanned the page, letting her gaze wander over the columns of names and figures and hastily scribbled pound signs. Each entry was a scrawl of accusation. Doug's hurried handwriting left no doubt that he had known what Elliot had been up to. Margery traced a line down the page to where Doug had circled vendors that had paid bribes for better places, her finger pausing over Jade's name and the amount scrawled next to it. It was not a small sum of money in anyone's book. She felt a shiver roll down her spine at the confirmation that Jade had been telling the truth.

'Could Doug have killed Elliot?' Clementine asked Margery, tapping her chin with her long fingers. 'It seems like a long shot, but weirder things have happened and he isn't around to ask, is he? Maybe Elliot found out Doug was onto him and confronted him, but… well… would he kill someone for that? That seems mad. But it explains why he's not here, he might have run afterwards.'

'This isn't good,' Margery said, realising as she said it how much of a massive understatement that was. 'Why did he lie to Kevin about Jade's money if he knew Elliot had stolen it?'

She tapped the page where Doug had written the amount Elliot had stolen from Jade. Clementine shook her head.

'I really don't know,' Clementine said with a sigh. 'Perhaps he's trying to protect the hall's reputation.'

She flicked through the pages of the book again as Ceri-Ann reached over to the laptop.

'I wouldn't bother with that horrendous chunk of metal,' Clementine said sadly. 'We're always being foiled by passwords. We'll need our computer experts, Sharon and Karen, and they're busy off doing, well, whatever it is they've been occupying themselves with.'

'Just because someone had a Myspace page in 2005 doesn't mean they're a computer expert,' Ceri-Ann said with a scoff. 'It means that they probably need to add retinol to their night-time skincare routine and there's 700 photos of them on Facebook from twenty years ago wearing ballet flats and a scarf as a belt.'

Ceri-Ann waved the computer mouse until the screen flickered into life. The computer loaded up onto the main screen immediately and they all exclaimed in surprise.

'No password?' Margery asked. Ceri-Ann was already tapping away on the screen and searching through the email account for the hall.

'None,' Ceri-Ann said. 'I guess that makes sense if it's shared between all the staff and whatever, but I bet it means we won't find much on here. Oh no, the Wi-Fi's down, isn't it? I can still look at saved emails and sent emails, though, in Outlook.'

Margery looked back at the disconnected router. That was odd too. It wasn't something that could happen on its own. Someone had come into the office and cut the cord.

'Not much here, really.' Ceri-Ann tutted. 'There is this random one from the council.'

'What does it say?'

'It's a reply sent to Elliot from environmental health confirming that all the vendors coming to the event have a five food-hygiene rating.' Ceri-Ann peered at the screen, scrolling back to the initial email. 'Basically Elliot asked them to check because he says he was sure that one of them only had a two.'

'Who didn't have a five?' Margery asked. Less than a five on a food-hygiene report was damning in her eyes. Two was an abysmal failing of management.

'Doesn't say.' Ceri-Ann shook her head.

Margery thought it over. Elliot had told them the night before that one of the food suppliers was not meant to be here and they had suspected earlier that it had been Jacob's stall that was unwanted. It must have been Jacob's stall with the low rating, that must be why Elliot hadn't wanted him there.

'Did you say you could see outgoing messages too?' Margery asked. Ceri-Ann nodded, opening the folder on the computer.

'Hmmm, let's see,' Ceri-Ann said, squinting at the screen. 'Ooh, yeah! Look at this one from Doug to some company telling them off… Ahh, it's from yesterday!'

'What do you mean?' Margery leaned closer to look at the email.

> To Elliot,
>
> It has come to my attention that several of next year's festivals have been amended to add your new catering company, Bell and Worthy, to the list of vendors. While I appreciate your ambition, removing previously booked vendors that have submitted deposits is a clear conflict of interest and goes

> against our company policy. As someone with responsibility for booking events and food vendors, you are expected to act in the best interest of the company, without personal gain affecting your decisions.

The rest of the email was an invitation to a disciplinary hearing for Monday morning. Margery gasped at the scandal of it. Bell and Worthy must have been the new business Mrs Bell had told them about, judging by the amalgamation of their surnames. Margery wondered if Mrs Bell knew what Elliot had been planning. This must be what Doug had meant when he told Kevin on the recording that he would 'deal with Elliot'.

'What are you three doing?' a voice called from behind them.

They nearly jumped out of their skins. Margery spun around to see who had interrupted. Sally glared at them, waving her hands in the air when she didn't get an answer quick enough.

'I knew I should have been on guard duty,' Ceri-Ann hissed under her breath. 'Can't go anywhere without a nosy busybody there.'

'We were just searching for clues,' Margery found herself saying, her voice weak. 'You know… for Elliot…'

'Clues!' Sally scoffed. She stormed over to them and slammed Doug's laptop shut with bony fingers. 'I don't know what the police are thinking, or Arthur for that matter. Letting you prance around pretending to be detectives – ridiculous.'

'Well, they've got a good track record,' Ceri-Ann said, glaring at her. 'That's why Symon wants them to help.'

'And we've got a website!' Clementine piped up.

Sally shooed them away from the desk and began to shuffle them all towards the door. 'Doug will be furious to know you've been through his things and I have half a mind to ban you from future events.'

'We don't want to come to any of them anyway after this debacle,' Clementine said as Sally escorted them out. 'We've spent enough time here as it is, and that's without a fire and a murder!'

'Not murder!' Sally gasped, shooing them with even more force. She managed to shuffle them back out into the hallway with rotating arms like a windmill, slamming the door behind them.

'That was rude,' Clementine said. 'What's she hiding?'

Margery wondered. Apart from her very understandable breakdown after seeing Elliot's body, Sally had struck her as a calm and detached sort of person. Nothing like the woman who had just thrown them out of someone else's office. Obviously, she had warned them off from asking questions, but Margery had thought that was so they didn't incite a panic, more than anything else. Sally certainly didn't seem the type to murder anyone, but Margery and Clementine had met more than a few murderers the very same.

Chapter Thirteen

'Well, that was suspicious, wasn't it?' Clementine said as Margery paced back and forth in the tiny cloakroom they had found Doug's phone and coat in. It was a massive understatement by any reasonable standard. Margery hadn't been able to stop pacing since Sally had rudely removed them from the office.

'She certainly didn't not seem suspicious,' Margery said, finally slowing down to a stop. 'But I can't put it all together yet. For one thing, why would anyone chop the tree down? To trap us all here?'

Clementine was reclining on a Christmas tree box, in what would have seemed a relaxed way if the entire weekend hadn't blown up into smithereens, running her fingers over her chin in thought.

'Elliot couldn't have suspected what would happen to him,' she said finally. 'Did one of Apex Void even chop the tree down? We don't have any proof that they did just because there was an axe in the van. Obviously we think one of them did, but no one will admit that, we'll have to see what the police say.'

'No,' Margery said. 'Do you think Sally knew about the money?'

Clementine sat up, her face the picture of surprised excitement.

'Yes, I bet she did!' Clementine exclaimed. She thought about it. 'Well, maybe she didn't know the ins and outs of it? It does seem strange, though. But then surely Elliot knew about what Doug had recorded and written? The computer didn't have a password, did it?'

'Maybe, and the Wi-Fi router was tampered with,' Margery said. 'Someone must have snuck into the office and cut the cord.'

'Probably Sally?' Clementine suggested. 'Judging by her reaction? She wasn't happy that we were in the office, was she?'

'Probably Sally,' Margery agreed.

'So, what now?' Clementine asked.

Margery shook her head. She really didn't know.

'If you think I had something to do with the Wi-Fi router then you're greatly misinformed,' a quiet voice said, barely muffled by the cloakroom door. In hindsight, Margery thought, it hadn't been a very private place for a secret conversation.

Margery reached out and pushed the door open, finding Sally standing on the other side of it.

'Were you listening to us the entire time?' Clementine accused.

Sally nodded back, hard-faced. 'Yes, I was, as a matter of fact. It's a free country.'

'I wouldn't say the hall is a country, shut away from the world like this,' Clementine scoffed. 'It's descending into more of a dictatorship.'

'Did you follow us?' Margery asked Sally.

'Of course I did,' Sally said. 'After I found you snooping in Doug's office, how could I not? And…' She spluttered to a stop, her mouth puckered as though what she was about to say might be physically painful. 'You seem to be making great strides in your little case and now you're still poking around, have you no shame?'

'We're trying to help,' Margery said weakly. She looked around the small space, begging for something else to say.

'I haven't even told Elliot's family yet,' Sally rasped. She wiped her eyes. Her voice cracked. 'I don't know what to say!'

'Why haven't you told his family yet?' Clementine said. 'They need to know. You can't hide this from them.'

'I suppose not,' Sally said. 'But I still don't know where Doug is.' She sobbed the last words in a great gasp. 'He's left me here to sort all of this out!'

They fell into an awkward silence. Sally finally broke it. 'I apologise for my reaction in the office. I was just surprised to find you all in there. I've… I don't know the code. Doug would never tell me.'

'Why not?' Margery asked.

'I don't know,' Sally said finally in a clipped voice. 'They were their own little boys' club, they never told me anything.'

Sally looked haunted by her own confession. It was as if she had never considered it before and had purely accepted the locked office as a fact of life. Maybe she was only now realising that Doug and Elliot had been hiding something from her. Or worse, actively conspiring against her. There was nothing to say that Doug hadn't been accepting of Elliot's schemes in the end. Jade certainly hadn't been given her money back, had she? Though perhaps he had planned to sort all of that out after Elliot's disciplinary meeting. Margery thought that the most likely reason that Doug hadn't been honest with Kevin was in an attempt to protect the reputation of the hall.

'Well, what do you have to say for yourself?' Clementine asked. 'You didn't know anything that was going on with Elliot and Doug?'

Sally's face fell.

'I didn't know there was anything going on,' she said. 'Not financially.'

'You're really telling us that?' Clementine asked, shaking her head. 'I find that hard to believe. You're the hall treasurer, aren't you?'

'Well, yes, that's true,' Sally said, folding her arms across her chest tightly. 'So, all the funds should have gone through me. I just don't know why they'd hide it from me. Elliot should have given me Jade's money right away. She should have paid it to me herself!'

'Did they have a reason not to pay you directly?' Margery asked. 'Did they not trust you for some reason?'

'Of course not!' Sally spluttered. She clutched at her chest like she might begin having a heart attack at any second. 'I've been in the post for a decade, why would I embezzle money now?'

Margery shook her head. She didn't know, but there was a puzzle piece missing.

'Well, you're telling us that you didn't know the door code,' Margery said. 'But someone's cut the Wi-Fi cord, so who else knows the code?'

Sally looked at her with surprise. 'Only Doug and Elliot knew it.'

Margery found that very hard to believe. It was too far-fetched. Sally didn't just have casual involvement with Doug and the hall, she was the treasurer. She should have been privy to codes and locks and how the hall worked. She had worked with them long enough. Margery had never been to an event at the hall that hadn't been graced by Sally's presence, for better or for worse. She didn't seem to be that upset by Elliot's death or care much about Doug's disappearance. In fact, the only thing Margery had heard her say about it was that she was in charge now, when she had been arguing with Arthur. It made it very difficult to believe that Sally hadn't crept into the office and cut their only link to the outside world.

They left Sally in the corridor and made their way back to the green room, though Margery wished they had some news to share. Ceri-Ann would probably have already passed on news of their discoveries, but it didn't help them. Especially if Sally was wary of them, Margery thought. They would have to be very careful not to be seen investigating under her watchful eye. Perhaps Sally had something to hide about Elliot's death. It certainly looked that way. But Margery kept remembering the way Sally's face had crumpled at the sight of his body. If she had been responsible for his death, she was certainly a brilliant actor. Still, there had probably been enough performance art and pantos put on in the community hall for her to have picked up some tips.

'Oh, Ceri,' Seren gasped, pointing to the toaster. 'I don't think that's supposed to smoke like that, is it?'

'Just a bit of smoke for extra flavour,' Ceri-Ann said, inspecting her nails as she leaned against the kitchen counter.

'Christ, it's on fire!' Gloria shrieked, wafting her hands over it to dispel the smoke. 'We're not trying to announce a new pope, what did you put in there?'

'Just a bit of bread,' Ceri-Ann scoffed. 'Well… maybe it was a piece of pizza. Couldn't be bothered to put the oven on.'

She unplugged the toaster and then picked it up using the tea towel, the flame much too close to her hair for Margery's liking. If it had been a normal day, things would have ended much more tragically. Luckily, none of them had brought any hairspray with them.

'Put it outside,' Margery said, jumping back so Ceri-Ann could pass her.

There wasn't time to try and find the fire blanket or risk their only shelter. There was no way she could face going back out in this weather for a fire alarm and they had already had such a close call with Kevin's coat and the candles. Also, she was sure that she had last seen Mrs Bell wearing the fire blanket as a sort of cape as she huddled down in Rose and Rhonda's makeshift den, where they were now selling single teabags without the mug for six pounds. The hall was descending into a capitalist *Lord of the Flies* situation before her very eyes. Though, even with their mad resource pooling, Margery couldn't see them having much left to sell soon. Rhonda was already trying to sell water in empty beer bottles, which she was calling 'God's wine'. Margery knew that the taps in the bathrooms and kitchens were all still running perfectly. There seemed no rhyme or reason to any of it.

Margery rushed to the fire escape and pushed on the handle. It didn't budge at all. She tried again, feeling weaker each time. Ceri-Ann began to hop back and forth, waving the toaster around dangerously. The smoke billowed out of it around their heads and burnt crumbs scattered all over the floor like tiny burning ants. Ceri-Ann puffed air over the toaster uselessly, like she was trying to blow out the birthday cake candles at her hundredth birthday party.

'Give me a hand here, Clem!' Margery called.

Clementine and the rest of the team all rushed over to join her at the door, putting their hands to the bar. Under the pressure of the group, the door began to slide open slowly, getting caught on something at the last minute. Margery could see something wedging it shut from the other side. Clementine reached out and gave whatever was in the way a swift kick, and the door opened just enough for Ceri-Ann to slide out with the toaster.

There was a brief moment where Margery looked around at the rest of her team, smiling at a disaster averted, but then Ceri-Ann screamed. Margery heard the toaster smash, the plastic and metal pieces clattering onto the tarmac with a thump as it hit the snow. Ceri-Ann slid back in through the fire escape, her face pale and her mouth hanging open in genuine fear.

'It's Doug,' she huffed, her breath coming in shallow bursts, her eyes glistening with tears.

'What?' Margery found herself asking, moving past Ceri-Ann and sliding outside herself.

She wished immediately that she hadn't. Doug sat frozen outside the fire escape door, wine bottle in hand still. His skin was pale blue and his closed eyelids had collected a layer of the recent snowfall. Frozen forever in place.

Chapter Fourteen

'That explains why no one could find him,' Clementine said a bit later as they sat back in the green room, huddled together for comfort.

At the beginning of their ordeal, Karen and Sharon had been so excited to use their Dewstow running club emergency survival kits, waving around bars of Kendal mint cake and survival blankets. Even they had finally had enough. The sight of Doug's frozen face had taken every last drop of excitement out of it. All that was left was fear. Margery wanted to run, but there was nowhere to go.

Ceri-Ann was recovering, sitting on a chair in the corner with a cup of tea, the warmth from the mug seeping into her hands. Gloria had a comforting arm around her and Margery could hear her voice, low and steady, reciting the bible verses in Tagalog from the well-worn book in her other hand.

Margery stood in the corner and watched Gloria speaking, listening to the words as they filled the room with a steady rhythm that matched the noise of the rain drumming on the hall's flat roof. A chair creaked as someone moved, their coat crackling as they pulled it tighter around them, but otherwise there was silence. Like the grief had somehow taken residence inside the walls. The hall should have only ever held happy memories and children's laughter, but it was becoming more a mausoleum as the days went on.

Margery could remember in great detail the first time she had seen a dead body, though she supposed they were old pros at it now. The first few times she hadn't been able to sleep after, the murdered person's face crawling behind her eyelids and playing peek-a-boo with her. Now, her brain moved on logically to the next thing. She wasn't sure it was a good thing to lose that part of your humanity, like cutting away at a bit of your soul with a jagged piece of glass and letting it drop down into the caverns below.

They had summoned Symon on the radio immediately, he would have no choice now but to speed things up. They needed to get everyone safely off site, though that would leave the killer out there somewhere still, Margery knew. But the police would have to deal with it from here on. It wasn't a job for dinner ladies any more, not now there were two bodies. Arthur had gone as white as Doug when he saw his body propped up outside on the step and they had decided between them to not announce it yet. His reasoning was that night was falling and it wouldn't do to incite any more of a panic if they could help it.

Margery wondered how Doug had felt as he died, remembering with horrible pickling dread that one day she would die too. She didn't know how or when, but it was certain. Perhaps she would die after a long illness, or in a nursing home or hospital. Maybe she would wake up one morning, choose what she was going to wear for the day and then drop down dead in front of the full-length mirror in their bedroom. No one could say.

It looked, to Margery and Clementine's untrained eyes, that Doug had been drunk and had gone outside for some reason only to find that he couldn't get back into the building. When he'd tried to leave the fire escape, he had fallen and broken his leg. Margery thought he might have tripped over the step down from it, judging by the way he had dragged himself back up. The bone had been visible through his trousers, jagged and white and disgusting enough to make Margery want to be sick.

'He wasn't even wearing a coat,' Clementine groaned. She fiddled with the walkie-talkie attached to one of her trouser belt loops like that would help speed things up. It dangled silently for now, but Margery dreaded when it would wake up again with more bad news from the police force.

He hadn't been wearing a coat, Margery thought. Which had been a dire mistake in the end. She supposed a coat wouldn't have saved him, though the phone in its pocket might well have. Maybe the coat alone would have given him some time, they might have heard him yelling when they were all up the next morning. She suddenly had the horrible recollection of the fire escape door banging and rattling all night that first evening. Now she knew it must have been Doug trying to get into the building. If any of them had gone out to investigate the noise then he might still be alive. The guilt consumed her for a moment and she allowed herself to wallow in it.

'Jacob said that he cleared up some wet footprints last night,' Clementine said, her brow furrowing as she tried to remember. 'Do you think someone purposefully shut Doug out, or knew he was out there?'

'Did Jacob actually see Doug?' Margery asked her. 'I swear he said he saw him come in. But he can't have because Doug was outside for who knows how long. They could have been anyone's footprints and if he's cleaned them up then we've got no way of finding out whose they were.'

'I assume the autopsy will confirm it, but I have my suspicions that Doug died not long after Elliot, at least,' Clementine said. She waved her hands in the air as she spoke as though she were trying to conjure up the image of what really happened. 'So does that put him out of the running for killing him?'

'Well, no, not at all,' Margery said. 'He could have killed Elliot first. We don't know the exact time of Elliot's death. We're not coroners or police officers. We'd need an autopsy to find out.'

There were certainly more than a few people who might have hurt Elliot. Jade for stealing her money, Kevin for similar reasons. Jacob couldn't be ruled out, not after his wishy-washy explanations about how he had known Elliot and how well. Margery couldn't be sure the killer wasn't sitting among them, although she didn't think Sharon or Karen had it in them. But Doug? She wasn't sure why anyone would kill Doug. Maybe it was a terrible accident. Maybe Elliot had shut him out after Doug confronted him about his schemes and then died before he could let him back inside. Perhaps Doug was involved in the scheming. None of that explained who had cut the Wi-Fi cord earlier. Elliot had been dead long before that. Of course it must have been the killer, Margery was sure that whoever had killed Elliot was trying to keep them disconnected from the outside world. But who was the killer?

'Did Jacob borrow our mop to clear the footprints up?' Gloria said, interrupting Margery's thoughts. 'This place is a pigsty and I couldn't find it anywhere earlier. I'm sure we mopped last night before we went to see the band play.'

'Oh!' Seren gasped, her cheeks flushing red suddenly. 'I took it out to empty the dirty water down the drain.'

'Well, where is it, then?' Gloria asked.

Seren grinned half-heartedly, twisting her hands together. 'It might still be outside.'

Gloria rolled her eyes, but she went to the back door of the green room anyway, opening it. The mop sat in the bucket outside where Seren had left it, the handle frozen stiff. Gloria didn't need to lift the bucket to bring it inside, the mop was frozen to it and it came with her in one piece. She went to put it down on the kitchen floor, but the handle came away from the mop and then the entire thing tumbled to the floor with a crack.

'If the mop has been out here since last night, then what did Jacob mop Doug's footprints up with?' Clementine asked suddenly, the question ringing around the room.

'Is there another mop and bucket?' Gloria asked. 'For the hall?'

'No,' Margery said, remembering the contract she had needed to sign that said they would provide their own cleaning supplies for the weekend. 'But maybe Jacob has his own mop?'

'I don't think any of the vendors had anything useful,' Gloria said, shaking her head. 'They were all asking me to borrow it on Friday. Obviously, I didn't let them because I didn't want it to get ruined.' She gave Seren a stern glare. Seren remained oblivious to it, lifting the frozen mop handle to look at it sadly, the mop ends twisted together like a wild tangle of tree roots.

'We'll thaw it out,' Karen said, giving Seren a gentle pat on the shoulder. Sharon had already jumped up to put the kettle on.

Margery got up from her seat and made her way into the hall, not waiting for anyone to follow her, but she could tell that Clementine had anyway by the footfall behind her. She didn't know what had come over her. Usually she was the one stopping Clementine from rushing off to apprehend a suspect. All she knew was that she was sick of being trapped in the hall, sick of having no answers, sick to her stomach thinking of the two dead men. She'd do anything to have an end to it. Even if other people thought she had gone mad.

Jacob looked even more bored than he had earlier and the hall seemed less vibrant somehow. It took Margery a moment to realise that more of the decorations had been stripped from the artificial trees. The plastic tree branches looked awfully bare without shiny baubles to line them. Margery shook her head in annoyance at the thought of Rose taking them, there wasn't time to wonder what on earth she must have taken them for. Jacob was sitting down in front of the floor-to-ceiling windows with his arms folded. His eyes were closed, he was dozing off even after all that had happened. It made her fume with rage, the very last straw after the bare trees, surprising even herself as she approached.

'Jacob,' she called to him before they even reached him. 'Jacob!'

His eyes snapped open in surprise. 'All right?'

'Yes,' Margery said, trying to keep the bite out of her voice and failing. 'Listen, what did you use to clean up Doug's footprints?'

Jacob looked confused for a moment. 'Oh, I used a tea towel.'

That stopped Margery in her tracks, the accusation suddenly deflating and falling flat. 'A tea towel?'

'Yeah, I didn't have anything else with me.' Jacob shrugged.

Margery didn't know what to say, so sure that Jacob would lie and say he'd mopped the floor and then reveal something that could possibly change their situation.

'Well, where is it?' Clementine asked curiously.

'The tea towel?' Jacob looked between them, bleary-eyed. 'Umm…'

He staggered up in slow motion and went to his stall. Jacob rummaged through the storage boxes behind it. He pulled out a dirty tea towel and held it up in triumph.

'Here you go!' he said, thrusting it into Margery's hand. She held it away from her and inspected the muddy patches on it. It was still damp from being put away without being cleaned and dried.

'Where did you say Doug came in?' she asked Jacob.

'Through that fire escape,' Jacob said. He pointed across the hall, before getting up. 'Come on, I'll show you.'

Margery and Clementine stumbled behind him, following to the fire escape where they had found Doug.

There had to be some sort of mistake, Margery thought, horror dawning on her as they stood on the other side of the door to where Doug's body still lay waiting for the police. Jacob pointed to the floor below the fire escape.

'The footprints were all through here,' he said, gesturing up the corridor towards Doug's office. 'Bit rude of him to not clean them up, I bet his office is a right mess.'

'Yes,' Margery said, at a loss for any other words. 'Were they coming in or out?'

'Oh… in. Look there's still a bit there,' Jacob said, pointing at the floor. 'Must have missed it.'

Margery and Clementine looked where he was pointing. Margery found her eyebrows raising at the sight of half a shoe print staring back at them. She couldn't believe they hadn't seen it before but realised that the halls were so busy at the moment that she hadn't thought to look. Could it in fact be someone else's footprint?

There was a noise from behind them, and Margery turned in a panic. Jade stood watching them from where she had appeared from the kitchenette, holding a cup of coffee she had procured from somewhere. Margery noticed that Jade was wearing an Apex Void long-sleeved T-shirt that was much too big for her from the band's merchandise stall. The sleeves were rolled up to her wrists.

She looked them up and down. Margery could feel the annoyance pouring from her in waves, though she saw a flicker of something cross Jade's face at the sight of the fire escape door. Margery looked away from her to Jacob, who was still holding the tea towel and had suddenly found something very interesting about the walls and ceiling.

'I'm off,' Jacob said, barely mumbling the words before he had disappeared, leaving them alone with Jade.

She glared at the pair of them. Margery thought that under the mask of her anger, she didn't look well. There was a grey tinge to her dark skin that hadn't been there earlier, she was sure of it.

'What are you two up to now?' Jade asked, but it was more of a demand than a question.

'Surely we could ask you the same?' Clementine asked in return. 'What are you doing?'

Jade shrugged, taking a sip from her mug.

'It's good you're here, actually,' Margery began. 'We just wanted to ask you—'

'A few more questions?' Jade said, giving them both a cold stare, which was intimidating even while holding a half-eaten custard cream. 'It's nothing but questions with you two. Have you found out who killed Elliot yet?'

'We thought you might know,' Clementine told her. Jade scoffed indignantly.

'Me!' she spluttered. 'Why would I know?'

'Shall we have this conversation privately?' Margery asked. She gestured to the tiny kitchenette behind her with its empty table and chairs.

'No,' Jade said. 'Whatever you want to say to me, you can say out here in front of everyone. I've got nothing to hide.'

Innocent people didn't say things like that very often, Margery thought with interest. Innocent people didn't usually realise their innocence was being questioned until you asked them something very directly.

'We didn't say you did!' Clementine said, holding her hands up in surrender.

Jade gave her a look before she put the rest of the biscuit in her mouth, her perfect eyebrows raising in a knowing way that told Margery that she knew exactly what they meant.

'Did Elliot take your money and then tell you he hadn't received it?' Margery asked her.

'You know about the money,' Jade realised, scowling at them. 'Who told you?'

'Does that matter?' Clementine asked. Margery realised how fortunate it really was that no one yet knew about Doug's untimely death. As horrible as it was, it gave them great scope for questioning.

'I suppose it doesn't,' Jade sighed. She sat back and folded her arms, leaning back against the wall.

'Why did you give him so much?' Margery asked.

'It was what he said I needed to secure the spot for my place on all the festivals for the upcoming year and the beginning of next year,' Jade explained.

'I don't understand why you need to pay a pitch fee,' Margery said. 'Surely you're here to provide a service, they should have been paying you. They paid us.'

'They would have paid you because the food is free for the artists, isn't it?' Jade said, suddenly becoming very interested in her own nails. 'It's different if you're selling food. All the best festivals have some sort of small pitch fee. Obviously, Elliot took it to the extreme.'

'But why pay so much for this one?' Clementine asked. 'Doug said you didn't pay the balance…'

'I have!' Jade yelled. 'I gave the money to Elliot, fat chance of getting that back now. This is why no one liked him. I'm not sorry he's dead, I don't care what that looks like. He took my money for himself and didn't even give me a good spot in the hall. I'm shoved at the back, aren't I? It's nearly as bad as Jacob's spot, and he isn't even supposed to be here.'

'You know about Jacob,' Margery said.

Jade spluttered for a moment, realising that she had said too much.

'Did you or Jacob ever confront Elliot about it?' Clementine asked, when she didn't answer. 'Surely he'd have had something to say to Jacob?'

'I couldn't get near him!' Jade explained. 'He avoided me all day yesterday and then obviously…' She waved a hand in front of her in the direction Elliot's body had been found. Margery found herself turning to look at the cardboard door to the Christmas grotto. 'Last night I went and made a formal complaint to Doug, but he told me it was "all in hand".' She lowered her voice to an eerily perfect impression of him.

'What did you do?' Margery asked.

'Nothing!' Jade said, much too quickly. 'I just told him to piss off.'

That was understandable, Margery thought. Given the circumstances. But it still left a lot of unanswered questions.

'Did you?' Clementine said. 'What did you say?'

'I...' Jade trailed off. Margery watched her eyes go to the fire escape door again and realised what it might mean.

'We saw you in the car park earlier,' Margery said, trying to sound light and casual. 'What were you doing?'

'I was getting some air,' Jade snapped, her mouth closing into a harsh line that didn't suit her face. 'Is that illegal now?'

'We saw you walk around the building,' Margery said. 'Towards the fire escape.'

She gestured to the door and Jade's eyes widened. Before Margery could say anything else she had turned and stormed into the kitchenette, seeming to have forgotten that she didn't care what people heard. They followed her. Jade slammed the door and then turned to glare at them both.

'You know,' she snapped. 'How do you know?'

'We found him,' Clementine told her.

'I didn't kill him,' Jade said, shaking her head so thoroughly Margery thought it might unscrew from her neck. 'You can't just go accusing people of things like that.'

Margery didn't think Jade saw the irony in that, even after she had accused Jacob of killing Elliot.

‘What do you mean by that?’ Margery asked. ‘We haven’t accused you of anything. What is it we’re supposed to know? How do you know he’s dead?’

Jade was stunned into silence. Margery watched her mouth opening and closing as nothing came out. She waited patiently for the words to return to her. Clementine did no such thing.

‘So, you didn’t kill him, but you know he’s dead,’ she said. ‘And you were just out in the snow having a little walk around the building to the fire escape, even though we’ve all been warned to stay inside…’

‘You were out there too!’ Jade roared, brandishing a finger at them. The hand shook even in her defiance.

‘We were trying to find out who killed Elliot,’ Clementine told her. ‘Not who killed Doug, we assumed he was just lying low somewhere.’

Margery took a deep breath, willing Jade to tell them what had happened without a fight. She suddenly realised that in their great search for the truth they weren’t being tactful at all. That was not an unusual occurrence, but in this circumstance, it made Margery feel awful. She might as well have thrown a glass made of pain and resentment at the woman’s head and watched it shatter against her skull. Margery saw the exact moment that Jade decided to tell them, the anger fluttering over her features and disappearing.

‘I locked him out,’ she whispered. She put her fingers over her face and Margery thought for a terrible second that she might draw her nails down her skin so hard that it bled. Instead, she just left harsh indents with her fingernails. ‘We had an argument, and he tried to get away from me by pretending he was going to check something outside and when he left, I locked the doors.’

‘The main doors?’ Margery asked. Jade nodded.

‘I thought he’d just bang on the window until someone let him back in,’ she said, her eyes welling with tears that didn’t quite fall. ‘But then he wasn’t around this morning, and Elliot was dead… I realised that maybe he didn’t come back in…’ She took a deep breath, steadying herself. ‘I found him on the step. I assume that’s how you know?’

Margery and Clementine nodded.

‘I didn’t mean for this to happen,’ Jade said, sounding angry again, this time at herself. ‘If he’d just stayed to talk to me then it wouldn’t have.’

Margery didn’t know what to say to that. Poor, poor Doug. The thought of him lying outside all night and most of the next day upset Margery in ways that she couldn’t even make sense of.

‘I’ll hand myself in,’ Jade said, ‘when the police get here.’

They would have to hold her to that.

Chapter Fifteen

That night was cold and the morning proved even more frigid. Margery had been glad that the dinner ladies could huddle together in the green room for warmth, though she couldn't say she had got much sleep. Even less than the night before, if that was possible.

Arthur and Sally might have been able to get the back-up generator working, but the heating wasn't what it had been now that the main door contained a van-sized hole. The heating was more of a vaguely warm breeze than a source of heat, a gust from a broken hairdryer even with the green room doors closed. Maybe it was gas central heating, Margery wondered, though it didn't really matter. There was nothing they could do to fix it. Still, it hadn't been reassuring to see everyone wearing their ruined coats inside. The candle wax had dripped down them all, leaving interesting patterns. That morning's breakfast had been an awful, cobbled-together affair again, but there were less complaints today. Even Mike had taken his plate without grumbling about the portion size. People were using their remaining energy to stay warm, huddling down in the hall in groups.

'Most people on Friday night were wearing some sort of boot or proper winter shoe,' Clementine whispered to Margery as they wandered the hallway back from the toilets. Washing in the freezing water from the bathroom taps had proved less than desirable, Margery didn't know if she'd ever feel warm again. The cold had seeped into her bones and rested there until the rest of her was numb. Clementine had been ruminating on the mystery of the footprint since they had left Jade alone the night before. Margery was becoming a bit sick of it under the circumstances but didn't have any better ideas.

'Yes,' Margery said, finding her voice. She examined the footprint as they passed it again, which was large with lines running across the sole in even spaces. 'Even Doug was wearing sturdy boots, wasn't he? That looks like a trainer to me, judging by the sole.'

'Yes, like a tennis shoe or something like that,' Clementine said, kneeling down to have a proper look at the shoeprint.

'Elliot was wearing tennis shoes on Friday night.' Margery suddenly remembered the red canvas shoes. 'Oh, Clem, did he know Doug was out there in the cold? Had he been outside with him?'

'I think he could have,' Clementine said. 'But why would he go straight to Doug's office when he got back in?'

'To do something on the computer?' Margery said, the idea dawning on her with horror.

'Yes, but what? Was he trying to delete Doug's notes about what he'd done? He didn't manage that, did he?' Clementine said, her eyes wide. 'Or… could he have gone in there to take something?'

They returned to the green room, where the team was still waiting and drinking the last of the tea.

'No word from Symon?' Margery asked as they approached the group.

'Nothing much more than last night.' Ceri-Ann gave Clementine the radio back. 'They've sorted all the gas and that now, though. They're just moving the tree. Symon's been told another five hours minimum, but he told me it's going to be much longer because the company that's supposed to be coming to move it hasn't turned up yet. Busy with everywhere else that got damaged in the storm. He reckons today, though. Probably.'

They all groaned at that. Five hours might as well be five years as far as Margery was concerned, and with the probability that it would be more, it was not looking promising. The only comfort in Margery's mind was that the killer hadn't seemed to deem Margery and Clementine a threat to be done away with yet. If Doug hadn't killed Elliot, then whoever had might be watching them, waiting to see if they'd be found. It sent shivers up Margery's spine, colder than the cool breeze that was freezing her fingers.

'At least it should be today,' Margery sighed. 'Come on, it's half ten already. We'll get lunch on for everyone, save a riot from happening.'

'Five hours, though!' Clementine gasped, though she had automatically jumped up to get the chicken from the van out of the fridge. They had saved it as long as they could before using it as their last resort. 'We'll all practically be frozen by then! We might as well wrap ourselves up in clingfilm and climb in the fridge to help things along. They can serve our bodies for Christmas dinner.'

'You know, Mrs Butcher-Baker,' Rose's voice boomed from the doorway, 'I'm so glad that you and your eternal optimism are here to help...'

'Nice of you to finally join us!' Clementine scoffed back. 'Have you finished selling everyone's cardigans and souls and tree baubles?'

'I haven't touched the baubles!' Rose said, before stammering the words back. 'I mean… no… I mean… oh, give it a rest, Clem. This is serious now. Ceri-Ann, are we actually getting out of here in five hours or not? We can't go on like this.' She waved a hand at Ceri-Ann's legs in a flapping motion. 'Can you shove over so I can sit down? Or better still, give me your seat, you've got young bones…'

'Have you never seen *Final Destination*?' Ceri-Ann scoffed. 'You're not supposed to swap seats with anyone. Anyway, you're not making anything any better, are you?'

Rose stared at her wide-eyed in shock. Margery found herself staring too. Ceri-Ann's temperament was usually so mild that it wouldn't have lit a tealight. Generally she was happy to bobble along with the rest of them, joking and not taking anything too seriously. It was odd to see the anger cross her face. Rose obviously hadn't been expecting it either by the way she goggled at her.

Ceri-Ann scoffed again in a harsh laugh. 'Why have you come crawling in here? Have you come to steal our teaspoons to sell? Just take it all, that's what you want!'

Ceri-Ann grasped for the teaspoons still lying on the Monopoly board and thrust them in Rose's direction. Rose's mouth opened and closed over and over but nothing came out. Margery suddenly realised that for all of Ceri-Ann's bluster and excitement over Whamageddon, it was probably a cover for how she really felt. It was surely easier to distract herself from how she was really feeling. Symon and Nicholas were at the top of the road, but they may as well have been on the moon.

'I'm missing the Christmas build-up with my son and you're here profiting on it all,' Ceri-Ann snapped, rising to her feet. Rose seemed to shrink and wither under her gaze even though they were the same height. 'What's wrong with you? Literally, what's your problem? You're supposed to be headteacher of a school or whatever. Is this what you'd want the students to act like? You want to have a word with yourself, mate, and Rhonda too. You can both get in the bin, acting like a load of kids. Worse than kids! My Nick knows how to share and he's a toddler!'

Gloria stood and took Ceri-Ann by the arm. 'Let's go and have a cup of tea, Ceri—'

'She's got all the teabags!' Ceri-Ann shrieked, flicking a finger at Rose like it was a weapon. 'And the milk and everything else. Even the tinsel!'

'Let's go and have a nice glass of hot water, then,' Gloria said soothingly. 'Come on.'

They slipped into the other room and Margery turned to Rose again. Rose's usually perfect complexion had turned the colour of Tippex. She blinked slowly, her mouth remaining open in surprise. Margery had never seen Ceri-Ann lose her temper before in all the years she had known her. Not even on the day that Seren had been showing off the shiny new plastic five-pound note she had received in her change and had managed to drop her entire purse into the huge pan of gravy Ceri-Ann had spent an hour making. Ceri-Ann had simply fished it out and then joked that it would give the gravy 'a rich flavour'.

'Is that what you all really think?' Rose asked after what felt like an age. 'All of you?'

Margery hesitated, then nodded, though she found herself feeling uncomfortable about it. She didn't know why. Rose had deserved to be called out on her actions, of course, but she had also seemed oblivious to how everyone else felt about them. Perhaps Margery should have tried to warn her gently when it had all started the day before. The thing was, Rose often acted in her own interests, or the sole interests of the school, that was not unusual. What was unusual was the situation. Being trapped together had drawn out the anger that wasn't always there.

Rose looked between them all, her face aghast. 'Seren?'

Seren went as white as Rose had. She wrung the tea towel in her hands, soapy water dripped from it onto the floor.

'Ummm…' Seren said, looking anywhere but in the direction of Rose's face. 'Well… yeah, I agree with Ceri. I don't think it's right…'

'Why didn't you tell me?' Rose muttered, the baubles that she was wearing as earrings clacking against her neck. 'You're supposed to be my conscience, Seren. I don't have my own!'

'It's just… taking the Christmas decorations down,' Seren said timidly. 'Isn't it depressing enough—'

'I haven't taken anything down!' Rose snapped.

Rose glared at Seren a second longer, before shaking her head and leaving. The green room door swung shut behind her and closed with a soft clack. Seren looked conflicted, but she returned to the kitchen and carried on washing up.

There was nothing else to it but to carry on with their lunch plans, things being as awful and confusing as they were. It had taken a short time to prepare the chicken and flatbreads and the very sad array of chopped lettuce onto trays and then Margery had asked Sally to let everyone know that they were serving. Surprisingly, once the green room was full of hungry people collecting plates of food or sitting down on the wonky plastic chairs to eat, Margery felt a lot better than she had since that first dreadful evening. Serving lunch felt a lot more natural than serving breakfast, after all.

If she closed her eyes tight then she could listen to the scraping of cutlery on plates and the hustle and bustle of people, the tap filling the sink with water to wash up afterwards, and imagine that she was at work. Of course, the water from the tap was ice cold because the gas was off and the people queuing for the mediocre amount of food were grown adults rather than spotty teenagers, but it was still nice to have some normality in the situation. Even if the electric oven was making a horrible buzzing noise and clearly on its last legs.

The queue had wound down and most of the hall's residents had left to go about their day, doing whatever it was that they had been filling the time with. There was a rumour that Mrs Bell had been handing out crosswords ripped from a puzzle book in the hall, and Margery was desperately hoping that there would still be some left when they finished cleaning the kitchen. It was much harder work without hot running water. They had needed to boil it on the induction hob and then add it to the sink. She would never complain about their basic school kitchen with its endless supply of hot soapy water and fully functioning dishwasher ever again.

If Rose hadn't been wearing her usual selection of brightly coloured taffeta scarves then Margery might not have noticed her slinking back into the room. She was holding a big silver platter covered in foil and looked incredibly sorry for herself. Ceri-Ann had noticed her immediately and had stopped washing up. Now that

Ceri-Ann had calmed down, she seemed a bit more sheepish about the argument, but she still looked guarded. Rose put the silver platter covered in foil on the nearest trestle table and turned to them all, clearing her throat.

'As you all know, I don't do apologies…' she began.

'That doesn't seem like a very good way to start an apology,' Clementine said. The rest of the dinner ladies shushed her. Rose gave her a glare that Margery had only ever seen her use at whispering students during GCSE exams.

'I don't do apologies, so this is very difficult for me,' Rose continued, wringing her hands. 'But I do sometimes have to get students to apologise to each other and I always say to them, "An apology is a fruit ready to flower," and of course, I'm completely correct. It is.'

There was a pause while the dinner ladies took that in. Margery could tell that Clementine was dying to say something, her face had practically gone purple from holding back. Margery didn't have the heart to tell Rose that her metaphor didn't make that much sense – surely fruit came after a flower – but before she could consider it any longer, Rose cleared her throat.

'Ceri-Ann, I am sorry,' Rose said. There was a communal gasp of surprise from the team. 'It was insensitive of me, and you're right. I should have been helping everyone band together. Not helping Rhonda carry out her schemes. She's merely a simple head of drama, head of the Ittonvale Thespian Society and the deputy head of Ittonvale school, isn't she? You were right, I'm the headteacher of the county's fifth best secondary school if you don't count the private schools. What would my students say? I have to hold myself to a higher standard.' Rose took a deep breath and looked around at the rest of the group. 'Ladies, I apologise to you all too. I've been… less of a help than I should have been. I hope… I hope that you can forgive me, all of you.'

Margery joined the others in turning to Ceri-Ann, who was considering Rose with her arms crossed.

'We forgive you,' Ceri-Ann said finally, giving Rose the first smile Margery had seen since they had found Doug's body. 'What's brought this on? Just me having a go at you?'

'I just realised that I might not be on the right side of history,' Rose said with a sigh. 'We're all suffering here, aren't we? I'm not making things better by raising money for a school concert, a quite frankly stupid school concert…' She slapped her hand over her mouth as if just realising she had said a terrible swear word and then looked up at the heavens. 'Please forgive me for saying that, Mrs Brewer…'

'Who's Mrs Brewer?' Ceri-Ann asked.

'My old school drama teacher,' Rose said. 'She'd be twirling in her grave if she knew I'd just blasphemed school plays like that. She'll be looking down at me from the heavens in outrage. Actually… I'm not sure she's even dead. Very old… yes, but I think she's in Maple Hill Nursing—'

'I knew Mrs Brewer,' Clementine interrupted. 'I'm not sure she's in heaven. When I was at school, she locked my friend Tabitha in a broom cupboard because she forgot her lines in *The Wizard of Oz*. No one found her until the rehearsal had finished.'

'You always said you didn't do drama.' Rose beamed excitedly at Clementine. 'I've got the perfect role for you in next year's summer show—'

'Well, now you've finished trying to flog desperate people deodorant, do you fancy helping us clear up?' Gloria interrupted before Clementine could be coerced into the starring role in *Grease*.

Rose looked suitably shamed for a moment, her shoulders sagging before she snapped back out of it. 'That's the reason I came, really, to see if I could help.'

'We don't need your help!' Clementine scoffed.

'We could use a hand clearing up and getting dinner sorted, actually.' Margery sighed. 'We're really behind organising it all.'

'Is there any point doing all of that now?' Karen asked. 'We could go and try and beat our 10k personal best instead? We can do laps of the hall!'

'I just feel like we should try and keep things going in here like we did at lunch and breakfast time,' Margery said. 'The rest of the place might be falling apart but there's no reason anyone should go hungry while we do it.'

Rose looked scolded for a moment. 'Well, point me in the right direction, then.'

Margery handed her an apron and Rose took it gingerly, holding it up awkwardly as if she didn't know which way to put it on. She flapped it at Seren, who rushed over to help her.

'We'll finish the washing-up and then we'll have to go through and plan what we'll do for dinner,' Margery said, tapping her lip with her fingers and thinking about it. There were a few packets of crisps in the vending machine and she was sure that there was a loaf of bread leftover somewhere. A crisp sandwich wouldn't exactly be sufficient for twenty plus adults, but it would have to do for now.

'What's this?' Karen called from behind them, interrupting Margery's thoughts.

Margery turned to see her begin pulling the foil off the platter that Rose had brought with her when she arrived for her bizarre apology. Rose looked pleased despite her best efforts not to.

'Oh, just a little friendship slash apology gift,' she said proudly, stepping over to Karen and whipping the foil off in one smooth motion. 'Ham, ladies!'

'Who are you calling ham ladies?' Karen said. 'We go running five times a week!'

Sharon burst into tears. Rose looked confused for a moment before rolling her eyes. The platter was laden with so much meat that the trestle table was almost buckling under the weight of it. They did have a small amount of chicken left for their own staff meals, but the ham was a welcome addition, even if the sight of it piled up like that made Margery feel a bit queasy for a moment.

'It's *jamón Serrano*,' Rose told them cheerily. 'From Spain, I assume! Only a very small donation to the Summerview school in exchange for a portion! I mean...' She snapped out of feckless salesperson mode. 'I brought it because I wasn't sure you'd have much to eat for lunch then I forgot about it all once we got going, you know... with my heartfelt apology.'

'I'll get the leftover flatbreads!' Seren gasped happily, leaping up from her seat in a rare burst of athletic achievement.

'Where did you get that from?' Margery asked Rose, as the others began to dive in.

'Spain!' Rose said again breezily. Margery found her eyes narrowing.

'You stole it,' Margery said. She suddenly realised where she had seen it before and found herself gasping for breath.

'The murder weapon,' she stammered, forcing the words out when they held in her throat as a gurgle, her brain thinking faster than she could say them. 'Stop, stop, you're all eating the murder weapon!'

The sight of the dinner ladies' shocked expressions with loaded plates of ham in front of them would haunt Margery until the day she died.

'Mrs Butcher-Baker,' Rose said, her voice low and surprised. 'How could a ham murder anyone? It's dead.'

'I—' Margery began but realised she must sound unhinged. 'The ham!'

'Yes, the lovely ham that Rose has kindly sliced up for us after Ceri-Ann reminded her that she was being a monster,' Gloria said. 'What about it?'

'Don't you see?' Margery said with a gasp. 'She stole it from Jacob. It's the giant Serrano ham from his charcuterie stall! Elliot had a head wound! The bone… what if Jacob killed him with the ham bone?'

The team gasped collectively. Clementine looked down at her plate with horror. Seren spat the ham she had in her mouth into the nearest bin.

'I didn't steal it,' Rose said with a roll of her eyes. 'I found it.'

'Oh well, that makes things so much better!' Margery said, feeling herself becoming hysterical and hot in the face as her voice rose to a wail. Rose went pale suddenly, all the colour draining from hers as she realised that Margery might be right.

'Where did you get it?' Clementine asked Rose. 'Tell us now.'

'It was just tucked away,' Rose said, her face falling. 'I assumed it had been forgotten about.'

'How was it "tucked away"?' Margery demanded.

Rose looked flabbergasted. 'Well, the slices of ham were just tucked away under a stall all cut up on the platter already. I just thought…'

'Whose stall?'

Rose had gone white, her eyes wide with horror. 'It was under Elliot's… I just thought… I don't know what I was thinking.'

'So, where's the bone?' Margery asked. 'This has all been sliced off the huge bone!'

Rose shook her head. Margery found her own whirling around as if the bone would appear in her desperate search. It was big enough and hard enough to have caused Elliot's head wound and they had nearly eaten the evidence of its existence. The team split up to look for Jacob, he had some questions to answer. If the bone had been his then had he used it to kill Elliot?

Chapter Sixteen

With the rest of the dinner lady team's help, they had secured Jacob's arms to the chair with clingfilm. The back kitchenette was possibly not the place for an in-depth interrogation while the rest of the team rushed around looking for the ham bone, but it would have to do. Jacob had gone down without much of a struggle, which Margery had found strange. He looked up at them both with slight amusement flickering over his features, even as the plastic dug into his skin. Margery hoped it wouldn't stretch enough to free him, and she breathed a sigh of relief that she had remembered to pack the extra-large catering-size roll of clingfilm at all.

It did make her feel like she had lost a slice of her humanity, stooping low enough to tie someone to a chair. In another way it reminded her of all the Christmas presents that were still unwrapped at home, hidden away in the back of the airing cupboard. Elliot would never get to open his, so she shook the guilty feelings away, even though Margery could see the red lines rising on Jacob's wrists already. They needed to find out why he had killed Elliot and stop him from killing again. Jacob had also known too much about Doug's whereabouts the night before for Margery's liking. For a moment, it all seemed quite simple.

'Well,' Clementine said, stepping back to look at him. Jacob did look out of place among the tea towels and clean teacups sitting on the draining board. 'This is certainly not what I thought we'd be doing today. I thought we'd be getting up bright and early to open my advent calendars before serving a simple roast at lunchtime.'

'There's still time for that if you untie me, love,' Jacob said. He struggled against the clingfilm as though he was testing it. They wouldn't be able to hold him here indefinitely. He was far taller and stronger than any of them, she could tell he was here because he wanted to see what they would say. Perhaps he was enjoying all of the attention. He wouldn't be the first.

'We can't let you go,' Clementine told him firmly. 'Not until you tell us how the ham ended up with us, getting eaten. Where's the rest of it?'

'What ham?' Jacob asked. Margery could tell from his sheepish expression that even he didn't think that they'd believe he didn't know.

'The ginormous massive Serrano ham you had on your stall,' Clementine said in disbelief, gesturing with her hands to explain how big it was.

'I sold it all,' Jacob said, his voice a little too bright. 'First night, sold out!'

Margery shook her head. 'That's impossible. I saw it still on the stand on Friday night, who could you have sold it to? There were about 300 portions on it.'

'All right, all right!' Jacob said, not stopping fighting the clingfilm for even a second. 'I didn't sell it, but I didn't cut it up either.' He had begun to pull at the clingfilm with his fingers, slivers of it escaping under his nails. 'It cost a fortune and it lasts ages. I wouldn't have sliced it all up and

I really wouldn't have given it to you all to eat. I'm a bit pissed off that you did, actually, it wasn't cheap.'

'We wouldn't be sitting here having this conversation if someone didn't cut it up,' Margery reminded him. 'And you've got to realise that it looks very suspicious…'

'No, it doesn't!' Jacob said with a chuckle. 'Why would that look suspicious?'

'Because of the man who died of a head injury caused by an unspecified murder weapon?' Clementine suggested. 'That could very easily be filled by the massive ham bone you had for sale?'

Jacob blinked at her, his mouth dropping open. 'Oh right, yeah… yeah, I guess that doesn't look like proper normal or whatever.'

'Understatement of the year,' Clementine said.

'But what, you don't, like, think I killed Elliot?' Jacob said, looking between them both in dismay. 'I didn't kill him! I already told you that…'

'What about the money he stole from Jade?' Margery asked.

'Why would I care about the money he stole from Jade? That's her problem, isn't it?' Jacob said, rolling his eyes. 'If he even took it off her.'

'You don't think he stole her money?' Margery said. 'Sally told us that Jade paid the invoice.'

'Well, maybe she did, why are you asking me?' Jacob said with a sigh. 'Look, she's my ex, isn't she? We don't always see eye to eye, and she wasn't exactly girlfriend of the year when we were together.'

'Well, were you boyfriend of the year?' Clementine asked.

Jacob paused at that. 'Well… no… not really. I bought her flowers once… look, Elliot promised me a good spot for cash. I didn't take him up on it, it's her fault if she did.'

'Is that why you set up your stall without permission?' Margery said, wondering how many people Elliot had offered the same deal to. 'He wouldn't give you a spot when you wouldn't pay?'

Jacob flushed, his cheeks turning red.

Margery suddenly remembered the email they had found in the office. 'Your food hygiene rating,' she said. He looked up, startled. 'Elliot tried to sabotage it.'

Margery felt a swell of interest as she watched Jacob react, the tips of his ears going as red as the tinsel attached to the kitchen cupboard behind him.

'How do you know that?' Jacob stammered, struggling against the clingfilm for a moment before giving up again.

'That doesn't matter,' Margery said. 'What matters is whether you killed him for it.'

'It's true that he did once threaten to set environmental health on me,' Jacob explained. 'He said he knew the inspector and they'd give me a bad review.'

'That's not a nice thing to do,' Margery said. 'Why would he?'

It would certainly have been devastating to Jacob's business as he would have had to display the food hygiene rating on his stand. The school kitchen had their five-rating sticker stuck proudly to the window of the canteen doors. Margery didn't want to think about what would happen if they ever got a worse score. Legally they wouldn't be allowed to hide it. Fingers crossed it would never happen.

Jacob shrugged again, his expression wary even half-hidden behind his handlebar moustache. Margery thought his shoulder would ache by the end of the day if he carried on being so nonchalant, and she couldn't think of anything much worse than a handlebar moustache.

'Because he didn't want me to be here,' Jacob continued, the words arriving in a babble. 'When the EHO lady turned up, I obviously passed, I'm a good chef and I know what I'm doing with the business. But I nearly failed.'

'Those two things are conflicting,' Clementine pointed out. 'Like when you said you didn't know him, but you also told us that you hated him. How did you nearly fail the environmental health if you're so good at what you do?'

'Because my paperwork was missing,' Jacob told them, looking between them both. 'I had it all in a folder at my kitchen unit on the industrial estate and it was just gone, months and months' worth. I think Elliot stole it, he's got the unit next door to mine doing Wrapmasters and whatever his new company is called.'

Margery knew from her own work kitchen that Elliot's entire food hygiene rating would revolve around his paperwork being in good shape. Her own paperwork going missing just as the environmental health officer arrived would make her angry, though perhaps not quite angry enough to kill someone.

'I didn't have any proof, so I let it go,' Jacob continued. 'But then I saw him come out of his unit when we were both leaving at the same time one day and he asked me why I'd got such a low score. He shouldn't have known about it, no one did. He said he'd seen them arrive and he was just joking, but I knew what he'd done.'

'That seems a very suspicious thing to keep quiet about,' Margery told him. Jacob rolled his eyes, the wisps of his moustache falling over his top lip as he groaned.

'Well, someone killed him, didn't they?' he said. 'I don't want people to think it was me just because I was annoyed at him. Anyway, I had the last laugh because I'd switched to a fully online system for the food management and I just showed her that. Kept my five rating.'

'So, you didn't plan to come here and kill him?' Margery asked. 'Even though you weren't on the books for it?'

'How did you know— Yeah, well, I did want to get back at him and he couldn't afford to make a scene by asking me to leave, so…' Jacob spluttered.

'So, you got away with that one,' Clementine finished for him. 'There's still some inconsistencies in your story, though…'

'My business is my livelihood,' Jacob said. 'I was angry… yeah, but he wasn't dead—' If Jacob could have clapped a hand over his own mouth, then he would have. His tied-down arms held him back, but the jerking motion his arms made gave him away. 'Like… um…'

'So, you did hit him with the ham,' Margery asked, finally feeling as though they were getting somewhere.

'No!' Jacob stuttered, then seemed to change his mind. 'Maybe a bit.'

'A bit?' Margery asked, almost having to hold back a laugh. 'His head had a huge lump on it!'

'Yeah, but it wasn't me who killed him!' Jacob said, his eyes wide with panic. 'I didn't kill him, I just hit him with it!'

'And killed him,' Clementine said, her tone announcing that she thought he was very stupid.

'No,' Jacob scoffed. 'We had a fight that evening because I wasn't supposed to be here and I just gave him a little bonk on the head, that's all. He wasn't even that hurt! He tried to punch me and missed, and then Jade came and interrupted us. I didn't see him again until the next day when that old lady found him.'

That was the argument Jade had seen them have, Margery realised.

'You realise that him being found the next day dead and with a head injury doesn't bode well for you?' Margery asked. Jacob's face fell. 'Is that why you sliced the ham and hid the bone? I think you didn't bin the meat too because it was too expensive to throw away. We already know you're in debt.'

'Yeah, I thought I could still sell it later, so I sliced it. There's nothing wrong with that, if anything, it's saving food waste!' Jacob didn't say anything more, his face had soured. Margery thought that maybe he had been enjoying the reprieve from boredom in the hall and hadn't realised that they knew all they did. Now that the odds had turned from his favour, he didn't want to play the game any more.

'I'm not saying nothing else,' he said firmly. 'Not without a solicitor or, like, a real police officer here or whatever.'

'That's fine,' Margery assured him. 'I think it would be best if you spoke to the police too.'

The kitchen door opened behind them, the hinges loud against the sudden forced silence.

'Found it!' Ceri-Ann announced as she appeared in the doorway. 'It was in the bin outside.'

She put the parcel she was holding down on the nearest kitchen counter with a clack. The bone rolled out of the plastic bag. It was a lot smaller than Margery had suspected without the added weight of the meat, but hefty all the same and with a hairline crack running through the centre of it like a squiggle of biro on an old piece of paper. Margery turned to see Jacob's expression. His face held all the doom and gloom of the weekend.

'I didn't kill him,' he said finally.

Margery looked at the ham bone again, tried to imagine it as a deadly weapon and found herself falling short.

'But you did hide this,' she said. It was not a question. She could tell by the look on his face that Jacob knew he was cornered.

He nodded, all the fight drained out of him.

'Yeah,' he admitted. 'But I knew what you'd all think if you found it once I saw his body. I had to.'

Chapter Seventeen

Jacob being apprehended should have been a comfort to Margery, but instead she found herself shivering with cold and exhaustion and nerves. None of this felt real any more. She felt like she was existing on a wave of single events clouded together in a fuzzy ball. Worse, if the ham wasn't the murder weapon, then what was? Margery didn't regret her reaction to the sight of the slices of meat, not for a second, but she was accepting that she was wrong in some way. Though she didn't know how yet. Jacob had twisted himself into knots with his half-truths and blatant lies, but she could feel that there was still an element of truth there somewhere. Enough to throw her off her original train of thought.

'He seems convinced of his innocence, doesn't he?' Clementine said, echoing Margery's own thoughts. They made their way through the hallway for what felt like the millionth time that day. 'Even after he admitted he hit Elliot with it, and Elliot had a pretty nasty bruise on his head, didn't he?'

Margery wanted to throw open the fire doors and run. She could feel her heart rate picking up as they walked. Claustrophobia was beginning to win out over all her other fears and hopes. She'd had enough of being in the hall, enough of being surrounded by people constantly. Margery tried to think of what they'd be doing at home and fell short, her brain too tired to even imagine it. Clementine sighed and took the Christmas lights they had found the day before out of her pocket, where she had been fiddling with the wire.

'Show me those lights again,' Margery said. She didn't know why she wanted to see them, she just felt like they were missing something.

Clementine handed her the Christmas lights and Margery turned them over in her fingers.

'Look,' she said, pointing to the end of the wire. 'It's melted. I noticed it before, but I didn't think anything of it then.'

'What do you mean?' Clementine asked, turning her head to look.

'I don't know,' Margery said. 'But the ham just feels wrong. I feel like we've jumped to conclusions.'

'You don't think the ham killed Elliot?' Clementine asked.

'There's a way to find out,' Margery said, feeling a bit sick. 'But I don't know if it's a sensible idea or even very ethical.'

'What is it?'

'I think we should go and look at Elliot's body,' Margery said, shuddering at the thought of it, but determined to put aside her nausea to do Doug and Elliot and everyone else some justice. 'If Jacob is sure that the ham didn't kill Elliot, then something else must have.'

'What?' Clementine asked, she didn't look convinced. 'I don't know, Margery. Jacob did confess to hitting him. You don't have to hit someone hard to kill them, do you? Lots of people have died from hitting their head wrong. You only have to slip in the shower once and then you get to spend the rest of your time relearning how to feed yourself. What if Jacob gave Elliot a concussion? That can kill you too.'

'I just… I don't know exactly, I just have a weird hunch that something else might have happened,' Margery said, trying not to think about her cold hands. The temperature had dropped considerably since the power had gone off and on again and there was no more kitchen service to keep her distracted. Perhaps the heating had stopped working or needed to be reset. 'Don't ask me exactly what, that's what I'm trying to work out.'

'Well, where did they put Elliot's body?' Clementine asked. Margery knew, she had watched them drag him there. 'Chest freezer?'

They reached the door to the freezer and paused. Margery tried to gather the strength to open it, putting her fingers to the handle and willing her hand to move down.

'Should we wait for the police?' Margery whispered, the sudden wave of fear overtaking her need to be reckless.

'Maybe,' Clementine said. She seemed just as conflicted for once. Clementine had managed to be quite reserved, all told, during the past few dreadful days. 'But when are they going to get here? There's another body lying outside, and they haven't managed to get him in yet. Anyway, we need to know, don't we?'

'That's true,' Margery told herself as much as Clementine in as firm a voice as she could muster.

'The thing is,' Clementine continued. 'Who else would have killed him? The general lack of other suspects does make Jacob look very guilty, doesn't it? Especially with the ham and all of that. I suppose Jade has confessed to accidentally killing Doug… Could Doug have killed Elliot? Hmmm… no, probably not, because Jacob found

Elliot's footprints after Doug had been locked out, probably. Ooh, maybe Sally's involved somehow? Oh, this is a mess...'

Margery nodded, it was a mess. Maybe they really couldn't wait for the police to get down here, whenever that would be. There was no telling what could happen in that time. The entire place could go to ruin, there could be another attack or death, though that didn't bear thinking about to Margery. Jacob couldn't be contained forever. For now, they'd had no choice but to untie him. They had left Gloria in charge, and she was forcing him to help with that evening's meal. Jacob hadn't seemed to mind, jumping into peeling and dicing onions with great gusto. Once a chef, it turned out that you were always a chef, even under suspicion of a murder charge.

'And Rose and Rhonda have lost their minds and dragged everyone else down with them,' Clementine reminded her. 'That's without us all running out of food. It's only a matter of time before people start eating the wallpaper. It's no good Rose having her change of heart hours after the last chocolate coins have been consumed.'

'I was thinking about that,' Margery said with a sigh. 'If we'd all pooled our resources in the beginning then we'd have had plenty to eat for a week at least, everyone just decided to be selfish. Except Rose for a brief second, and even that was with stolen food.'

'I'm sure we'll be wanted for a study on human nature after this,' Clementine said. 'Hopefully they'll take some scans of Rose's brain to see what's wrong with her. Though I suppose we can't be too harsh on her seeing as she did accidentally find the murder weapon. Possibly.'

There was a noise behind them down the corridor and they jumped away from the freezer door. Margery breathed a sigh of relief when she realised it was only Mrs Bell, shuffling towards them with her arms full of squished mince pies.

'Do you need a hand, Beryl?' Margery asked.

'Oh no,' Mrs Bell said, her voice a fragile croak. 'I'm taking these to the girls watching the ham man.' She looked Margery in the eye. 'I told you it was him. You can't trust a man who'd own such a big ham, it's illogical. No one should aspire to that.'

'I suppose that has proved itself to be true,' Clementine said with a shrug.

Mrs Bell gave her a soft smile and then carried on her way. Margery watched her go, hoping Mrs Bell was all right. She certainly seemed physically fine, but you never knew with these sorts of things.

Clementine had obviously had enough of talking about the freezer and the rights and wrongs of their search. As soon as Mrs Bell was far enough away, she reached out and touched the handle, pulling at it hard. The freezer door rose with it, the cold air inside billowing out into the hall. Margery closed her eyes for a moment, willing herself to continue. Years ago, they had been trapped in the walk-in freezer that their former kitchen manager Caroline had died in. Since then, Margery hadn't liked the feel of the cold and the dark and was only just able to step foot into their walk-in freezer at the school to do the stocktake, claustrophobia getting the better of her. It did occasionally make using lifts at airports difficult, but it also meant that dying underground in a caving accident wasn't written in her future. That was comforting in a morbid sort of way.

Even now, she always had the freezer door wide open and the light on while she did the stocktake. Some days she couldn't face it at all. She wouldn't be able to breathe in there, her hands and legs would itch to find the exit and her heart would palpitate like it was determined to leave her chest. She'd be terrified that someone would swing the door closed behind her, though she knew that none of her staff would ever even think to do that.

The thing was, she knew the fear was silly now and even if by some chance someone did shut her inside the fridge by mistake, the door exit button worked correctly now. Margery would have never let it get into the state Caroline had. Even so, some days she would still ask Clementine or Gloria to count the food instead. She was glad that she had known Rose for so long – another headteacher might not have been so pleased to sometimes have to wait for the stocktake result. Rose gave her as much time as she needed to finish her work, she wasn't afraid of being questioned at a governors meeting. It was what made Rose a great headteacher, although Margery suspected that her willingness to voice her unedited thoughts might well get her in trouble at some point in the near future.

Margery opened her eyes as Clementine peered down to see what she had uncovered. She followed her eyes reluctantly, deciding that if Clementine could be brave then so could she, and found herself shivering at the sudden drop in temperature. Still, it wasn't anywhere near as cold as her freezers at work. Perhaps it had gone off when everything else had. She knew that it was very unlikely she'd be trapped in it either, she'd have had to fall into it and Clementine would have to slam the lid shut.

At the bottom of it was Elliot's body, wrapped in a tablecloth that had a pattern of cartoon mince pies with smiling faces. Arthur had tried to preserve Elliot's dignity and had instead managed to make him look like something you might find under the Christmas tree at a vampire's castle. His tennis shoes stuck out of one end of the tablecloth and his head the other, his knees bent upwards, as tall in death as in life. His feet lay at an angle that surely would have been uncomfortable if he'd still been able to feel anything.

Margery tried not to look directly at the face still hidden under the fake Father Christmas beard. She pulled the tablecloth down over his chest and inspected his clothing, looking for pockets. His arms were blue as Clementine shone the light from her phone over him, his fingers unnaturally rigid. The Santa outfit he wore wasn't a one-piece as Margery had originally thought. It was just a red fleece coat that Elliot had pulled on over his skinny jeans and T-shirt. There was no Santa hat to be found, which made the outfit look a bit lacking.

The pocket of his jeans contained a rectangle that Margery assumed was his phone. She slid it up and out of his pocket and into her hand. She turned the object over in her palm, realising it wasn't a phone at all. But it was certainly an electronic device of some kind and as hefty as his phone would have been. Still, it might be useful. She slid it into the pocket of her cardigan for later. It rested against her side, the cold metal burning through the material of her T-shirt underneath.

Clementine had moved up to inspect the horrible bump on Elliot's head, which had not gone away even after being iced. It looked strange under the soft glow of the phone light. There was something else strange as well, Margery thought as she stared at Elliot's face, trying to look at it in the way she would inspect a packet of raw chicken or a cut of beef, to keep her sanity. The cold helped slightly. Elliot's skin was tinged blue and no longer looked human at all. Margery reached out a gloved hand and moved the Father Christmas beard slightly, pulling it across by the elastic attached around Elliot's ears. It was not an easy task. The beard had frozen to his face.

'Look, Clem,' she said, her breath rising in the air. 'His hands…'

Clementine stepped closer, unable to hide her grimace. 'Not a pretty sight, is it?'

'No, but look,' Margery said. She lifted the sleeve of the jacket fully, and they both gasped in surprise.

There was something wrapped around his right hand and it had dug into it, leaving purple lines. Red beads of blood had bloomed and were frozen along the paths of them. Margery realised what the strange marks had been caused by at the same time as she realised where the wire wrapped around his fingers was from. They were burns. Before she could stop herself, she reached out and lifted his arm by the sleeve so she could see his hands. The burns lined his palms too.

'The Christmas lights,' Clementine said. 'The skull ones that I found in the wall, do you think that was what killed him? The melted wire…'

'I think so,' Margery told her. 'That's why the lights had been hidden there, probably. They electrocuted him.'

'Jacob was telling the truth, then,' Clementine gasped. 'Who'd have thought it?'

'Possibly,' Margery corrected her. 'We don't know everything yet, but… well, it does look a bit more unlikely.'

They both stared at Elliot's body for a moment longer. Margery's heart raced terribly.

'Do you think there was an argument?' Margery said out loud finally. 'Surely he would have fought back? In which case, we should look for someone with scratches on them.'

Clementine nodded. 'Unless they were wearing gloves or a coat. It's winter, everyone's got their winter things on.' She waved her own gloved hands.

Margery hadn't considered that. It was the season for gloves, after all, thick and insulated ones at that. You would certainly be covered enough to save you from the wrath of someone else's nails. An autopsy would be able to tell them, but they didn't have the privilege of one. Margery knelt down to inspect the man's nails, there was a distinct layer of blue thread under a few of them. Perhaps the fibres from his attacker's jumper.

'Maybe it was an accident,' she said finally.

'His death could be an accident.' Clementine nodded. 'But do you not remember Kevin saying that he'd seen Elliot lying dead in the hall? He was found in the Christmas grotto. Someone had to have moved him.'

'Obviously, we won't know until there's an autopsy,' Margery said, trying to think even though her fingers were beginning to freeze. 'But, I mean, we know he fought with Jacob and those lights are from an Apex Void music video. Could someone from the band be involved?' She stopped to think about it. 'Maybe Mike? He certainly flew off the handle before, remember how angry he was when no one could find Kevin? He practically threatened to beat up Arthur. Arthur of all people! Arthur's never had an argument with anyone in his life, which is a great achievement considering his wife loves to meddle in everyone's affairs.'

'I think it's entirely possible,' Clementine said. 'Back to the drawing board, then.'

Margery could tell she wanted to close the freezer door. Her arms were folded tightly around herself like that would help keep the warmth in and the death out.

Margery covered Elliot back up gently, pausing for a moment to pay her respects. For once Clementine didn't rush her, standing back behind her with her head bowed.

'All right,' Margery said finally.

Clementine pulled the freezer door down gently, shutting the cold air away. It made the freezing hall seem practically toasty warm in comparison, though Margery knew that it couldn't be.

'What now?' Margery said with a sigh. 'What do we know? Elliot came back in from being outside at some point and Jade had shut Doug outside and left him to freeze. Did Elliot know that Doug was out there? Maybe came in to get help? Then when he came back into the hall, Jacob attacked him with the ham and then, somehow, he was electrocuted. Why? How?'

'To frame Kevin and Apex Void? The lights were used in their music video, like you said,' Clementine suggested. They wandered through the halls back to the green room. 'Or maybe it was Kevin or a member of Apex Void.'

'Maybe.' Margery nodded, though another person's face had swum to the forefront of her mind. 'The killer didn't want to be found out, so they hid the lights. Was Elliot always wearing that Santa costume?'

'Do you think it could have been put on him after he died to cover up what had happened? Or did the killer force him to put it on?' Clementine asked with a surprised gasp. 'This is worse than anything we've dealt with before, I think, Margery. Way above our pay grade. We're more entry-level murder solvers, aren't we? If only there was a crash course we could do on solving them and not being murdered ourselves.'

'I don't think you can call us entry-level at this point,' Margery said quietly. The words were a knife in her throat at the memories of all they had been through.

They had been witness to so many terrible things over the last few years that for a second it was hard for Margery's brain to focus on an exact memory. There had been blunt force trauma before, of course. They had only dealt with one poisoning, but Margery wished almost constantly that they had never been at the hotel at the wrong time. Out of all the horrible things they had seen, the mayor of a small town turning blue and then purple, with his hands wrapped around his own throat, was one of the worst. Sometimes she thought that, given the chance, she'd swap her eyesight for the choice never to have seen the man gasping for air through his closing windpipe. This was still worse somehow even though they hadn't witnessed it, possibly because it was fresher and somehow more surprising.

'I'm sure the police do courses on things like that,' Margery said finally. 'We're just not really supposed to be involved in these things. Saying that, though, how do you not get involved? I couldn't ignore that this was happening any more. I feel like we have a duty to investigate now.'

'One step closer to opening the detective agency?' Clementine asked.

Margery smiled despite herself at Clementine's insistence that one day they would finally open their own detective agency in Mr Fitzgerald's old shop. She could never say never, but it wasn't the time. The school still needed them, in Margery's opinion. 'You'll definitely have to stop mentioning our entry-level skills if we're going to market that properly!'

Clementine laughed, then her expression soured again. 'I had been thinking that the Christmas event might be boring, but there couldn't be much more excitement of a day than being murdered, could there?'

Margery agreed. It seemed so strange that a day or so before, Doug and Elliot were with them in the hall, full of life still, even if it was a boring one. Perhaps not as boring as they had previously thought, though.

Margery put her hands into her cardigan pockets to warm them and flinched when her fingers touched the cold metal rectangle that she had taken from Elliot's body.

Chapter Eighteen

They returned to the safety of the green room and the dinner lady team. Rose had joined the dinner ladies properly for the time being and had brought Jason with her, along with her handbag and all sorts of oddities Margery thought she had probably been trying to sell. Jason was sitting on Seren's lap with his eyes closed as she stroked his tiny head with one hand and held up cards with the other. Rose, Ceri-Ann and Gloria were playing cards for the grand prize of a few pennies, a brand-new permanent marker and a battered tin of mushy peas.

'Anyone good with technology?' Margery asked. 'Or, well… whatever this is.' She took the strange metal box out of her pocket. The metal was slowly leaching the warmth from her fingertips.

'Let me see.' Rose got out of her seat and reached for it. Margery noticed that her usually impeccable gel manicure was beginning to wear. One of the gel nails had chipped off, leaving her real nail at its original length. It made Margery feel sick with the mundanity of it. 'Whose hard drive is this?'

'Quick, get it back off her before she makes us trade our last bags of crisps for it!' Clementine yelled. The other dinner ladies looked as though they might be about to obey. Gloria certainly looked as though she wanted to lunge at her out of principle, and Jason nearly fell off

Seren's lap as she put a defensive hand over the bag of Skips next to her.

'Get away from me, I'm redeemed!' Rose screeched, shaking Clementine off. It didn't make her seem any less suspicious at all. 'Why have you got a hard drive?'

'Is that what it is?' Clementine asked in interest. 'I thought it was a pencil sharpener… look, it's got a hole to stick pencils in…'

Rose looked at her as though Clementine had arrived from the Stone Age and was asking how wheels worked.

'Forget how we got it,' Margery pleaded. 'How can we look at what's on it? Sally is in Doug's office, we saw her on our way here and I'm not sure we should trust her with it. The less anyone knows about what we're doing the better.'

'I agree,' Gloria said. 'We can't be too careful here. Everyone's mad and weird. Aren't they? Present company included.'

'Hey!' Sharon spluttered. 'All we've done is suggest a few warming runs around the building…'

'In the middle of a weather warning with a killer on the loose,' Gloria reminded her. 'Not even you can outrun the wind.'

'We could give it a good go!' Karen scoffed as Sharon burst into tears again at the mention of the murderer. 'Anyway, if a murderer came, would being a well-practised runner be a bad thing? No, we'd run circles around you all while you stood there and got murdered.'

Rose gave them all such a well-practised and stern glare that Margery suddenly pitied her less well-behaved classes.

'You don't need a computer,' Rose explained, turning to Margery. 'I've got a hard drive that Seren downloads films onto for me… I mean, that I use for work. You can plug it in on the TV.'

She gestured with the frayed fingernail to the television hanging on the wall above the folded-up trestle tables. The dinner ladies oohed in excitement. 'I tried to charge my phone using the TV once on holiday and it took two days to get a full battery, but this should work?'

'Well, put it on, then!' Clementine said, clapping her hands together in excitement. 'Let's see whoever's holiday photos and illegal downloads!'

'My downloads are perfectly legal, aren't they, Seren?' Rose asked. Seren smiled toothily, but in a way that told Margery exactly where she had downloaded the films from.

Rose connected the USB to the TV and began to search for it with the remote. It dangled precariously from the wire but didn't fall, it just swung in an awful way that reminded Margery of a hangman's noose.

'Well, there's not much on here,' Rose scoffed as she flicked through with the remote. 'I thought you could put lots of things on these, but there's only one folder on here. Not like mine with my full seasons of *Kath and Kim* and every episode of *Coronation Street* since 1997.'

'All legally downloaded, obviously,' Seren said much too quickly, clutching Jason tightly to her chest. He looked overly warm in his tiny Christmas jumper. 'But if the BBC ever came to your house, you should tell them you don't have a TV. Just, you know… for good measure.'

'What is it, then?' Clementine asked, jabbing her finger towards the hard drive. Rose opened a folder on the screen and they all gasped as it loaded.

Margery realised that they could be in big trouble depending on who entered the room next and saw what they had. 'Quick, Sharon, close the door.'

Sharon leaped up from her seat to close the green room door, leaning on it with her arms outstretched as if that would hold back anyone trying to enter.

'The CCTV,' Clementine breathed as they watched the screen. 'From the whole day?'

'It certainly looks like it,' Rose said. Her eyes were wide as she flicked through the footage.

The camera showed the car park, directly above the main entrance. Margery hadn't noticed it before. It must have been hidden up in the rafters of the vestibule.

'Oh wow!' Margery gasped. 'But I thought there wasn't any CCTV? Sally said—'

'Sally says a lot of things,' Rose said, her face darkening. 'Whatever the person she's talking to wants to hear, mostly, which isn't very useful, all told.'

Seren nodded heavily. 'This is great news for Kevin's car insurance, though, isn't it? He'll have footage of him crashing the van into the hall. His premium won't go up.'

'Yes, what absolutely brilliant news, Seren,' Gloria said with a scoff. Seren beamed, the sarcasm zooming over her head at 500 miles an hour.

'Sally did say there definitely wasn't any, though,' Clementine exclaimed. She thought about it. 'Well, maybe Sally didn't know that Doug had a camera?'

'Maybe,' Margery said. 'But it seems odd, doesn't it? She's here all the time. Would she not have spotted the camera at some point? She said it would have been useful in the past. I bet she would have used some of the footage if she knew it existed.'

Margery suddenly felt vindicated for not telling Sally what they had been doing after they had searched Elliot's body. It was becoming obvious now that the woman knew more than she was letting on.

'That's just one of those cameras you can get from the internet,' Ceri-Ann explained from behind them. 'A bit like your camera to check the cats are okay, but posher. Maybe Doug bought it and didn't tell anyone.'

'Well Elliot must have known about it,' Clementine said. 'Do you think we'll be able to find out who pulled the tree down?'

'No, it doesn't quite cover that bit of the car park, it's facing towards the hall,' Rose explained. 'But there's one inside the hall entrance.'

Rose began to flick through the footage of the last few days from the outside camera, all of which had poor visibility from the storm outside. The camera was indeed attached to something, giving a good view of the hall. Margery assumed it must be attached to the lamppost nearest. Nothing of note happened that Margery could tell, until she noticed the man fighting against the wind. His clothes billowed out behind him as he struggled and the camera's microphone was barely able to pick anything up over the noise of the weather. It rattled around him, whipping leaves into the air.

'Doug,' she gasped, despite knowing the end of the story.

He made it to a car and tried the door handle, but it didn't open. It must have been locked. Had he forgotten the key? Margery asked herself as they watched him go back the way he had arrived, the wind blowing him faster than his legs could keep up. He didn't have his coat, the car keys were probably inside it.

'What was he doing?' Clementine asked. 'Is this after Jade locked him out? Did he forget to take his car key?'

That was what it looked like, Margery thought as Doug reappeared. This time he didn't go to the car but instead he began to walk around the side of the building, disappearing again. Margery knew from current events that he wouldn't be returning. She wanted to scream at him to go inside and get his coat or stay inside and hide somewhere. Though there weren't many places to hide, even Kevin's hiding place underneath the stage had been found eventually.

'What happened in the hall entrance at that time, then? Is there any footage of that?' Margery asked Rose, who dutifully loaded the next camera roll and began to search for the correct time. 'We should probably see if there's footage of Jade to show Symon later, if he ever manages to get here. It'll help the case.'

'You need to stay after school one evening and do Mr Worle's computer course for the elderly... I mean, computerly challenged persons,' Rose said as she scrolled. 'Honestly, then you can do your own dirty work.'

'Is this not a nice change from robbing people?' Clementine scoffed. 'Doing some honest work for a change?'

'Helping the aged, you mean? Do I look like a charity?' Rose said. 'Anyway, sometimes you have to steal from Peter to pay Paul, or whatever, Mrs Butcher-Baker!'

'Stop there!' Ceri-Ann called as Doug appeared onscreen. Rose gasped and then rewound the footage slightly so they could watch him enter. The timestamp read that it was just past three in the morning, not long before Margery had been woken by the mysterious figure rushing down the hallway in the Santa hat.

Doug looked concerned, Margery thought. He was pale, visible even on the poor-quality camera footage. He paced the vestibule of the hall, wringing his hands together alternately with running them over what was left of his hair. It brought images to Margery's head of someone trying to shine a bowling ball, her mind hysterical with surprise and fear. She suddenly didn't want to see the argument with Jade. She wanted to pretend it had never happened and wait for Symon without seeing the events that led to Doug's death instead. The team watched, quiet for once. Margery realised that Doug was wearing a blue jumper under his Christmas waistcoat. Was that where the fibres under Elliot's fingernails had come from?

'I want a word with you!' a woman's voice called from offscreen. Light flooded the video for a moment as the doors to the main hall opened and then closed again. The cacophony inside the hall reverberated through the vestibule for a moment and then disappeared with the light as the door slammed shut again.

Onscreen, Doug turned panicked for a moment, then his expression twisted into something jovial, as fake as the plastic reindeer littering the main hall.

'You want Elliot, you mean,' Doug said, a hint of laughter in his voice, though Margery knew instantly that there couldn't possibly be any from the anxious husk of a man who had just been pacing the room.

Jade didn't let him get away from her that easily. She grasped for his arm. He jumped backward as if she'd burnt him. It was late at night, the party was beginning to wind down, and Jade had been drinking. Margery could tell by the way she carried herself. No wonder Jade had felt guilty enough to tell them what she had done. It had probably been a split-second drunken decision.

'Elliot said to speak to you! So, which is it?' she hissed. 'He said he gave you the money!'

'I don't know what to tell you,' Doug said as he shrugged, but the tremor in his voice gave him away. 'But I'm quite busy, you know, police matters, getting everyone out of here alive.'

'I can't survive the summer without that money,' Jade said, her voice rising. 'I need to do that festival. You've got to get me on the bill.'

'Unfortunately, all vendors have been finalised,' Doug told her, waving a hand firmly. 'You should have got your deposit in faster, that's a lesson for you for the future.'

Jade paused at that, her fists clenching. 'Are you joking me?'

'No, I—'

'Wait till everyone finds out how much debt you're in,' Jade said. Margery couldn't see her face, but she could imagine the smug grin that had crept upon it.

'I'm not—'

'You know anyone can have a quick look at Companies House,' Jade sneered. 'See how many late filings there are. You're in trouble, aren't you? You've stolen my money to cover it up!'

'If you'll excuse me…' Doug reached for the front door switch behind him, lunging for it and leaving through the doors. Desperate to get away from her questioning.

The wind blew Jade back and for a moment, Margery thought she might rush after him, even though she knew Jade wouldn't. Instead, she reached forward and pressed the automatic door switch, the inner hall doors slammed shut. Then she stormed back the way she'd come without even a second look.

'So, she really did lock him out,' Clementine said quietly. 'She really killed him.'

'She said she didn't mean to kill him, but didn't she realise it would?' Margery wondered. She suspected that Jade hadn't even thought of it until Doug had not reappeared the next day. They had seen her searching the car park in a panic, after all.

Rose wound the footage forward, until Doug reappeared. He pounded on the glass window with his fist over and over again. The hall remained dark and still. Margery felt unease run through her at the thought of it.

'How did the camera film anything anyway?' Ceri-Ann asked. 'The power was on and off all night.'

'It might run on the emergency power with the fridges,' Gloria whispered from behind her. 'The door must run off it as well if he couldn't open it.'

There was something to that, Margery thought. The automatic lock switch was still lit by its own green light, shining like a beacon of torment in the dimly lit vestibule.

'Do you think Jade might have killed Elliot too?' Clementine asked. 'The fact is, she killed Doug and managed to keep quiet about it for a long while. What if she killed Elliot too, but is using the Doug thing to hide the greater crime?'

Margery wasn't sure. On one hand, it would be easy to waltz over to Jade and accuse her, but that might not help their cause. There was a lot to think about.

'Why didn't Doug go and bang on one of the hall windows?' Margery asked. 'I don't understand why he didn't.'

Clementine thought about it. 'Maybe he couldn't because of his leg. It was broken, wasn't it? He must have gone to try the fire escape first.'

That did make sense, Margery thought. She imagined he had turned to go back the way he had come and slid off the step.

'Why did Elliot have the CCTV on him?' Clementine asked. 'Did he delete it from the computer? Why keep it on this hard drive thing?'

Margery thought about it. 'Perhaps he wanted it to prove his innocence.'

'But all it proves is that Doug was outside,' Clementine said. 'And Jacob said he cleared up footprints and the one we saw was clearly from Elliot's trainers. Did he go outside to help Doug?'

'Or to taunt him?' Margery asked. They shared a worried look.

'Why didn't Doug just knock on one of the hall's windows?' Margery thought out loud. 'Why walk around to the fire escape?'

Her question was answered. The shadow appeared on the screen first and then the man followed. Elliot in the Santa outfit. He went to the window and Margery sucked in a breath as he began to chuckle.

'Locked yourself out, have you, mate?' he called through the glass to Doug. Doug yelled something back, his voice muffled.

Doug gestured frantically to where the automatic lock button was on the wall. It must have been freezing outside.

'No can do.' Elliot shook his head. 'Not until you promise me you won't fire me.'

Margery heard a horrible, strangled noise and realised it was her own surprised yelp. She couldn't quite make out what Doug said in return, but it didn't sound polite.

'Don't be like that!' Elliot cried. 'Look, if you can't take a bit of friendly competition…'

Doug had obviously had enough. He pounded against the window again, then he stormed away from the doors, disappearing into the night. Elliot waited a moment, then he pressed the automatic lock button. The main doors opened, the wind whipped Elliot's hair backward into a fin. He waited for a long moment as if he was deciding what to do. Then he slapped the door switch and quickly stepped out into the weather as the doors slid shut behind him. Locking him outside with Doug.

'Any more tape?' Clementine demanded.

Rose's hands shook as she sped the footage up again. People came and went through the hall entrance as they passed in a blur of party hats and tinsel, the last stragglers left from the party. Margery found herself holding her breath. Somehow in her imagination she had decided that Elliot would return with Doug and help him. Though she knew that wasn't what would happen at all. She put her hands to her face and grimaced as the doors stayed firmly shut. But then, at least ten minutes after he had left, Elliot returned from the opposite direction. Appearing as if by magic inside the building again. That explained the footprints leading from the fire escape, Margery thought.

He rushed into the hallway, no longer calm and collected. He paced back and forth by the front door, running his hands through his hair. He turned to stare directly at the camera, seeming to judge them all down the lens. He knew its exact location.

'Don't turn your back on me!' A voice came from offscreen and Elliot jumped. Jacob appeared, pointing a finger at Elliot in anger. 'I've got a bone to pick with you.'

'Yeah, literally,' Elliot scoffed. 'Give it a break, will you!'

'What's that Jacob is holding?' Gloria asked from behind her in a hushed whisper. 'Is that a baseball bat?'

Margery peered closer, almost laughing out loud at the sight. 'No.'

The dinner ladies began to murmur as they realised what he was holding. Jacob brandished the ham as though it was a weapon.

'You're not supposed to be here,' Elliot snapped. He looked fraught, his eyes scanning the phone screen in his hand. 'Leave me alone.'

'No,' Jacob said. 'Where's Jade's money?'

'It's in a Christmassy place,' Elliot said with a nasty laugh.

Jacob had obviously had enough of arguing, he lunged forward with the ham and cracked Elliot over the head with it. Elliot reeled backward, clutching his head. Jacob stuttered apologies. He reached out to try and inspect the already forming bruise on Elliot's forehead.

'Get away from me!' Elliot shrieked at him.

He used the glass in the main windows to inspect the bump. Jacob stood frozen for a moment before turning and rushing away with the ham down the dark corridor. Elliot sighed and then turned back to his phone, shaking it with anger. Margery had seen that frustrated look on many of the others' faces recently, the phone was evidently out of battery.

He looked up at the camera again, staring them out down the lens before disappearing through the hall doors. They waited. The main lights came on in the vestibule and then Rose wound it forward again until there was movement. Someone was leaving the hall, only visible from behind. It took Margery a few moments to realise that whoever it was, they were dragging Elliot's body out into the vestibule, their hat pulled low over their head. The bobble of the Santa hat dragged behind Elliot's head as they disappeared offscreen. Margery gasped at the sight.

There was not much more until Mrs Bell shuffled into view from the way the killer had gone. She looked up at the camera for a moment, seemingly staring them down. Then she shuffled away, mumbling to herself absent-mindedly.

Chapter Nineteen

Jade hadn't killed Doug. Elliot had. Margery thought about it as she stared off into the abyss. Or in the very least he had known that Doug was outside in trouble and hadn't helped. Did Jade know what Elliot had done? They had to find out. It would drive Margery mad if they didn't. Not when Jade and Elliot might have been in cahoots the entire time. Elliot knowing that Doug was outside didn't make Jade look any more innocent in Margery's eyes, not yet. There were more questions to be asked. Margery couldn't stop wondering about the footprints Jacob had cleaned up. They were certainly Elliot's now, but who had let him back into the building? Someone had to have, he hadn't come back through the main entrance on the footage. Jacob had initially seemed the most likely suspect for that, but now she wasn't so sure.

Jade wasn't acting at all like Margery thought someone being crushed by guilt should. She was an eager participant in Rhonda's get-warm class, which entailed a lot of vigorous jumping up and down on the spot interspersed between mindless hopping. Ada Bones was now asleep on the chair behind Rhonda, who was leaping into the air with her hands on her hips. Rhonda had obviously decided to turn over her own new leaf, just as Rose had, and with it had decided to reenact an eighties workout video. She probably thought that was a way to give back after portioning out the teabags and rationing deodorant. Margery and Clementine had no plans to join in the festivities.

Jade noticed them and immediately looked upset, pausing for a second before the usual annoyance at the sight of them returned to her features. She made to carry on following Rhonda, but Rhonda had stopped jumping after seeing the look on Margery and Clementine's faces. Reluctantly, Jade turned to see what they wanted.

'We need to talk,' Margery told her.

'I don't think we do,' Jade said, looking her up and down. She tried to go back to the class, but Rhonda had made herself scarce, taking her boombox with her.

'It's about Doug,' Margery explained. 'We have footage of the night he went outside.'

Jade's face hardened.

'I told you I'd hand myself in when the police arrived,' Jade said. 'I'm not going anywhere with you, you've got no authority here at all—'

'You didn't kill him,' Clementine blurted at her. Jade blinked in surprise. 'So you don't need to hand yourself in.'

Jade froze.

'Oh,' she said after a long moment. 'Well, who did?'

Margery and Clementine exchanged a worried look.

'We think Elliot did,' Clementine told her. Jade's eyebrows almost met her dark hairline at the revelation.

'Elliot,' she said with a tut. 'Yeah, that makes a certain amount of sense.'

'We need to know who else you saw that evening,' Margery pleaded. 'Did you see anyone let Elliot in through the fire escape?'

'No, but Jacob said he saw him.' Jade sniffed. 'Why don't you ask him?'

'Are you sure you didn't see anyone?' Margery prodded, not willing to tell her that they had already questioned Jacob thoroughly or what they had seen him do in Jade's defence.

'I don't know,' Jade said.

She looked as though she might have more to say, but to Margery's surprise, Sally stepped in between them both. Margery hadn't seen her sneak up on them at all. She must have been listening, they hadn't been very subtle after all. There was something odd about Sally, though Margery still hadn't managed to put her finger on quite what. She reminded Margery of being at school and being told on by another student. Sally seemed sneaky enough to have done that during her time.

'Now, now,' Sally said, waving her hands as though she were wafting away cigarette smoke. 'Let's be reasonable about this. How about we all go and have a cup of tea and calm down, hmmm?'

'They're accusing me of helping someone kill someone and you're telling me to calm down?' Jade spat. Margery could almost see the steam coming from her ears.

'I'm telling you that we all need to pull together until the police get here,' Sally said, stroking her arm soothingly. Jade flinched away from it. 'If you're as innocent as you say then you've got nothing to worry about, have you?'

She was deflecting, Margery thought. She didn't need to be involved in this, and Margery found her insistence at getting involved suspicious. Though maybe she shouldn't – after all, Sally certainly had her finger in most of the hall's goings-on. But that made her exclusion from Doug's office even more suspicious. Perhaps Sally had used to use the office all the time but was lying about it to keep something concealed. There was certainly no one left to tell them otherwise. Elliot and Doug weren't up to saying anything. Several things Sally had done now struck her as suspicious, and Elliot's murderer was still roaming free.

'Give it a rest, Sally,' Jade snapped. 'If you were being accused of helping someone kill Doug, you wouldn't just get on with it, would you?'

There was a pause. Margery watched as Sally's face paled and turned ashen, her knees practically buckling underneath her. When she finally spoke, her voice was the quiet whisper of a frightened child. 'What do you mean?'

Even Jade paused at that. Margery watched Sally carefully, what she did next might give away if she was Elliot's murderer. If she was lying, then she truly was a tremendous actor. Her face had fallen, crumpling under itself as though it were made of tissue paper.

'Doug's dead?' Sally repeated. They all nodded. 'But how?'

'We found him outside the fire escape,' Margery explained.

'Doug can't be dead,' Sally said, waving a hand through the air, her voice frothy and light, the laughter bubbling to the surface. 'Don't be so silly. If he was dead the police would be on their way.'

'They are on their way,' Clementine reminded her. 'They just haven't managed to get here yet.'

Sally shook her head again, a smug smile appearing on her face. 'No, no, you've got it all wrong.'

'It's true,' Margery assured her.

'Well, where is he?' Sally snapped. 'Let's see what stupid joke you're all playing. You think this is funny, do you?'

Before anyone could stop her, she launched herself across the room and through the doors into the corridor, the tails of her cardigan flapping behind her. Margery and Clementine chased after her, but it was too late to reach her before she made it to the fire escape. Gloria had left the green room at the commotion, but even she was too late. She reached for Sally's arm, but her hand slipped over the smooth material of Sally's raincoat and before anyone could stop her, she had pushed the door open. Margery thought that she would hear Sally's scream whenever she closed her eyes from now on. It was guttural and pained. The noise of someone who was being sliced to death by barbed wire.

–

Margery didn't know what to do now. Jade was 100 per cent correct, in that they weren't really the police – they couldn't hold anyone here if they didn't want to be held. Though there was still no way to leave yet. A bleak sadness had taken over the hall since Sally had discovered Doug's death. Margery wondered if that was the only reason she seemed rattled. Obviously, Margery had not known her before all of this, so it was hard to say if that was just how Sally usually acted. From the little they had seen, she did not think it was. Margery found herself wondering if Sally was the one who had hidden the Christmas lights behind the loose skirting board. Sally had been the one to get the lights back on each time they went off and she knew the hall better than anyone else. Could she have used that information to kill Elliot? Maybe one of the plugs in the hall had been faulty and Sally had set it up for Elliot to go to unplug the lights. For all they knew, she could have asked him to tidy up.

Sally did seem genuinely upset by Doug's death and Margery felt a wave of sadness for her each time she caught a glimpse of her across the hall, where she was being comforted by Rose and Rhonda. She was squished between them with a cup of something in her hands. Margery suspected whatever it was, it was stronger than coffee.

'I keep thinking, where's the money?' Clementine asked, interrupting Margery's thoughts. 'Jade's money. Whoever else's money. In that video, Elliot said… what did he say?'

'He said, "It's in a Christmassy place,"' Margery reminded her. It had seemed strange at the time and hadn't got any less strange at all.

Clementine snorted with laughter. 'I bet he posted it off with a Christmas card or something.'

'Or maybe it's closer to home?' Margery asked, thinking of a box of Christmas crackers she had seen in the storeroom, though she couldn't imagine he would be foolish enough to stuff it inside them. Not with Santa's grotto due to have been open the next day.

'Ceri!' Gloria cried, interrupting Margery from her thoughts. 'Are you all right? Where have you been?'

'I've been…' Ceri-Ann panted. She tried to catch her breath while simultaneously signalling with hand-waves that whatever she wanted to say next was incredibly important. Gloria rubbed her back as Clementine tried to offer her asthma inhaler. Ceri-Ann shook them both away. 'In Apex Void's van.'

'What were you doing in the van?' Margery asked. 'Listening to Wham!?'

Ceri-Ann nodded furiously. 'Yeah, listening to Wham!'

Clementine looked mystified. 'Are you really telling us that you've been in Apex Void's van, just to listen to Wham!? How did you get in through the broken glass without getting scrammed?'

'I climbed in through the back because the doors are jammed,' Ceri-Ann said brightly, no longer so winded. 'And I found a dashcam!'

The dinner ladies all oohed at that in excitement.

She pulled the camera out of her coat pocket and held it up with a flourish.

'And it was worth it too, cos as soon as I put the radio on, "Last Christmas" was playing, I just knew it would be!' Ceri-Ann punched the air in a fervour. 'Take that, Chantelle!'

'I think you mean Wham!,' Clementine said. 'But it's of no consequence to us at all, is it? While you were enjoying the soothing tones of George Michael and Andrew Ridgeley, we were here confronting nearly accidental murderers.'

'Actually, mate, it's very important to your case,' Ceri-Ann said with a grumble. 'The dashcam is bound to have something on it.'

'Well, why didn't you say so?' Clementine exclaimed, clapping her hands together.

'I literally just did!' Ceri-Ann countered.

'Wait, what do you think it'll have on it?' Margery asked.

'I think we might be able to see who pulled the tree down,' Ceri-Ann said smugly, her mouth pulling up into a wide grin.

Chapter Twenty

Ceri-Ann didn't wait for even a moment before she rushed off again. They all stumbled after her, tripping over each other in their eagerness to see what was stored on the camera. They huddled together in the green room again, but this time Clementine made sure the door was firmly shut behind them. Ceri-Ann fumbled with the dashcam, the buttons clacking as she fiddled with it.

She gasped with excitement, the words coming out of her mouth almost too quickly for her to speak clearly. 'The band's van was facing the tree, wasn't it? Obviously, it's not now that it's in here with us and whatever. It would have seen loads of stuff.'

'That's not very useful, is it?' Clementine asked quizzically, taking the camera and giving the power button a jab with her index finger. 'It doesn't seem to be working.'

'It needs to be plugged in for the power to work and the van was knackered,' Ceri-Ann explained. 'Oh... shit...'

Clementine visibly flinched but didn't make a remark. Ceri-Ann held the lead up and glared at the cigarette lighter plug attached to it. 'It won't work without being plugged into a car, will it? The van's dead.'

'Well, it might not have anything interesting on it,' Margery consoled her. 'If it's anything like our car then it'll just be videos of them driving around Tesco car park while they sing along to the radio and I'm not sure anyone wants to hear that. Even if Apex Void are supposed to be good singers.'

'Yeah, maybe. It's just that the van was facing the right way to see who cut the tree down, wasn't it? I thought it might be one of those ones that captures movement. It looks like the one my mum has.' Ceri-Ann waved a hand over the now useless camera. 'You need an adaptor thing to watch the memory card inside it on a laptop, so we can't even do that.' Her face brightened as she thought of something. 'Ooh, why don't you go and have a look at it in our minibus? All you've got to do is plug it into the cigarette thingy.'

'The weather's still bad—' Margery began.

'Another brilliant idea!' Clementine interrupted. 'No wonder Symon passed his detecting exams, you probably snuck him all the answers!'

Clementine clapped Ceri-Ann on the back in triumph much too enthusiastically, leaving Margery to wonder for the hundredth time that day if their unexpected imprisonment was making them all lose their minds. 'Come on, Margery, a little bit of wind can't slow us down.'

Margery thought about arguing that it wasn't just 'a little bit of wind', but Clementine was probably right for once. They had already been outside when the weather was much worse than it was now, what was the worst that could happen? They bundled up warm again, borrowing scarfs and gloves from the dinner lady team. They couldn't use the main door this time, the van was still firmly wedged in place. Even though Ceri-Ann had somehow managed to climb into the front of the vehicle for her love of George Michael, Margery didn't fancy their chances among all the pieces of shattered windscreen and doorway.

They were thirty years older than Ceri-Ann and were sure to get caught on all of the bits of broken glass. Using a door seemed like a much better idea.

They couldn't use the closest fire escape to the green room either, as Doug's body still sat on the other side of it. There was no choice but to go through the hall and hope no one asked too many questions. Luckily, the dinner lady team were more than bored enough to cause a distraction. Karen and Sharon had dragged the karaoke machine into the main hall, and music was blaring from it.

'Who wants a mince pie?' Gloria called from the other hall as Margery and Clementine stood tucked away by the large plastic Christmas tree in the foyer. 'We've got brandy sauce and coffee too!'

It was a lie, but Margery was hoping that they would be able to make it outside before anyone realised that the cups of coffee Gloria was handing out was really gravy granules mixed with the last bit of decaf coffee from the tin. Seren was already wringing her hands at having to lie. It had taken a moment to get the gravy's thickness correct. Anyone who had been paying attention over the past few hours would have realised that they had long ago run out of coffee and the mince pies were simultaneously very squashed and stale now, but there was still almost a stampede as the group all rushed from one hall to the other.

Feeling a bit like a wrapped Christmas present with how many layers she had on, Margery followed Clementine through the other hall and over to the fire escape along the back wall. Clementine paused after pushing the door bar and opening the door. She looked around desperately for a moment before spotting someone's shoe. She picked it up. They stepped out into the cold and

Clementine wedged the shoe in the doorway as the fire door closed. Margery breathed a sigh of relief at Clementine having the foresight to avoid the same fate for them as Doug had faced, wincing as the cold air filled her lungs.

Clementine gasped in excitement when she saw the spare box of biscuits left abandoned on one of the back seats of the minibus. In all the panic of the last few days, Margery had forgotten about it entirely. Clementine immediately opened the box and found them each a single-serve packet, custard creams for Margery and bourbons for herself. Margery took the packet, not entirely sure that she would be able to eat it anyway. Things were much too stressful.

'Right,' she said, as Clementine tucked in. Crumbs flew all over the seat and dashboard and Clementine wiped them away. 'Let's see what we can find, then, shall we?'

Margery plugged the dash camera into the minibus cigarette lighter and held her breath. The screen burst into life.

'Right, how do you work this, then?' Clementine asked. Margery shook her head.

She really didn't know and wished that they had brought someone slightly younger out with them. Still, how hard could it be? She pressed one of the buttons, gasping when a symbol of a dustbin appeared onscreen.

'Don't press that!' Clementine cried. 'Or… is it the bin? That might be a good sign. Maybe that's where we're supposed to look?'

'I really doubt it,' Margery said, trying again.

This time she managed to find the camera roll and began to click through it with the arrows on the camera.

'There,' Clementine said, jabbing a finger at the screen in excitement.

They watched the last clip of footage, which was from when Kevin had unceremoniously crashed through the hall doorway backward. Margery kept flipping through until she found something of interest. A man set off the camera as he walked past the van, his head covered by his coat hood. In his hands he held an axe.

'That's Mike,' Margery whispered. 'Look…'

'How can you tell?' Clementine asked. She squinted at the screen. 'That stupid Santa hat is covering his face.'

'Look at the shoes,' Margery said, pointing to them on the screen. It was very hard to tell on the tiny screen exactly what brand of shoes the man was wearing, but Margery recognised them well enough. The big black motorcycle boots under the dark trousers. Margery couldn't see for sure, but she would have put money on them being Mike's. She had noticed his concealed heels the day before and they were obvious to her now.

'So he tried to cut it down with an axe?' Clementine breathed as they watched Mike disappear up the road. 'What possible reason could he have had?'

Mike rushed back down the hill, passing the van on his way, the axe still in his arms and his face very visible. The camera cut out again, only recording the snippets of movement for a few seconds at a time. A moment later he reappeared, carrying a large towing chain, and began heading up the hill again. To Margery's surprise, someone else rushed up the road after Mike. She realised with a jolt that it was Doug. They were arguing as Mike stormed back down the hill towards the van pulling the length of chain, though it was impossible to work out what was being said over the noise of the wind already whipping through. The van door finally opened a few minutes later and they heard Mike's heavy breathing as he climbed in and started the engine.

'Bloody camera!' Mike yelled, then the screen went dark. He had obviously turned it off before he used the van to pull the tree down.

To them in the hall the commotion of it all had probably been covered by the wind, or the band who had gone on before Apex Void. Doug had known what Mike had done and hadn't said a word to anyone.

'Maybe Mike wanted us to all be trapped in the hall so the murderer could kill Elliot and Doug,' Margery suggested. 'But I don't know why either. Perhaps it's something else to do with the money? Everything always seems to be about the money.'

'That still doesn't explain why he killed either of them, if he did,' Clementine said with a sigh. 'This is such a mess. Why was Doug there? You're telling me that Doug knew all about the tree from the get-go?'

'I think we're missing something here still.' Margery found herself massaging her temples. 'I can't believe Doug would allow him to do that.'

The lack of sleep and decent meals was beginning to wear her down. Her back felt like all the bones of her spine weren't slotted together properly, like a jigsaw whose pieces had been chewed by an overenthusiastic puppy.

With her eyes closed, she could picture the dining table in their cosy kitchen, one of the cats curled up on the rocking chair next to it as Margery and Clementine tucked into a late supper. A wedge of cheese each and some crackers, a few pickled onions and one of Gloria's homemade chutneys, served alongside a slice of turkey or two and some fresh salad. All that was waiting for them back in the hall was a pack of pot noodles, of which none of the good flavours remained. Margery scanned the car park for any sign of Symon and his team, they had to be almost on their way. It was only the thought that they were that was keeping her from sheer panic.

'Come on,' Clementine said, looking at Margery fondly as though she could tell what she was thinking. 'Let's go back.'

Margery packed the dash camera carefully, ready to give it in as evidence later, and then they climbed out of the minibus.

'Who would kill Elliot?' Margery said as they crossed the frozen car park. 'It looked like he'd been electrocuted. It's not like loosening part of a stage light or putting poison in something, it could certainly be accidental.'

'I agree,' Clementine said. 'You'd have to really have no conscience if you planned something like that.'

'Would Mike do that?' Margery offered as the solution. 'He did chop the tree down and trap us all here…'

Clementine reached for the fire escape and made to pull it open, scrabbling at the closed surface.

Margery looked down and realised in horror that the shoe Clementine had placed there carefully to keep the door open was gone.

'Oh!' Clementine cried, scrabbling at the door again and leaving long scrapes in the icy door with her nails. 'We're stuck outside!'

Margery felt a rush of fear that made her ears ring. She reached out and tried the door as well, her gloved fingertips sliding over the cold surface. It didn't budge at all. They stood there stupidly for a moment, Margery opening and closing her mouth, but none of the obscenities in her head would come out.

‘It’s okay, we’ll go round to the green room fire escape,’ Margery told Clementine, reaching for her arm. ‘Let’s not panic.’

‘But Doug’s body…’ Clementine wrung her gloved hands together. ‘I don’t want to have to step over it…’

Margery shook her head. ‘There’s nothing else for it. Anyway, the police are coming soon, aren’t they? We’ll knock on the door and get the dinner ladies to let us in if they aren’t here in time.’

Clementine opened her mouth to speak, but her attention was stolen by something happening inside the hall. Her jaw dropped open. Margery looked too. Sally was standing in the window watching them. For a second, Margery thought she might be about to open the door and a surge of relief raced through her. It disappeared as quickly as it had come when Sally slid the hall curtains closed. Margery and Clementine rushed along as the curtain blocked them from sight, but Sally drew it all the way shut, obscuring them from view completely. They waited for a moment for her to return, but she didn’t. Instead, music had begun to play, so loudly that Margery knew they’d be drowned out even if they banged on the doors and windows. ‘Last Christmas’ blared from the hall’s PA system and Margery lost all hope of rescue.

Chapter Twenty-One

Lost for words for once, Clementine followed Margery back to the minibus and they both climbed back in. Margery put the key in the ignition and turned the heater back on, unable to think in the cold. The cacophony from the hall was audible even inside the vehicle. Sally was using the music as a distraction so they wouldn't be rescued from outside, Margery knew. She must have turned it up even louder than Karen and Sharon had the volume initially. But Sally couldn't possibly think that she could keep them out forever. What was her plan really? Was she trying to buy time for something? Maybe she was about to hide some evidence, Margery wondered.

'I knew she was up to something!' Clementine said with a scoff, warming her hands on the heater. 'Well, she won't get away with it. The others know we're out here. They'll come and get us soon.'

'Will they?' Margery asked, her voice feeling very small. 'They might not for a while. Ceri-Ann and Gloria will probably continue the ruse because they think we need more time, and that's if they aren't dancing to Wham!' Her hands were already beginning to feel frozen stiff, and it was getting darker the longer they stayed outside. Her breath filled the damp air of the minibus with clouds of steam. 'We could just go and wait in the minibus? The police can't be that far away—'

'But the murderer is still in there with our friends, and Sally is looking the likeliest suspect at the moment, isn't she?' Clementine said. She looked around desperately. 'Have you got your phone? We could try and charge it with the cigarette lighter.'

'I didn't bring the charging cable with us,' Margery groaned. Clementine groaned too.

Clementine hadn't brought her charger cable either and they hadn't been able to use Ceri-Ann's because she had a different type of phone. Clementine tapped her finger to her lip as she thought.

'Let's drive up the hill and meet the police,' Margery said, shaking the idea away in as firm a voice as she could muster with her nerves as shot as they currently were. 'Symon will know what to do, won't he?'

'Surely if the police could get down then they would already be here,' Clementine reminded her. 'The road must still be blocked.'

Clementine must be right, Margery felt her heart sink down to her shoes.

'Maybe we should go back and try the fire escape door?' Clementine offered. 'We'll knock, they have to turn the music off eventually.'

'Will they hear us?' Margery voiced her fear. 'The party last night went on for hours, we might freeze to death by then. Or Sally might have struck again. The rest of the team is in there – they don't know about her! She's probably dangerous. I bet they'll be her next target!'

'It's okay,' Clementine said, reaching over to pat her hand soothingly. 'Gloria's got her guard up, I'm sure she'd notice anything weird going on. Shall we try?'

Margery couldn't shake her worry that the others might well not hear them through the hall or that the dinner ladies might be the next targets. As far as they all knew, Margery and Clementine were still looking at the camera footage in the van. They would all still be in the hall trying to flog gravy granules as coffee. Ceri-Ann would probably be ecstatically dancing to Wham! while ticking another listen off on her score sheet. Sally knew exactly what she was doing when she had put the song on. Margery briefly thought about trying to climb in through the band van's broken windshield, but Ceri-Ann had already been very lucky not to cut herself when she had climbed into it from the back. The side doors of the van were wedged shut by the doorway and Margery didn't think she was acrobatic enough to leap up through the windshield anyway. Clementine was gazing off into the distance through the bus window.

'You look like you've had a very bad idea,' Margery said. Since they had met over thirty years before, Clementine had come up with a veritable wealth of terrible ideas. In the days before they had somehow ended up solving murders, it hadn't been so much of an issue. Living with bright orange wallpaper that had been put up at the spur of the moment, or stepping around the cat-sized water fountain that Clementine had plugged in on the hallway landing was one thing, a split-second decision when a murderer was loose was quite another.

Clementine looked down at the minibus keys in the ignition then back at the hall windows, now covered by the curtains. A determined look crossed over her face.

'No,' Margery said adamantly.

'Oh, come on!' Clementine pleaded. 'It'll be fun!'

'We'll end up decapitated!' Margery said. 'And Mr Evans will be furious if we scratch the minibus.'

'It'll have insurance!' Clementine said. 'Anyway, the school could use a new one. This one barely made it here, didn't it? It can't possibly be safe for children to travel in, the mince pies barely made it. And the thing is, Sally won't be expecting us, will she?'

Margery begrudgingly agreed that Clementine was probably right. Sally would certainly not be expecting them to careen through the window in a vehicle. The fact of the matter was, you didn't shut someone out into the cold and cause a distraction unless you were doing it maliciously, and Sally had seemed tricksy since they had met her. Perhaps Sally had facilitated Doug's death somehow, maybe she had been in on it with Elliot and was trying to now cover the last of her tracks. Either way, they needed to get back into the building. There was no telling how long the police were still going to be, and the road was still impassable. There was no way to get home without calamity.

'I'll try and get their attention with the horn first,' Margery said, Clementine shrugged. She pressed the horn as hard as she could, and then again and again, until her ears rang with the noise of it. No one came out of the hall and the curtains didn't so much as twitch. The volume inside must have been deafening.

'Back to plan B then,' Clementine said, Margery could tell she was trying to hide a grin.

'Should we swap seats?' Margery asked her, clutching the steering wheel so tightly that her knuckles were pale, and simultaneously trying not to sound as nervous as she felt. 'It was your idea, so you should probably drive, do you not think so?'

'Good Lord, no!' Clementine said with a chuckle lacing the edges of her tone. 'Have you never seen *Final*

Destination? We'll have to stay in the same seats now we've got in them so that we die in the correct order… I mean…'

'When have you seen *Final Destination*?' Margery asked, feeling her eyebrows raising of their own accord.

'Ceri-Ann made me watch it once because I said I didn't think a film from the 2000s could be the best film of all time. I'm still not entirely sure what her point was and we were on break so she just showed me what she thought were the best bits,' Clementine sighed. 'Look, just gently manoeuvre the minibus into the window enough to get inside the building. Just a quick little tap, it'll practically be like opening a dippy egg!'

'I think I'm going to try and aim the bus at the main fire escape,' Margery said, her voice feeling weak in spite of her decision. 'The one that leads into the hall, not the one Doug is still sat by.' The thought of running the bus over his body made her feel tremendously queasy for a moment. 'Or should I try the window?'

'We could try one and then the other. Why not, eh? We've got time!' Clementine breathed breezily from beside her as if Margery had just suggested knocking on it gently, not careening into it in a big chunk of metal. Though Margery noticed that Clementine was holding on to her seatbelt tightly and her face had gone as pale as Margery's knuckles wrapped around the steering wheel. 'Now, just aim it at the door and we'll give it a little tap with the bus, just enough to get into the building.'

Margery nodded, gripping the steering wheel tight with one hand as she turned the key in the ignition with the other. It didn't burst into life as quickly as it had on Friday afternoon, but the engine did eventually turn over. She fought for a moment with the gearstick, which was much harder to use than her automatic Nissan Figaro. She had needed to take a practice run around the school car park before they had hit any main roads the day they had arrived, but there wasn't time for that now. She slipped it into first gear with a horrible crunch and then eventually found the bite point with her foot.

As the minibus began to roll through the car park, several things happened at once. Firstly, the minibus wheels lost traction on the icy ground almost immediately. Margery only remembered that the car park had not been de-iced for days as the minibus began to slide sideways. They careened towards the hall, Margery letting out a frightened yelp as she tried to turn the steering wheel back the way they had come. It was too late, the wheels were locked in place and the minibus continued on its own trajectory. She slammed on the brakes, unintentionally putting the bus into a spin.

'What should I do?' Margery cried to Clementine, who was ashen-faced on the seat next to her and holding on to the dashboard for dear life. She turned to share a horrified look with Margery.

'Maybe we shouldn't have tried something so drastic,' Clementine called back unhelpfully as they spun. Time had slowed down to nothing, the clock moving in slow motion as the wheels skidded over the frozen tarmac. 'This is Dawn Simmonds' pond all over again!'

It was in a way, but in another Margery thought that this was definitely worse than the time they had plunged into their across-the-road-neighbour's pond in her car. For one, that time there had been water to break their fall. The only thing that would stop the minibus now was the glass of the community hall. With the last of her might, she turned the wheel and held it there, forcing the minibus towards the only thing that she could see might break their landing – the band's van was already wedged between the doors, there was nowhere to go. Margery had a split second to hope that no one was standing near it, then the fear overtook her.

The minibus continued to gather speed, though Margery kept stamping on the brake with all her might. It didn't make any difference as they careened towards the doors. She closed her eyes, preparing for the collision, gripping the steering wheel and letting fate decide their course. The crash that followed was so deafening it made Margery feel confused, a horrible scraping noise followed by the minibus coming to a sudden stop.

Chapter Twenty-Two

Margery opened her eyes to find that amazingly they were alive and, even better still, unhurt. Somehow the minibus was still mostly intact too, the windshield even containing glass somehow, though the door windows were both gone. Margery gasped in surprise at the luck of it all. She had been sure their time was up. The band's van hadn't faired quite as well. It had careened through the vestibule on impact and smashed into the back wall.

On hearing the commotion, the dinner lady team had rushed to the main entrance, along with a number of others, and a crowd had already begun to gather. Seren and Gloria had reached them first, leaning in through the shattered minibus windows to help pull Margery and Clementine away from the vehicle. It didn't seem too much worse for wear, there was no smoke from the engine that Margery could see. They certainly hadn't thought about that before ploughing into the building.

'You trapped us outside!' Clementine yelled at Sally as soon as she had crawled out of the passenger side door. 'Were you trying to kill us? Do you want us dead like Elliot and Doug?'

Margery had escaped the minibus in much the same way and was torn between staring at it in shock and watching the confrontation between Clementine and Sally happen. Sally stared at them both with wide, worried eyes, her mouth had fallen open. She had flinched at the mention of Elliot's name.

'I didn't—' she began, but Clementine didn't let her get another word in.

Clementine existed on the edge of anger most of the time, but she almost always managed to keep a lid on it. Usually, Clementine dealt with her emotions using sarcasm or very gentle annoyance. Margery very rarely saw the rage boil over, in fact, she could count the number of times she had seen Clementine truly, madly angry on one hand. The altercation with Sally had sent Clementine over the edge into a wild fury Margery wasn't sure she would ever see again.

'You could have killed us,' Clementine screeched, waving wildly at the minibus and the crumpled front of the van and all the smashed glass. The wind whipped through the broken windshield. It gushed through Clementine's hair, a visible embodiment of her fury. 'Look what you made us do!'

Sally puffed out her chest. 'I'll have you know I didn't force you to drive through a doorway! Look at the property damage you've caused.'

'Who cares about property damage?' Clementine wailed. Gloria was helping Ceri-Ann hold her back, though Ceri-Ann looked like she would like to let go and see what happened. 'It's freezing out there and you shut us out.'

'What are you talking about?' Sally waved a hand in a fleeting way at the window that made a rush of rage arrive in Margery's brain. 'Surely you'd get back in the way you went out there…'

'You hid the shoe,' Margery protested. Sally looked genuinely confused for a moment before bristling again in anger.

'It's kept you on your toes, hasn't it? All of this,' Sally sneered. 'You'll have to pay to have it all fixed. When Doug finds out, you'll be in terrible trouble—' She gasped in horror, putting her hands to her face, and Margery realised that Sally had briefly forgotten that Doug was dead.

A worried hush rolled over the gathered crowd. Margery bitterly hoped that their confrontation was enough of a spectacle for them. Sally gasped again, holding a hand to her mouth. Margery heard someone murmur about Doug's death. Arthur hadn't told anyone. He had probably not wanted to start a panic, but the panic was arriving anyway. Margery could see it on the horizon.

'Oh, we need to get out of here,' Sally said.

Margery found herself wanting to reach out and help her, but she didn't know how to. She lifted her arm to reach out and steady the woman, who had begun to back away from them. Sally snatched her arm away, lifting a finger and pointing it at Margery and Clementine as if it were a knife.

'How do we all know that you didn't kill him?' she said, her voice a cold snap. 'You seem to know so much about everyone else's comings and goings. Who put you in charge?'

'Well, actually—' Clementine began.

'You're both in here, rootling around in things you don't understand,' Sally snapped.

Margery shook the confusion away. 'What do you mean by that?'

'You know what I mean,' Sally said.

She glared at Margery and then stormed away, so eager to get across the hall that she nearly tripped over Ada Bones on her way through. Ada yelped and scuttled behind the safety of Rhonda's legs. The crowd began to disperse now that the show was over. Margery wondered if they ought to follow Sally, and what good it might do if they did.

'Daft old bat,' someone said with a laugh. Margery turned and saw Mike grinning at Sally's departing back.

'You can't be serious?' Clementine spluttered. 'After what you've done.'

Mike folded his arms over his chest and leaned back in the fold-up chair he was sitting on. 'She's obviously lost it, being in here. Poor old girl.'

'And whose fault is that?' Margery asked him, trying to stay calm and feeling her anger rushing up through her body and into her chest. Her hands pulled into fists, the nails digging into her palms. 'You're the one who trapped us here in the first place, and anyway, need I remind you that you and Sally are the same age!'

Clementine was staring at her open-mouthed with a look of wide-eyed awe on her face and Margery realised that they hadn't discussed when they would confront Mike with what they had seen on the dash camera. The crowd that had begun to disperse had returned, sharks that could already taste the blood of a fight. Margery paid them no mind.

'So what if I did!' Mike said. He folded his arms even tighter to his chest, his face taking on a hue only usually seen on ripe summer tomatoes. He glared around at everyone. 'I had my reasons!'

'So, you admit that you pulled down the tree?' Margery asked.

Mike nodded. 'And I'd do it again!'

There was a collective gasp from all around them. Martha and Arthur stood clutching their hands together, their mouths hanging open, Gloria and the rest of the dinner ladies looked furious. Margery took it all in. Even Rose and Rhonda had angry, reproachful expressions, and they had made a profit from their entrapment. It seemed like everyone except Sally was here to watch, and Mrs Bell, who Margery hadn't seen for a while. She made a mental note to check on the elderly woman at some point.

Margery hadn't even needed to pry much to get the confession out of Mike, it had rolled off his tongue like water. It was as if Mike had been wishing someone would ask him so he could confess to it all. Mike got up and tried to saunter away, but Margery moved to stand in front of him, blocking his path.

'But we don't understand why,' Margery said, her head swimming with confusion. 'Why did you pull the tree down?'

'Rock and roll's all about making a statement,' Mike sneered. 'Why do you think I'm always wearing leather trousers? It's not because they're comfortable, let me tell you!' He chuckled at his own comment. 'I had a big statement to make.'

'You trapped us all in here,' Clementine reminded him, her eyes wide at his audacity. 'Two people are dead and we're all lucky it isn't more, with the dwindling food supplies and the cold weather. There's no heating and we've got elderly here!'

'I wouldn't call yourselves elderly,' Mike said kindly. Margery joined Clementine in glaring at him. 'Middle-aged, yeah, but we're nearly the same age and I'm not old… do you think an old man could wear these trousers—'

'I meant Mrs Bell,' Clementine snapped. 'And you're too old for pranks like cutting down trees. You wouldn't see me out there with an axe or using our car to pull down a tree, of all things!'

'Well,' Mike said sulkily, folding his arms over his chest. 'I just drove off a little bit, it went down like a sack of spuds. Rotten inside. I thought just a bit of it might fall. I didn't know all of it would!'

To be fair to him, Mike couldn't have known that the tree would come down quite in the way that it did that before he had done it. She didn't expect that his years of singing in a band had given him much experience in tree surgery.

'I had to do something,' Mike said with a shrug. 'The band's been doing my head in and Kevin won't talk to me about any of it. I thought it would be a little bit of a disturbance, you know? Just enough that I'd have a few hours to confront Kevin before it was cleared. I didn't know the gas lines were underneath it or the tree roots would bring half the road up, did I? How could I have known that! Doug should be in big trouble for that really, he's in charge of maintaining the grounds. Surely having a huge rotten tree hanging over a car park isn't ideal. I've done everyone a favour.'

'You did that?' a voice whispered from the side of them all. 'Why?'

Margery turned to find Kevin standing off to the side, staring at Mike. The hurt was visible in his eyes alone, but it radiated to the rest of him as well. His arms slumped at his sides in defeat, his brow furrowed under the weight of it all.

'Oh, come on, mate,' Mike said, his voice rising in a nervous manner Margery wouldn't expect from him. 'You've got to have known that things aren't going to plan, and every time I bring up my contract issues, you run off.'

'Obviously things have been a little bit wonky, but no more than usual,' Kevin spluttered. He looked genuinely upset. 'I thought we were past that. I thought we'd agreed to carry on till the end of the contract.'

'You agreed that,' Mike said, pointing a finger directly at the man's chest. Kevin flinched as if Mike had stabbed him with it. 'You! That contract has got another four years on it. Where am I going to be then? Basically a husk… I'm getting on, Kevin. I haven't got the energy to go prancing about like a teenager, we can't keep up with the social media stuff! I feel like I'm starring in a new *Spinal Tap* film every time we get together.'

'You were the one just talking about your love of leather trousers.' Clementine laughed. There was no happiness in it, just anger and annoyance. 'So which is it?'

Mike ignored her. For a moment he looked like he might drop to his knees in front of Kevin and beg to be freed from the contract, but instead he sat down on the nearest folding chair.

'Just let me break the contract,' Mike said.

'You shouldn't have signed the new one in that case.' Kevin scowled. 'We could have parted ways when the old one expired. I've been managing you for thirty years, Mike. I helped you through rehab, all of it!'

Mike worried at his lip. 'I needed the advance, you're not the only one with a mortgage.'

Margery realised then why Mike had pulled the tree down, and it had nothing to do with rock music or anything of the sort. Simply his anger at Kevin and his need to try and escape his contract. Another thing that Mike might be responsible for came to mind. Putting two and two together wasn't always wise, but at this moment, she knew that she had a good enough chance of being correct to risk asking the question.

'Did you kill Elliot?' Margery asked out loud after considering it for a moment longer.

Mike looked genuinely startled for a second before he managed to pull himself back together. 'No, why on earth would you think that?'

'The Christmas lights—' Margery began.

'Oh, come off it,' Mike said with a snort of laughter. 'What are you on about?'

'Elliot wasn't killed by a head injury,' Margery told him, watching his face closely to see his reaction. 'We think he was killed using the skull Christmas tree lights that were in your music video. And now you've admitted chopping down the tree that caused all this trouble, you've got to admit that it doesn't look good for you.'

Mike looked horrified. He turned to Kevin. 'Did you know about this?'

'No,' Kevin said, his eyes wide with shock. 'No, I didn't.'

Margery didn't know if she should believe them or not. For all they knew, Kevin and Mike were in cahoots.

'You can't believe we had anything to do with that. You want to go and chat with your mate Sally,' Mike said, pointing to the hall door, which Sally had left through. 'She's who's been acting mad.'

'I think she's just traumatised,' Clementine said. 'You've got to remember that two of her colleagues are dead and we're all trapped here.'

'She needs to get over it.' Mike grinned at her with veneered teeth. Margery had the ridiculous urge to hold a piece of printer paper up to them and see which was whiter, though she knew the answer already.

Chapter Twenty-Three

The argument with Mike had taken every little bit of energy Margery had left, and judging by Clementine's face, she felt the same way. Margery imagined her spine crunching with every step and winced.

She remembered the sight of Mike's wet leather jacket dripping onto the hallway flooring before he yelled at poor Arthur. 'Let's recap for a second. Mike, obviously we know he's the reason we're all trapped here… he was very forthcoming with that information, wasn't he? He was almost proud of himself. We don't even need the video for evidence, we could have just asked him.'

'Yes,' Clementine said, her brow furrowing darkly. 'And I'm still not entirely sure why he did it anyway.'

'No,' Margery said. It had certainly been dramatic. She was sure Mike would face some charges even if just for the tree once the police had dealt with the more important aspects.

'Sally knows something else,' Clementine said with a firm nod that told Margery she had decided on that.

'I agree,' Margery said, playing with the sleeves of her cardigan as she thought about it. 'But where is she?'

A lightbulb seemed to go on in Clementine's head at that, Margery could almost hear her thinking. Margery looked to where Clementine was staring and saw that the office door was open. As they reached the door, Margery peeked her head through the gap between the open door and the door frame. Sally was inside, pulling things apart. The office had been a bit messy before, but it had been more an extension of what went on inside Doug's brain. Sally had torn the place in two. Margery watched as she opened the next desk drawer and began pulling things out, barely looking at them before she discarded them onto the floor. The floor itself was littered with files and papers and the random items Doug had obviously had inside his desk. A stress ball fell from Sally's groping hands and bounced towards Margery. She stopped it with her shoe just as Sally looked up.

Sally wore the horrified look of someone who had been caught stealing their grandmother's pension out of her purse, stopping mid-rummage to stare at them both boggle-eyed.

'What are you—' Clementine began. She was cut off as Sally stormed towards them.

For a moment, Margery thought she was going to try and pass them, but instead Sally gestured to the mess.

'Just looking for our insurance documents,' she explained breezily, her voice strained and fake. 'We'll need them if we're going to replace the flooring that caught fire in front of the stage and now the hall doorway. It's a very expensive automatic door system, I'll have to make sure that it gets replaced with the right thing.'

'Are you sure that's all?' Margery asked, looking around at the chaos.

'What other reason could there be?' Sally said through clenched teeth.

Sally reached out and slammed the door behind her, closing herself off from the world. Margery and

Clementine shared a confused look. Margery thought she could hear Sally sobbing behind the door.

'Now what?' Margery asked Clementine.

Clementine had a dazed, far-away look in her eye.

'I think I might know where the money is,' she said. 'Elliot said it was in a Christmassy place, didn't he?'

Margery followed her along the corridor until they reached the Christmas grotto. Clementine paused there too. The grotto seemed more than slightly cursed. She pushed aside the cardboard door and crouched down to clamber in through the archway behind it. Margery followed, propping the cardboard door open so they had some light.

Inside, the air was thick. It was so dark Margery felt as though they were being entombed. The cardboard and glue were comforting, like a brand-new book. The grotto hadn't been as exposed to the elements as the rest of the building and it had been kept insulated by the cardboard. Margery found herself feeling along the walls, her fingertips dipping into the ridges of the cardboard. Clementine didn't waste any time. She began to rummage through the sack of wrapped presents sitting next to the throne.

'I thought...' Clementine began, unwrapping a present and finding a soft toy. 'Oh, well...'

'Did you think the money would be in the presents?' Margery asked. 'I had that thought too earlier, but I think they were definitely planned for the children. He wouldn't have put the money in with them.'

'Yes, it seems silly now,' Clementine said with a sigh.

'It was a good enough idea,' Margery said soothingly.

'You know what,' Clementine began. 'Let's forget all of this. Let Sally have her mad moment and then let the police deal with it all, shall we? They should be here soon enough and you look exhausted.'

'I am tired,' Margery said, realising it was true as she agreed.

'Let's go and have a rest, then,' Clementine said. 'What's the worst that can happen now? Everyone's on edge, aren't they? Whoever killed Elliot would be mad to act again now that everyone's on high alert.'

'You're probably right,' Margery said, rubbing her hands over her eyes.

'You could stay in here for some peace and quiet,' Clementine said. She looked down at the floor. 'It might be nice in here, you know? I might join you in a bit, but I think I'm going to go and help Gloria pack everything up ready for when the police finally get here.'

'That's not a bad plan,' Margery said agreeably. 'Are you sure you don't want me to come and help?'

Clementine shook her head and then reached over and kissed her on the cheek. She left Margery alone, shutting the cardboard door behind her. Margery sidestepped behind the tinsel-covered throne made of egg cartons. She knelt and pushed the presents out of the way, leaving a space on the floor to lie down on her back. The relief was instant.

It was comfortable on the floor, and the room was so dark, she found it easy to begin to drift off, promising herself that she'd only close her eyes for a moment. Then she would drag herself back up onto her legs and get on with it, even though her legs and back may as well have been filled with concrete for all the use they were. She tried to keep her thoughts steady, but they began to disappear in waves, floating her to the place where memories of people lived. She thought vaguely about her mother and her father, the space in between sleep and awake the only place she could think about them in detail without getting too upset by their absence.

Her mother had been reserved, but still defiant in her own way, Margery could never have lied to her, even if she had wanted to. Once, they had stopped at a fish market one morning on a seaside holiday somewhere Margery could no longer picture the name of. Margery had been too overwhelmed by the smell of the place to notice her mother staring at the sole lobster still left, alone on a bed of ice with its claws taped shut. Before Margery could fixate on anything more than the dirty water pooling around her best patent leather shoes, her mother was paying for it and guiding her out of the building. Her father had roared with laughter when he saw the poor creature in the plastic bag, but he had played along. Margery had a flickering memory of driving to park up by the pier and then watching her mother fight with the binding over the claws before she dropped the thing back into the sea where it had come from.

Margery always thought that the thing about happiness and the people involved in yours is that you can't possibly realise how good it all is until you see the absence of the same in someone else's life. It made her grateful for what she'd once had, though desperately sad that it was all over. The thoughts slipped away like the waves under the pier and the lobster disappearing into the water below, leaving her with nothing but the comforting darkness.

Chapter Twenty-Four

Margery didn't know how long she'd been asleep for, but she startled awake. Light washed over the ceiling for a second and then plunged her back into the darkness. She lay quietly, listening to her own shallow breathing as her head swam with confusion. There was a creak, and the cardboard throne to her side moved slightly. It knocked against Margery's arm as the weight of whoever it was settled onto it. The tiny grotto filled with the gentle rap of someone tapping their fingers against the arm of the chair in annoyance or boredom. There was a soothing rhythm to the noise and it was hard to blink her eyes open when the room was so dark.

Margery was about to sit up and announce herself, not willing to startle anyone, it might have been Clementine, though surely Clementine would have come to lie down with her. She was about to call Clementine's name when the grotto door opened again, and then closed as tightly as before, the cardboard scraping against the carpet softly.

'Took you long enough,' a woman's voice said.

There was a cold snap in her tone that took Margery by surprise. She found herself wincing, even though it wasn't aimed at her, but at whoever had just arrived. Margery tried to lie perfectly still and keep her breathing even and measured, her fingers clutching at the cardboard floor to steady herself. Her surprise at hearing Mrs Bell's voice in the confined space was only surpassed by hearing a man sigh with annoyance in return.

'You need to stop asking me to meet you,' Kevin said. Margery could imagine his face twisting into annoyance even though she couldn't see it.

'Oh, Kevin,' Mrs Bell said quietly. 'You know I can't do that. That wasn't part of our deal at all.'

'I've got you what you wanted.' His voice rose into a wail. Margery heard something thump down onto the floor. 'You've got to leave me alone now. The less we see of each other, the better. You need to leave me alone if we're going to get out of here. Those *dinner ladies*...' He spat their title as though it were the most disgusting of swear words. Margery clasped a hand over her own mouth at the change in Kevin's tone. This version of him was hardened and detached. Margery could hear him pacing the small space.

'What about the dinner ladies?' Mrs Bell asked, sounding confused. 'They're all right. I know them, they're fine.'

'They're meddling in everything,' Kevin wailed. 'I don't know what else they know but I reckon they'll figure it all out eventually. Mike's an idiot for starting all this. I should have known it was him who'd pulled down the tree. And I've just found out that Elliot shut Doug out, not Jade. Why did you tell me Jade did that?'

'I didn't know,' Mrs Bell snapped, interrupting him mid-rant. 'I didn't know he was outside when I let Elliot in, if I'd known...'

She paused and Margery heard Kevin's breath hitch. Kevin had always seemed a bit aggressive when they had spoken to him before so it shouldn't have been surprising, but somehow it was.

'I didn't know what was going on,' Mrs Bell said, in a small voice that loomed large in the confined space anyway, even muffled by cardboard. 'I didn't know that Elliot had killed him.'

'Well, I didn't know about the lights,' Kevin insisted.

'They were your lights, how could you not know?' Mrs Bell snorted. Margery found her blood going cold at the idea that anyone could find any of this funny at all.

'I didn't kill him!' Kevin cried. 'You know I didn't!'

Mrs Bell laughed again, a dark, humourless laugh. 'Let's not forget that I found you dragging his corpse into this very room!'

It had been Kevin dragging Elliot from the hall on the camera footage. Margery clapped a hand over her mouth so she wouldn't gasp out loud at the same time as she heard something skitter along the floor. Whatever it was didn't sound heavy, it clattered over the floor rather than thumped.

'Don't kick that!' Mrs Bell hissed in warning.

'Or what?' Kevin said, the attitude from earlier returning. 'You'll blackmail me again? What have I got to lose?'

'Ooh let's see,' Mrs Bell sneered, unfazed by Kevin's own anger. 'Your job, your house, your wife… namely everything. So, we're going to stay nice and quiet until this is all over and then we'll never speak of it again. Do you understand?'

'I can't believe you,' Kevin said. 'You're evil.'

'I'm not evil!' Mrs Bell said in a horrified voice. 'You aren't innocent here, and look, you'll get your money back now and Jade's! The band will be able to put out a few more terrible albums and then you can retire. Do you think I want to do this? Resorting to stealing money that a dead man stole against my will?'

'I don't believe you,' Kevin told her firmly. 'You both would have stolen the money anyway… I know what you were doing with that new company, poaching all the good spots at festivals. Doug knew what was going on, he told me all about it in the end.'

'Well, Elliot's getting what was coming to him now, if you believe in all that,' Mrs Bell said. Margery could almost feel her shrugging. 'Because you killed him.'

'I didn't kill him!' Kevin stuttered.

'Then why are you here?' Mrs Bell said. Margery could feel her smirk sucking the air from the room.

'You know why I'm here,' Kevin said, the noise filtered through gritted teeth. 'You've got CCTV footage that shows me hiding his body. Where is it? Tell me, it's over…'

'No,' Mrs Bell said. 'Listen, if you didn't kill someone, you don't move a body, do you? I'm keeping that footage safe until I'm well away from you. I don't know how dangerous you are, do I?'

Kevin gasped and stammered, but he didn't have a retort. Margery found herself gripping her nails into the cardboard floor below her as she realised that they had completely overlooked Mrs Bell's absent stare into the vestibule camera footage. She had gone into the office and taken the footage. But how had it ended up in Elliot's pocket?

'You dragged him in here,' Mrs Bell said in a quiet voice that contained layers of despair and sadness. 'Then when you realised I'd caught you, you hid under the stage! Well, you can't get away with it that easily.'

'I've told you over and over, it was the lights, not me,' Kevin pleaded. 'Sean must have hit them too hard the night before when he was drumming, there was something wrong with them.'

Mrs Bell scoffed and Kevin continued. 'It's true! I was trying to sleep in a chair next to the stage. I saw Elliot come in. When the power came back on, they electrocuted him. I couldn't leave him there to be found next to the band's drums, could I? It was lucky that it was three in the morning and everyone else was still in the other hall—'

'Well, why was he near them in the first place?' Mrs Bell asked. Margery could hear the triumph in her voice.

'He was trying to plug his phone into the socket behind Sean's kit that the PA system and the lights were plugged into,' Kevin explained. 'It was a freak accident!'

'Well, you're too deep in to get away with it now. You made it look like it wasn't an accident, which is as good as intentionally killing him,' Mrs Bell told him firmly. 'How did you know he was even really dead? That's all there is to it.'

'I don't… I didn't… I've never seen anyone die before!' Kevin groaned. He collected himself. 'Well, I think we've done a pretty good job of the cover-up, they all think it was Jacob who killed him with that ham. I heard them all screeching about it.'

'The dinner ladies have already realised that's not how he died. I saw them go and look at Elliot's body in the freezer,' Mrs Bell warned him. 'If they've managed to work that out, do you not think the police would work it out in about three seconds? They'll do an autopsy and find out what happened immediately.'

'I hid the lights,' Kevin said, his voice returning to smug very briefly. 'We'll get rid of them before the police get here. Anyway, the police will realise that they're from Apex Void's music video and they'll think Mike did it.'

'They've already got the lights,' Mrs Bell told him. 'It took them hardly any time at all to find them. I watched Clementine pull them out of the skirting board.'

Kevin began to stutter out an answer, but Mrs Bell laughed again, her cackle drowning him out. 'It's not looking good for you, is it? Who hides under a stage when they haven't killed someone? That's not suspicious at all, is it? I wonder what they'd think of the camera footage…'

'You need to tell me where it is!' Kevin spat in anger.

'Of course,' Mrs Bell said. 'As soon as this is all over.'

Kevin spluttered, but Margery didn't think he had much of a retort. Mrs Bell wasn't wrong in what she was saying.

'What if I just killed you?' Kevin said, his tone cold. 'You seem so sure that I killed Elliot… I could easily kill you. You weigh about three stone and I've just proved I can drag a man's dead weight all the way down a corridor…'

'Oh, sweetheart,' Mrs Bell whispered, the chuckle coming from deep in her throat. 'You really are a terrible man.'

Margery realised that she should really be recording the conversation as proof, but she didn't have her phone with her. Even if she had, the battery was long dead. Instead, she tried to focus on remembering every word of the conversation. Anything she heard now would be helpful for the report she would give the police. What had Kevin done for Mrs Bell? That was what concerned Margery now. Mrs Bell couldn't possibly want anything nice from the situation if she was already involved in a takeover with Elliot before. What more could she want from Kevin?

'Where's the money?' Kevin asked, sounding sulky and scorned. 'Have you found it yet? You've got me running around collecting trinkets.'

'Wouldn't you like to know,' Mrs Bell said, a hint of a smirk in her voice.

'Yeah, I would,' Kevin snapped. 'I want my money back and I want to know where you've hidden that camera footage and I want to be adequately compensated for what I've done for you, traipsing around getting all of these for you even when I'm innocent. You said you'd split the money with me, where is it?'

The cardboard throne moved backward slightly. Kevin must have kicked the bag of whatever it was he had brought into the grotto again and Mrs Bell had risen to her feet in anger. Margery gasped quietly in surprise as the cardboard touched the skin of her arm. There was a pause. The energy in the small room shifted.

'Is there someone there?' Mrs Bell asked softly.

There was a rustling and then a click as the room exploded into colour for a second. Margery froze. The fairy lights that ran along the ceiling had all switched on and left her exposed underneath them, lying down behind the children's presents foolishly in the pink and blue glow. She blinked at the sudden change in lighting.

'Well, well,' Kevin said. They both eyed Margery curiously from over the throne. 'Isn't this a surprise?'

His eyes were almost twinkling as much as the Christmas lights. Margery had seen that look before. It was the look of a killer who was winning a game that Margery didn't even want to play, and it made her regret every moment she had ever written Kevin off as simply the band's bumbling manager and Mrs Bell as only a frail old lady.

Chapter Twenty-Five

Kevin and Mrs Bell fell into a two-step each side of Margery and they marched down the hallway and out of the fire escape. Kevin moved with much more ease than both Mrs Bell and Margery put together. He must have been at least ten years younger than her, Margery thought as she risked a glance over at his face. His lips were drawn in a way that told her that he wasn't happy about this new development in their plans, yet he didn't stop the march.

Margery looked around desperately for an escape route, hoping that a dinner lady would come out of the kitchen and spot them and ask them where they were going. She had no such luck. Kevin grimaced as he shoved the door past Doug's body, hefting it out of the way with ease. Doug fell to the side and collapsed to the floor in a horrible heap. Margery tried not to gasp as she caught a glimpse of his blue frozen body from the corner of her eye. Mrs Bell barely reacted as the three of them skittered past him. Instead, she jabbed Margery in the side with the handle of the knife that Kevin had given her. Margery wasn't sure it was entirely intentional but thought it best to keep her mouth shut on the journey. Her brain raced as she thought of escape routes. She thought that she probably had more strength than Mrs Bell, but she couldn't risk acting on it. Not with Kevin whispering threats.

'Remember that it'll be much worse for you if you scream for help,' Kevin had hissed as Margery had stood to a crouch in the grotto, his hand around her wrist. 'She used to be a nurse, she'll know exactly where all your arteries are. You'll be dead in a second. You won't even have time to think about it before every drop of blood in your body is on the floor.'

The knife was from Margery's own colour-coded set that she had brought from their work kitchen. She knew that it was stupid, given the circumstances, but she wished that Kevin had deigned to use the red-handled raw meat knife for the purpose, instead of the green-handled salad knife. If it did end up killing her, the kitchen team wouldn't be able to slice cucumbers with it any more.

'This is all very inconvenient,' Kevin sighed. 'If you hadn't been sneaking around listening to things then we'd all be out of here in a few hours, probably.'

Kevin led them across the car park, his smart leather shoes sliding on the icy ground. Mrs Bell didn't fare much better in her slip-on flats, weighted down with a heavy bin bag, full to the brim with something Margery couldn't see, but imagined it was the bag that Kevin had been kicking in anger. Whatever it was rattled as they walked. Margery thought that might give her an opportunity to run, but Mrs Bell's knife remained firmly wedged against her neck. Margery had thought for a brief moment that Mrs Bell was going to try and escape Kevin's clutches too, but she could feel the nick the knife was beginning to make in her skin, a drop of blood running down to her cardigan.

'You let Elliot in through the fire escape door,' Margery accused as she was marched along. She didn't dare turn back to look Mrs Bell in the eye, but she answered her anyway.

'I did,' Mrs Bell admitted. She didn't seem particularly concerned about the confession.

'Why did Elliot kill Doug?' Margery asked.

'Spur of the moment, I think,' Mrs Bell told her. 'I didn't realise that Doug was still out there in the cold and I don't know if Elliot had managed to finish the job before he came in. I killed Doug, if we're being correct about it, by not realising.'

'You didn't tell anyone about Elliot,' Margery found herself saying, though she couldn't bring up any anger to go with the comment. Everything felt flat and hopeless.

'I didn't,' Mrs Bell agreed cheerily. 'Too late to do anything about that now.'

She tutted at the memory like she was telling her about a naughty cat that had brought a dead mouse into her kitchen. It made Margery feel sick.

'You have to see what it would look like to the police,' Mrs Bell explained. 'Elliot dead, Doug dead, and me setting up a company with Elliot that was already suspected of theft. There would be a lot of questions for me.'

'You could have done your little old lady act and fooled them all,' Margery said.

'Maybe. But I didn't need to once Kevin and I made a little deal,' Mrs Bell continued. 'The plan was just to hang on till we could get away. I need the money, Margery, why do you think I was going into business with Elliot in the first place? I'm struggling by on pennies day to day. This was a way to fix all my financial woes. I'm getting on, I don't own my house – you can thank my ex-husband for that… I'll need care at some point and I'll be damned if I don't have the money to pay for good help.'

Margery would have shaken her head if the tip of the knife wasn't still biting into her skin. 'You can't think it wouldn't eventually all be pieced together.'

'Who's to say?' Mrs Bell said. 'If the police ever asked, well, I'd have to tell them my memory hasn't been quite right for a while…'

'You're a liar,' Margery snapped. Mrs Bell didn't reply and Margery didn't dare to turn her head to look at her.

They arrived at Mrs Bell's car, and she flung the bag she was holding into the back seat. It rattled away and hit the passenger door with a clunk. There was a noise from behind them and Margery turned just in time to see the police cars careening down the hill. They poured down it like an errant train. Her heart soared at the sight of them.

'Get into the car,' Kevin told her. 'Quickly.'

'What's your plan?' Margery asked them both. 'You can't get away without being seen and what are you going to do with me? You can't keep me forever.'

'We don't need to keep you forever,' Kevin said. 'We just need to keep you long enough to convince you that you shouldn't say anything to the police.'

'But where will they think we've gone?' Margery asked, feeling her voice rise in pitch. 'Clem will be looking for me. She's probably already looking for me…'.

She made to turn towards the hall, Kevin gripped her by the arm. His fingernails dug into the thin material of Margery's cardigan and etched themselves into her skin.

'Unfortunately, you were hurt as you tried to take Beryl away as a hostage after we realised that you killed Elliot,' Kevin explained with a shrug towards Mrs Bell. 'She's just an old lady and she's not all there. Nothing much more to it. You died attacking her.'

'No one will believe that,' Margery said, but she realised that there was a good chance that it might be believed by some people. The residents of Dewstow did enjoy even the simplest of gossip. This would be at least a year's worth of excitement. Margery and Clementine might even have believed it themselves if they had been on the other side of the fence. Mrs Bell would have been the last person they'd ever have suspected to be involved in it all. 'Why would I kill Elliot? I'd only met him once!'

'She's not wrong,' Mrs Bell said at the same time as Kevin groaned.

Kevin ignored her and gestured for them to get into the car. Margery did so begrudgingly. Mrs Bell followed her into the passenger side and Kevin clambered into the driver's seat in front of them. The bin bag sat between them as the only witness.

They watched the police go streaming into the hall through the fire escape. Margery watched through the windscreen as Ceri-Ann gasped and rushed over to them before they had even entered the hall. It was only as she threw her arms around the tallest in the group that Margery realised that it was Symon. She let out a huge sigh of relief that she hadn't known she had been holding. The cavalry had finally arrived and at least the others in the hall were fine, they were much safer than Margery, who was sitting in a car with Kevin, who seemed to have lost his mind. Through the glass hall windows, Clementine peered around the room, looking for Margery, and she felt her heart jump with fear. If only she could get away from Mrs Bell for a moment.

'What's the plan now, then?' Mrs Bell asked Kevin. 'You're just going to drive away in my car with us in it?'

Kevin rolled his eyes, finally deigning to say something. 'You can't really pretend you're not a willing participant in this.'

He had a point. Mrs Bell gripped her nails into Margery's arm, the other hand still on the knife. She had taken it from Margery's neck, but now the point of it was sitting just under Margery's ribs. She could feel the prick in her side, waiting to slice through the material of her cardigan.

'Well, I don't want to go to prison!' Mrs Bell snapped, but she still paused, thinking it over. She smiled as she thought up an idea. Margery watched her mouth curl upwards like an unwanted cursive letter, the font used for the grade on the front of a particularly hard maths test. 'But we won't after we frame Margery for the murder.'

'You are joking?' Margery heard herself scoff. 'You can't be serious. I was with my team for the entire evening of Doug and Elliot's deaths...'

Kevin gasped in triumph, turning around to stare at Margery.

'Your team were living it up at the party,' Mrs Bell reminded her. 'The only ones who weren't there were you and your wife. I know that everyone in this town holds you in their favour, Mrs Butcher-Baker, but there will be undeniable evidence of what you did. We'll make sure of it. You and your wife found the very Christmas lights that electrocuted him, and you haven't been quiet about parading them around.' Kevin looked on with glee, very pleased with Mrs Bell's fruitful scheme. 'You've been showing them off ever since and you haven't been subtle.'

Before Margery could ask what Mrs Bell even meant by that, the woman jabbed Kevin in the leg with the point of the knife. He screeched and clutched the wound as Mrs

Bell pulled it away. It was just a nick with the point that had sliced open his trousers, but Margery knew Mrs Bell wouldn't have hesitated to plunge the entire knife through his leg if she needed to.

'Why did you do that?' he cried, bringing his hand up to look at the blood that had collected on it.

'Why did Margery do that, you mean?' Mrs Bell said, with a grin. 'Now come on, what are you waiting for? Get on with it! They're all distracted by what's going on in the hall. If you want to leave, let's go… keep the headlights off.'

'You can't run from this,' Margery said. 'You could just let me go. I didn't suspect you'd had anything to do with it at all. Until I heard your confession, that is. I'm sure no one else has any idea either.'

Margery had a terrible feeling that the surprise of finding Margery listening when they had thought they were alone had propelled Kevin into the next idea he could think of. If there was anything she knew from the last few years, it was that panicked people don't make good decisions. Mrs Bell had joined in the panic, it hadn't taken her long to turn.

'Start the car, Kevin,' Mrs Bell bellowed. Kevin rolled his eyes again, but he obeyed anyway, one hand still clasped to his bleeding leg as he turned the key in the ignition.

The car engine spluttered and then fell silent. Kevin tried again.

'Something wrong with the engine,' Kevin said with a shrug as the engine died a third time.

'It's this old engine,' Mrs Bell said with a sigh. 'My poor car doesn't do well in the cold and I didn't have her cover with me to put over her, poor dear!'

'Well, can you get it going?' Kevin spluttered.

‘I’ve got a battery charger, let me go and have a look—’

‘No,’ Kevin said quickly. ‘Just tell me where it is.’

‘It should be in there,’ Mrs Bell said, pointing to the car dashboard. Kevin began to rummage around inside it, finding nothing but used tissues and parking receipts.

‘Where?’ he called. ‘I can’t find it in here—’

‘Let me have a look,’ Mrs Bell said impatiently. ‘Come and open this door.’

Kevin hesitated, but he obligated, getting out of the car and opening Mrs Bell’s door. Mrs Bell got out of the car, slamming the door behind her, the child locks trapping Margery inside. Mrs Bell looked through the dashboard compartment too and then sighed.

‘I think it’s in the storage compartment in the boot,’ she said. ‘Under the spare tyre.’

Kevin rushed around to the boot, the cold air chilling Margery’s face as the breeze blew into the car from behind her.

‘Watch her!’ Kevin screeched, pointing a finger at Margery through the window. ‘Don’t let her get away.’

Margery wasted no time in trying the doors anyway, even though she knew that they would be locked. She climbed over the centre console with great difficulty and lunged for the driver’s side seat, almost getting wedged between the seat and the steering wheel. She managed to fumble for the car door, but that was locked too. Her fingers grazed the unyielding surfaces of the interior desperately. Mrs Bell sat down next to her in the passenger seat.

‘Please don’t do this,’ Margery told her. Mrs Bell lowered her eyes but didn’t say a word. ‘Please,’ Margery continued. ‘You’re right, you can’t get away with this. You’ve got to make Kevin see some sense. The police will be able to put it all together. You'll get caught, they aren't stupid, and they've got a full team of forensics and evidence and all sorts of things. There's no way you'll be able to get back into the hall to plant evidence that I did it. They're already here…'

Mrs Bell raised her head to look over at the hall, where the police were gathering outside. If the weather had been better or it had been earlier in the day, Margery thought that they might have been noticed by now. As it was, the sky was darkening rapidly and swallowing them with it. They were half hidden from sight by the row of police cars sitting in front of the hall windows. She had never felt more alone.

'Why are you helping him? I thought you were supposed to be blackmailing him?' Margery tried one last time. Trying to find the person underneath. 'You didn't kill Elliot.'

To her surprise, Mrs Bell threw her head back and laughed.

'Oh, Margery, I'm in much too deep now,' she admitted. 'I knew about Elliot's scheming, of course, I wasn't innocent in that, and then when I saw Kevin dragging his body into the grotto… it just seemed like the way to go about it so I could still get my money. It wasn't hard to blackmail him, once he'd been found under the stage anyway. For a minute there I thought he was going to get away.'

'Did the lights electrocute Elliot?' Margery asked, to confirm it for herself. They had suspected as much. 'Kevin didn't really kill him?'

'I saw it happen,' Mrs Bell said. 'Not that Kevin knows that – don't tell him. It really wasn't his fault, but you can't blackmail someone who knows you know that they're innocent.'

The silence passed between them. Mrs Bell cleared her throat and continued. 'The thing with Elliot's scheming is that most of it was my idea. The guilt's heavy, Margery, it's like it's weighing me down. It was a good scam, he was always really convincing, but I think Elliot wanted out of it and I convinced him just to get the business up and running… this is all my fault.'

Margery found herself scoffing. 'Elliot's dead, Doug is dead. Who else has to die?'

'Well, I think you know the answer that he would have for that, don't you?' Mrs Bell said, as if it were a very simple matter. 'Thing is, I've been seeing the writing on the wall all day. He thinks we'll get away with it, but it's not the old days, is it? Even if we didn't kill Elliot, well, we haven't exactly helped anything. I've been blackmailing Kevin and Kevin moved Elliot's body. You know, I keep thinking… I'm old enough that my prison sentence wouldn't be very long, would it?'

'Then why are we here, then?' Margery asked. 'If you know you won't get away with it?'

Mrs Bell turned to her and seemed to see her properly for the first time.

'Where is it!' Kevin yelled from behind them. Margery could hear him throwing things out of the boot, they clattered onto the cold ground and smashed.

'You know, people's motives are never as interesting as you think they're going to be,' Margery finally said. 'You were working with Elliot to steal people's money and promote your own new business and Kevin tried to cover up Elliot's death to protect the band. And Elliot killed Doug in a fit of rage because Doug knew what he was doing and was going to fire him, or maybe Elliot didn't intentionally kill him… just left him to die, which is even worse! All this for a few thousand pounds and the reasons are as inane as any case I've seen.'

Mrs Bell managed a small smile at that. Kevin continued to search for the car battery charger, becoming angrier and angrier, hidden behind the parcel shelf. Margery watched the spare tyre bounce past them and roll away. Mrs Bell sighed, rubbing her hands over her face.

'He'll be there a while,' she said.

'Oh?'

'Yes, the charger is at home in my garage,' Mrs Bell admitted. 'I knew the car wouldn't start, it never does when the engine's too cold. I wasn't lying about the cover. Would you get up easily if you hadn't had your duvet overnight?'

Margery turned to stare at her open-mouthed and then somehow, they were both laughing. Margery didn't quite know why. Maybe at the absurdness of it all, or at Kevin's anger. The car locks clacked suddenly, rising out of the doors. Margery turned to look at Mrs Bell in surprise.

'Quick,' she said. 'Go… before I change my mind.'

Margery didn't wait to be told twice. She reached for the door handle, it opened and she slid out.

'Get her, Beryl!' Kevin screeched from the boot of the car as he noticed Margery.

Margery felt a wave of fear wash over her for a minute. Mrs Bell wouldn't be able to take her down on her own if she tried to run from her. For all that her cluelessness over the weekend had been an act, and for all that Margery wasn't much younger, she still felt as though she would be able to fight her off. Kevin was another thing altogether.

He would have no problem attacking Margery and over-powering her instantly.

Mrs Bell still looked conflicted, but she didn't move, her hands firmly wrapped around the steering wheel. Margery didn't hesitate again. She turned and began to race towards the building as fast as she could, slipping on the ice and stumbling, losing precious seconds to get away. Kevin yelled after her, his voice captured by the wind. Something hit her on the back of her leg and she stumbled, arms flailing before she hit the ground hard. All the air sucked from her lungs as if from a set of bellows. The knife lay on the ground next to Margery where Kevin had thrown it.

Margery held her hand to the back of her leg and brought it away to find blood streaming over her fingers. The back of her trouser leg flapped open where the knife had caught her, leaving the slick cut exposed to the cold. The heat from her warm blood rose into the air and the icy wind burnt the cut raw. She raised her head and saw the warm lights of the hall, glowing golden through the window as the last of the winter sun disappeared. She thought she could hear the sound of people's excitement at being rescued. The happiness and laughter at being safe at last. As her heart pounded in panic, it almost looked like the scene from a Christmas card, peace and joy to all mankind. Margery pulled herself back up, chancing a look back at Kevin, who was grinning at her gleefully. The knife gleamed between them and Margery's hand twitched as she wondered if she could reach it before Kevin did. Mrs Bell was getting out of the car and rushing over. Kevin reached out and grasped her by the arm. She stumbled and fell to the ground, landing hard on the ice.

'You'll have to do better than that,' Margery gasped, her breath filling the air with steam.

Kevin smiled coolly, his eyes locked on Margery as he crossed the car park towards her. Mrs Bell lay motionless on the ground and there was no time to check on her. Margery grimaced as she grasped for the knife, her leg burning with pain as she twisted. She stood to full height and turned to Kevin again.

He smiled as he continued to approach.

'Don't come any closer,' Margery said, though she couldn't bring herself to hold the knife up.

Kevin wasn't deterred. He stepped into Margery's personal space like he owned it and then crumpled to the ground like a marionette with the strings cut, clutching the leg that Mrs Bell had nicked with the knife.

'Help!' Kevin cried. Margery's brain froze with confusion. 'Help, she's trying to kill us!'

Chapter Twenty-Six

There was a noise behind her. Margery turned her head to see a crowd gathering inside the hall and realised what Kevin was trying to do. A dozen faces stared back at her. None of them saw the real Kevin, who had moved a body in order to protect the reputation of a band, or Mrs Bell, the person who had orchestrated the events that led to Doug's untimely demise and the cover-up of Elliot's death. Everyone saw Margery clutching a blood-covered kitchen knife, towering over Kevin while he bled, and the tiny elderly woman who still lay unconscious on the cold ground. They would all think she was the killer, and she had attacked poor, confused Mrs Bell and Kevin in a fit of rage. Panic rushed through Margery's mind and into her body, her legs felt weak with it.

Margery could admit that it didn't look good. Any casual onlooker would decide that she was guilty, purely based on the sight of her.

'Drop the knife!' a voice roared from the fire escape door behind her: a police officer. Margery recognised her as Symon's work partner, Officer Perkins. They had met before at baby Nick's birthday party. The recognition wouldn't help her. The shout cut right into Margery's nerves, her hands began to tremble. The knife shook.

Margery's grip went slack, her mouth opening and closing as her mind fogged over with indecision. Kevin continued acting, collapsing in on himself like crumpling paper. The knife slipped out of Margery's fingers and clattered to the floor. She kicked it away instinctively and watched as it twirled, gleaming over the ice until it disappeared under a car, and then turned with her arms up in surrender. At the very least, Kevin would struggle to reach it to act.

Margery turned around and found herself spluttering as she looked to Officer Perkins. Symon wasn't far behind, and neither was the rest of the force. He was looking at her in surprise. Margery would have bet all the missing money that the spectacle was the best the hall had ever seen, even beating Apex Void in their glory days or next week's panto.

'You can't think I did this,' Margery pleaded on deaf ears.

For once, she couldn't think of a way out of it. She was going to be arrested, and in the chaos Kevin would escape, getting away with his crimes forever if he had his way. Mrs Bell lay motionless, her legs twisted horribly underneath her where she had collapsed like a broken deck chair. There was no one to back her up and no one to believe her.

Officer Perkins raised her arms up at Margery like she was trying to soothe a wounded stray cat and lure them to the vet's. 'Just stay there, Mrs Butcher-Baker, don't make any sudden moves. We can sort this all out…'

Clementine had escaped from the hall somehow, making it past the officers trying to keep her in. She whipped past Officer Perkins, who spun around, nearly losing her balance. Somehow she still managed to grasp Clementine firmly by her cardigan collar before she could get to Margery. Clementine struggled against her.

'Margery wouldn't have killed anyone, and she wouldn't threaten anyone without reason!'

'She would!' Kevin protested. Officer Perkins continued to hold Clementine back. 'It was her knife, from her kitchen!'

'Anyone could buy those knives!' Clementine scoffed, wriggling in Officer Perkins' arms. 'They were half price at the kitchen supply shop in Ittonvale. You'd have been a fool to miss the sale!'

Kevin threw his hands up in outrage. 'She attacked poor Mrs Bell!' he yelled across the car park at Clementine. Officer Perkins lost her grip on Clementine's cardigan for a minute but then regained her hold on her arm. On the ground, Mrs Bell stirred. 'And she killed Doug! Tell them, Beryl!'

'You're a liar!' Clementine cried back. 'And I bet Beryl Bell is too if she's got something to do with this. She shouldn't have a superhero name!'

'What?' Perkins asked in confusion, still straining to hold Clementine back. Mrs Bell groaned and began to get up. Margery felt a rush of elation at the signs of life.

Clementine kicked furiously, losing a shoe in the process. 'Get off me, Officer Idiot, if that is your real name!'

'It's obviously not,' Officer Perkins muttered, out of breath and red in the face.

The other dinner ladies had arrived behind where Clementine and Officer Perkins were twirling.

'Symon, tell her to let Margery go,' Ceri-Ann called back to him. Symon looked bewildered in a way Margery hadn't seen since they had first met him all those years ago. Gloria grasped for Seren's hand and between the two of them and Karen and Sharon they formed a human wall between the police officers and Margery.

There was nothing left to lose. Margery felt it in her chest with certainty that she knew the only way to prove her innocence. Clementine's struggle with Officer Perkins was keeping her distracted for the moment. While she didn't think the dinner lady team would be able to keep anyone back for very long, the rest of the force were far enough away that Margery thought she might make it if she tried for the car. She looked over to it, the driver's door was still hanging open.

Margery didn't know if the police were armed. She presumed that they probably had tasers and batons, seeing as they were stepping onto a murder scene. Kevin was still doing his act and Mrs Bell was only just getting to her feet, clutching her head. Margery just had to get out of reach long enough to get to the vehicle and then she would be able to prove that she hadn't orchestrated it all.

She didn't think about it any longer, clearing her mind as she got shakily to her feet, ignoring the blood pouring from the back of her leg. Without turning back, she launched herself across the car park, slipping and stumbling as she went. She thought she heard Clementine's voice call for her, but her focus narrowed to the car door handle. Kevin had been expecting her to go for the knife, Margery had been counting on that. She was pleased to be correct. He didn't react until Margery had already rushed past him.

He yelped as he realised what was happening. He lunged back towards the car. Margery reached the door handle first, the world slowed down as her cold fingers slipped from it. She tried again, the door swung open. Inside the car, Margery reached into the bag and plucked a bauble out of it, already knowing what she would find. The bauble had a clear line running around it and Margery gripped both sides and twisted it as though she were opening a cut avocado. Bank notes propelled out onto the car seats.

'What are you doing?' Kevin yelled, trying to wrench the bauble away from her in confusion. 'What… what is this?'

'The stolen money,' Margery said. Kevin took a step back, scratching his head.

'Get away from there!' Mrs Bell cried from nearby, but Margery wasn't paying attention. 'That's mine!'

Margery gasped in gleeful surprise as the next bauble split into two as well and the bank notes inside it joined the others. She reached down to pick up some of the money, inspecting it closely. Before Mrs Bell and the police officers could reach them, she wasted no time in taking out another bauble and cracking it open too, finding another great wodge of money. Kevin gasped.

'That old witch,' he seethed. 'She had me collecting the money right under my nose!'

'Look!' Margery called to Officer Perkins over Mrs Bell's shoulder as she arrived at the car at the same time, Clementine still in her wake. Margery flapped a handful of notes in the air, a laugh forcing itself from her throat. She dragged the rest of the bag out and let the baubles roll along the tarmac. Mrs Bell lunged for one as it arrived at her feet, dropping to the ground to scrabble for them.

'They're yours?' Symon asked Mrs Bell.

She stood upright, looking between him and the baubles in her arms.

Mrs Bell realised her mistake and dropped them to the ground. 'No! Margery stole the money… I…'

'That's your car, though,' Clementine said, pointing to it. 'Your car and you just said it was your money.'

Mrs Bell screeched with the fury of being caught out. Margery's heart sang with relief. To his credit, Kevin had realised the game was up, hanging his head at the sight of the arriving officers.

Chapter Twenty-Seven

'Thank God you got here when you did,' Clementine told Symon as he approached them finally. 'Rose was about to make us eat a stolen pig leg and Margery was nearly murdered by a one-hundred-and-six-year-old woman and a man who needs his driving licence revoking.'

'Hazards of the job, I suppose,' Margery joked, though she didn't feel much like laughing. It had been much too close a call. 'You should definitely arrest Rose for stealing the ham, though.'

It had taken Symon and his team a long time to get all the witness statements needed. After all, it wasn't just one statement for the last few hours, but days' worth of crimes that needed piecing together. An officer had patched up Margery's leg, but she would have to go and have a tetanus jab at the hospital before they went home. She didn't mind, a hospital visit meant that it was really all over. The cats would be glad to see them and she would be glad to sit down for a bit and do nothing.

The knife lay in a plastic evidence bag with the Christmas skull lights and all number of other things. Once the police had begun digging, they had found all sorts of evidence in with Mrs Bell's things. Margery couldn't believe she had ever thought she could get away with it. There was months of correspondence from Elliot on her phone describing their plans in great detail. How they would take the money, who they would take it from, how they would make sure it wasn't found. Elliot had obviously wiped his phone clean of messages from her, but Mrs Bell had either been so cocky that she didn't think she would ever be found out or she hadn't known how to delete her messages.

'Yeah, I think we got here just in time, to be honest,' Symon said. Ceri-Ann wrapped her arms around him again.

He looked relieved, Margery thought, and as tired as she felt. Whatever the car park looked like at the bottom of the hill, it couldn't have been easy to get down to, and the weight of knowing Ceri-Ann was down here must have been heavy. Margery would have felt the same if it had been Clementine separated from her by gas works and the curled and cracked limbs of the old tree. She supposed that Symon had at least had some control over the situation, which she might have not.

The police had immediately begun the slow process of dealing with Doug and Elliot's bodies. They had also brought a hot water urn with them and a selection of teabags and biscuits and had been making hot drinks and instant noodles. It was a much-needed sight, nearly bringing a tear to Margery's eyes. She had seen enough of the hall for a lifetime, and vowed to herself that she would never take on anything as ambitious ever again. They would stick to the relative safety of the school, she decided. Even if it made for a less exciting life. They had had enough of that for one lifetime now.

Mrs Bell was being bundled up in a foil blanket, handcuffs around her wrists with the fuming expression of someone who had finally been called out on all of their nonsense. Margery hoped that she would be evacuated first but selfishly hoped that they would be second. Kevin sat across from Mrs Bell with his own matching set. Mike would be able to get out of his contract now, Margery thought. It was a shame it had needed such an extreme series of events for that to happen.

'How's Nick?' Ceri-Ann asked Symon. 'Is he asking for me?'

'Yeah, of course,' Symon said. 'But he's fine. He's having a great time with your mum. She let him eat a bag of chocolate coins before bed last night.'

'What?' Ceri-Ann asked, her eyes widening in bemusement. 'He can't have that much sugar, he's three!'

'Yeah, and then she asked me if he usually went to bed after ten,' Symon said, his grin threatening to spill into a laugh. 'She let him stay up to watch a film with her.'

'A kids' film, I hope?'

Symon grimaced. 'I think it was *The Nightmare Before Christmas*. She said it was okay because it's a cartoon.'

They were interrupted by Sally appearing in the doorway behind them. Margery watched her with interest. She stormed straight over to Symon.

'Detective!' she called over the crowd. 'I need to speak with you right away.'

Ceri-Ann and Symon both looked over at her, confused, as she approached. Ceri-Ann stepped back to give Symon room to work. Symon shook his head at Sally. 'I'm sorry, but we've got a lot to get on with. We need to speak to each of you in turn.'

'It will only take a minute,' Sally insisted.

Symon looked like he was debating simply ignoring her, but begrudgingly he followed her out of the hall. Margery and Clementine exchanged a confused look as he slipped away with her.

'Sorry,' he said to Ceri-Ann more than anyone else. 'I'll only be a sec.'

'No worries,' Ceri-Ann said. 'It's time for me to try and Whamageddon again anyway.'

She slipped away as he followed Sally, leaving Margery and Clementine alone again. Margery found Clementine's hand resting on the arm of her chair and took it. Clementine squeezed hers back.

'No harm done,' Margery said, though she wasn't sure she meant it.

Clementine chuckled. 'There's always next year to get it right. We'll have to offer to run Mrs Bell's stall too.'

'I think we can just pretend it never existed at this point,' Margery said with a sigh. Clementine squeezed her hand again, harder this time, in the unspoken love language of their marriage. Margery wondered if other couples had similar. There were certainly a few staff their age still working at the school who hated their other halves, or certainly seemed to if the dark jokes they made about them were anything to go by. Ceri-Ann called it 'Boomer humour', but Margery thought it was something more depressing than that. After all, it was a free country: you could divorce whoever you wanted. She knew it wasn't that simple, really, but she also knew that Clementine was more likely to write her a sixteen-page sonnet about how much she liked the shape of Margery's earlobes than make a joke about her being a ball and chain.

'How did you know the money was in the baubles?' Clementine asked her.

Margery found herself smiling, despite it all. 'Elliot said they were in a "Christmassy place" and I reasoned that Mrs Bell knew where that was. Then the decorations in here kept disappearing, didn't they?'

Clementine nodded. 'When Seren said about it to Rose, Rose denied taking them, didn't she? And she'd have made horrendous earrings out of them, or something like that, wouldn't she?'

'Yes, exactly!' Margery exclaimed. 'And Mrs Bell was lugging around a huge bin bag and she had got so angry when Kevin kicked it. I thought at first it was just things from her stall that she wanted to take with her for their grand escape, but then I realised how ridiculous it would be if that's where the money was. She must have been planning to take them all home and not give him a penny.'

'You were right,' Clementine said.

'A broken clock is right twice a day, or whatever it is,' Margery said, suddenly feeling very tired.

'Don't put yourself down,' Clementine said. 'You've just single-handedly solved a man's murder. Well, a murder and an accident. Crikey, I'd better solve a murder to catch you up...' Margery gave her a stern look. 'Well, maybe we'll just hope that there aren't any more instead.'

'I'd like that,' Margery said. She leaned over to rest her head on Clementine's shoulder, closing her eyes for a moment.

Symon reappeared in the doorway, looking more annoyed than concerned.

'What did Sally want?' Margery asked curiously. Sally had since disappeared, whatever conversation she had had with Symon seemingly enough to get out of the way and let the police do their jobs.

Symon chuckled in a way that told Margery he was laughing at Sally's audacity more than anything else. 'I probably shouldn't tell you this, but it's so mental... She wanted to tell me that the entire thing's been blown out of proportion and that I shouldn't tell the public anything until she's had the hall checked for electrical safety, as that's how Elliot died.'

'What!' Margery and Clementine cried in unison.

'I know!' Symon laughed again.

'How is that possible?' Margery asked as Clementine continued to splutter at Sally's ginormous understatement.

'I don't know what she was expecting me to do,' Symon said. 'I feel like she wanted me to just drop the entire case. I told her I can't do that. Two people are dead, I don't know how much more proportional it could be. I think she's just worried about the hall now that Doug and Elliot are gone.'

'Surely she could probably take it over now?' Margery suggested. 'She was the treasurer anyway.'

'Yeah, I bet she will,' Symon said with a nod. 'I'm sure she's just worried about negative publicity, not safety or whatever.'

'I imagine people won't forget any of this in a hurry,' Clementine said, looking around the hall. 'We certainly won't be in a rush to return. Well, maybe it'll all be forgotten by next Christmas.'

'They'll have to find a new Santa first,' Margery said, grimacing.

Symon didn't look like he was listening. He was staring over at Ceri-Ann, his eyes soft.

'Sorry,' he told them, beginning to slip away towards her. 'I've got something to do.'

'Dealing with Kevin and Mrs Bell?' Margery asked.

'Yeah, I'll get to them after.' Symon smiled in acknowledgement.

He slipped away before either Margery or Clementine could say anything else and approached Ceri-Ann, who was standing over with the other dinner ladies with her back to him. Before Margery could wonder what was going on, he had dropped to one knee in front of her. Clementine almost deafened her with the shriek she let out. Ceri-Ann stared down at him in confusion as Gloria, Seren and the rest of the dinner ladies began to clap in excitement like performing seals.

'Ceri-Ann Reynolds, how do you feel about becoming Mrs Nowak?' Symon began.

'Don't you dare.' Ceri-Ann laughed. She gave him a gentle shove to the shoulder, but she didn't really seem displeased. 'You haven't even got a ring!'

'Take one of mine!' Rose stormed over, desperately pulling at the excessive amount of costume jewellery she wore on both hands. She thrust a handful of it at him. He froze in panic for a second, staring down at the replica of Princess Diana's engagement ring and Rose's own humongous diamond wedding band, before delicately picking out the least offensive piece of jewellery. He gestured with it to Ceri-Ann, who shook her head, but let him take her hand again anyway, a smile playing on her lips.

'Ceri,' Symon began again. The tips of his ears had gone bright red and the stammer he'd had when Margery and Clementine first met him had returned in force. Ceri-Ann beamed down at him. 'Ever since I met you, I always felt like we were two peas in a pod or… er… something more poetic than that.'

Ceri-Ann chuckled, but Margery saw the happy tears welling in her eyes. She could feel her own arriving, her hands went to her mouth as she watched.

'I'm sorry I haven't asked you before,' Symon continued. 'I just always thought it needed to be at the right time, and I had to do, like, a huge engagement plan but I… after the last few days… I can't… I can't do any of it without you.' He stuttered off, words failing him.

'I know how you feel,' Ceri-An said softly, taking both of his hands. 'I don't need a massive engagement ring or a big party, I'm not Rose… I mean…' She looked at Rose, who rolled her eyes. 'I love you. That's special enough.'

Symon rose up from his knee and kissed her as the entire hall whooped with glee.

'We'll play at your wedding!' Mike yelled from somewhere in the crowd. 'If I'm not in prison for pulling down a tree!'

The lights twinkled and Margery found herself relaxing after the stress of the past few days, leaning back in the chair and enjoying it. Symon and Ceri-Ann twirled together and she watched them sway. Something good had come of a horrible weekend.

Epilogue

'I keep telling you, marriage isn't as glamorous as we've all made it look,' Margery heard Clementine telling Ceri-Ann. They were talking so loudly that she could hear them even over on the other side of the table. 'Look at Seren's marriage as well, she's got to live with Gary and iron his absolutely huge socks. What kind of life is that? You've got a son as well, and Symon's so lanky, I bet it'll just be ironing extra-long trousers for years and years…'

'Gary does all the ironing, actually.' Seren beamed with a toothy grin, holding up her glass of Prosecco in excitement. 'I bought him a Tefal steamer for Christmas, he loved it!'

The guidebook she had bought the moment the trip had been mentioned was in her other hand. She had gone through it and marked things she wanted to do on the holiday, it was weighted down with sticky notes. Margery hadn't had the heart to remind her they were only going for a few days and that their hotel was so far from the beaten track there was very little chance they would go to the nearest town at all.

'Marriage is fine, especially if you book a lot of girls' trips to get away from them,' Rose scoffed. 'And by girls' trips I mean five-star spa weekends, not whatever this horrendous ordeal is going to be like.'

'The hotel's got six five-star reviews,' Clementine said with a laugh.

'Yes, out of a thousand. We should have just stayed in the country and gone to my little holiday home again,' Rose said.

'Little' was an understatement for Rose's ancestral country pile. Still, she was correct that it would have been the cheaper option. Margery hadn't realised how expensive it would be to go abroad during a summer break, and even then, the hotel in their price range wasn't what you would call five-star, or even two-star. She was sure it would be worth it in the end. Rose had paid for Seren's passport, as she had never been abroad before, and had bought them both matching passport cases. Seren had been so thrilled to have one that she had worn it around her neck in a holder for days before they had even got to the airport.

'Mate, I want a little bit of a glow for the wedding day, save spending money on fake tan,' Ceri-Ann said. Her best friend, Chantelle, nodded grimly. Neither of them had wasted any time getting into the hen party mood, both wearing sashes that announced what part of the bridal party they were. Rose had refused to wear hers when Chantelle had handed it to her when they picked her up in the brand-new school minibus, saying that they would be kicked off the plane if they caused too much of a ruckus. Margery could see it sticking out of the top of her carry-on bag, though, ready to be worn.

'Listen,' Chantelle said, staring Rose directly in the eye, her voice low and serious. 'Do you want Ceri to be a pasty bride?'

'Well, of course not!' Rose stammered. 'But we're only going for three days, haven't you seen the weather report? Clouds the entire week.'

'The UV rays will be enough,' Chantelle said knowingly. Ceri-Ann nodded along.

Karen was laughing along, but she suddenly gasped. 'Before I forget! I've done our travel insurance policy.' She reached down into her bag and pulled out a thick folder.

'Did you need to print it off?' Clementine asked, her brow furrowing. 'I thought you were supposed to do everything by internet now.'

'You can never be too careful,' Karen said in earnest, Sharon nodded along vigorously. The brim of her huge sunhat wobbled back and forth. Karen turned to Ceri-Ann, her face even more serious. 'Ceri, I had to put you were a smoker. I know you said you were a non-smoker on the form, but I saw you smoking a cigarette last week and you can't lie in an official capacity...'

'That was a cigar,' Ceri-Ann said with a smile. 'Doesn't count.'

Margery's phone buzzed from its place on the table, and she peered down at it to see that she had a new email. She was looking forward to the moment she could put the phone on airplane mode and be done with it, but while they were still in the country, she'd felt the need to have it on while they waited. She didn't know why, everyone who might usually call her was with her.

'What's that?' Gloria asked as she brought another tray of drinks over. At this rate they would be lucky to be allowed on the plane. At least they had already been through the duty free, which had been an ordeal in itself. Margery thought that there was probably a 50 per cent chance that they wouldn't make it on time.

'Is it Sally again?' Clementine asked from the other side of the table, her brow furrowing in annoyance. 'Tell her we're not doing it.'

'I have,' Margery groaned, 'but that's easier said than done.'

'Doing what?' Gloria asked, all the glasses of Prosecco forgotten.

'The catering for Ittonvale hall's harvest festival green room,' Margery admitted. 'I just don't think it's a good idea. We haven't been back since, have we? I've managed to avoid answering so far, but now it's August she's really ramped up.'

'Well, I guess there couldn't be many more murders,' Gloria said, tapping her fingers to her chin.

Margery wasn't so sure on that one. Murder seemed to follow them, and she wasn't sure it was all over yet. It didn't feel like the final time that they would be plunged into the deep end with their kitchen shoes on. She didn't fancy returning to the scene yet, even for something as innocent as a festival.

'That's the gate!' Karen shrieked, jabbing a finger towards the big screen outside of the bar. 'They've announced our gate! Quick! Quick!'

She jumped up and began trying to squish the folder back into her handbag at the same time as Sharon burst into happy tears.

'We've got an hour yet!' Rose said, but she got up as well, gathering her many duty-free bags. Seren took her carry-on luggage dutifully. 'Thank you, Seren. I'll get you a pot of Pringles on the plane.'

Margery slid down from the bar stool and followed them, taking it all in and unable to hide the smile that had arrived on her face. Clementine took her hand, and they sauntered along through the airport as the rest of the team ploughed ahead in excitement. It was enough, she realised. As sure as she was that the bad days weren't over, she could feel deep down in her bones that there were just as many good ones to come.

Acknowledgements

Hello again! Sorry if you're getting sick of me! Though I suspect if you've made it this far then you don't mind me continuing to put Margery and Clementine's stories out into the world.

I wanted to go in a slightly different direction for this book. When I wrote book three in the series, *A Terrible Village Poisoning*, I really struggled with the lack of school setting. But I've always wanted to write a locked room mystery, so I thought I'd give it another go. I enjoyed writing this a lot and I hope you don't miss the school too much. I suspect it will be back in the next book!

It's the usual suspects who have been elemental in keeping this going. Robyn, Emily, Mum, Jim, Dad, Kirstie, Bethan, Jon, Teresa. My publisher Canelo and audiobook publisher Saga Egmont. Of course, my wonderful agent Francesca Riccardi, who puts up with so much nonsense from me! Thank you for always replying to my weird vague WhatsApp messages. Ami Smithson for another excellent cover. 'How does she do it!?' I hear you cry. (I don't know either!)

Siân Heap was my editor at Canelo for the first half of the series and I was so pleased to be able to work with her again for this book – thank you for all your help, Siân. I couldn't have done it without you, excellent copy editor

Becca Allen or brilliant proofreader Millie Godwin. Any weird spelling mistakes left over are unfortunately mine!

Also, a big thank you to Wham! for writing the best Christmas song of all time. (It's between 'Last Christmas' and 'Christmas Time (Don't let the bells end)' by The Darkness for me!)

While I'm here, I also wanted to say thank you to all the hosts and staff of the events I was invited to last year. It's nice to be able to say thank you in permanent form! A huge thank you to all involved at Harrogate Festival, Crime Cymru Festival, Carolynn Bain, Afrori Books and everyone else at Brighton Book Festival, everyone at East Riding Libraries Festival of Words and The Beverley Bookshop. I know I've forgotten someone/several people, so I apologise if that's you! It's been wonderful to meet you and the people of your communities, who I equally need to thank! We all share the same love of books and writing, what a lovely thing that is.

Lastly, thank you to *you* for reading this! As always, I owe the success of everything to the people who read my books and I can't thank you enough for picking this book up.

Until the next time!